T0082208

Otto Lehrack

BEAR AGAINST THE SUN

Bear Against the Sun

Print ISBN: 979-8-35093-760-2
eBook ISBN: 979-8-35093-761-9

Printed in the United States of America

For Jan
and for Anna Appleby

NON-FICTION BY OTTO LEHRACK

No Shining Armor: The Marines at War in Vietnam

Operation Starlite: The Beginning of the Blood Debt in Vietnam

America's Battalion: Marines in the First Gulf War

Newspeak: Orwell's 1984 in the Age of Obama

Road of 10,000 Pains: The Destruction of the 2nd NVA Division by the Marines, 1967

TABLE OF CONTENTS

PROLOGUE

BLOOD ON KHODYNKA MEADOW, MOSCOW, 1896

The day began peacefully enough; it was a day of hope, of promise. The crowd started gathering before dawn, dozens of people at first, then hundreds, then thousands until nearly a half million people stood on the meadow. Spirits were high, the crowd joyous, the day bright with sunshine. Strangers struck up conversations and chattered cheerfully. Here and there, children frolicked. All waited for a glimpse of the new tsar.

The small girl in a ragged dress bounced on her toes, arms raised. "I can't see, Mama."

"Tatya, you are getting too big for this," Olga said, lifting up her daughter with a grunt.

"I did not know there were so many people in the whole world, Mama. Can we get closer?"

"Be patient, child. We'll see the new tsar and someday you can tell your grandchildren about this.

"He has gifts for us, Tatya. After he leaves, we will get bread and sausage and a souvenir mug to remind us of today. Look!"

Olga pointed at the enormous piles of gifts in center of the field, roped off and guarded by a dozen Cossacks. Hundreds of burdened wagons lined up as far as the eye could see, ready to replenish the goods.

Olga watched as a dirty young boy led a score of urchins toward the prize. He clearly planned to get his comrades close to the mountain of food to make sure they got all they could carry. Each had a cloth bag tucked under his shirt to fill with booty. The boy looked about him, and then, satisfied they were ready to go, waved his cloth cap above his head—the signal.

The boys leaped over or under the rope barrier from several directions at once, baffling the Cossacks. Those nearest the center began tossing bread and sausages to their confederates.

The Cossacks' shouting set off a tide of confusion and noise that rippled through the crowd toward the perimeter. One voice after another added to the chorus.

"What is going on?" "Is he here? Is he here?" "Are they giving out the food?" Heads swiveled this way and that.

As the guards tried to stop them, the boys, laden with loot, slipped between the legs of some, around others, and made for the edge of the crowd. A Cossack grabbed the leader by his collar and was enthusiastically hitting him. Another boy fell under the feet of the crowd but most of them managed to escape.

Olga felt the crowd surge forward, eager to not be left out when the goods were distributed. The ranks nearest the center moved first, and then those behind them pushed from every point in the compass, compressing the mass of human bodies, and so compacting the mob that no one could move without those around them moving too. People fell beneath churning feet. The old, the sick, and children were the first to tumble and be crushed; then stronger adults and even some of the outnumbered Cossacks fell victim. In just a few minutes the giant gathering became a roiling mass. Tatya shrieked in Olga's arms as arms and legs snapped, ribs cracked, faces became unrecognizable, and many were trampled to death. Screams of pain, panic, horror and despair overwhelmed the few voices of reason; the air thickened with smells of blood, of voided bowels, of unwashed bodies.

The human maelstrom carried Olga in one direction and then another. She nearly lost her daughter as she hugged her tightly and made a desperate attempt to carry her back through the surging crowd. Impossible! Tatya slipped out of her grasp and fell down.

"Mama, Mama!"

Olga yanked her up just in time. Behind her a row of a dozen people holding on to one another tumbled to the ground together. Unhesitatingly, Olga stumbled over them, kicking at those arms and legs and heads that got in her way.

"Out of the way! Out of the way! I must save my child!" She gained a few yards before the crowd closed in again, threatening her hold on her daughter. Tatya screamed. Blood flowed from her nose and from a cut on one leg.

The fallen were done for. There was nowhere for the others to stand but on top of them and the churning feet slowly ground them to bloody pieces. The eyes of the people were wide with terror. like those of horses trapped by fire. Slowly, the living mob paused and breathed like the ocean on a shoreline at slack tide, and then, like the tide, resumed its movement. On the fringes of the crowd, the outer layers peeled away as people hobbled, crawled or limped away from the horror behind them.

Olga yelled at those nearby, giving orders and trying to get them to stop pushing. Her voice was strong, and a small portion of the crowd in her immediate vicinity stopped surging. "Take my daughter," she commanded to a couple behind her. "Pass her toward the outside, away from the crowd."

"Mama, Mama! Hold onto me!"

Olga pried her daughter's fingers loose from her dress and passed her to the dumbstruck couple.

As if grateful to have something sane to do, the man grasped Tatiana, held her on his shoulder and yelled to the people behind him. They too, seemed to seize on the thought of doing something rational, any relief from the madness. A tiny current of sanity coursed through that sliver of the mob as one person after another passed the struggling girl from hand to hand until she disappeared from Olga's sight, the crowd thinned, and she was put down. The small droplet of reason quickly evaporated, and the crowd resumed grinding and surging. Tatiana struggled against the mob to fight her way back and find her mother but person after person ran past her, running or staggering away from the slaughter at the center. Several knocked her to the ground. Defeated and bleeding she walked to the edge of the field, sat down and cried. Blood from her nose and from a scalp wound ran unnoticed down her face.

Dozens of carriages bearing nobility approached the field and stopped. The meadow looked like a battlefield. Some of the wounded staggered off without assistance. Family members and strangers carried many of the dead and bleeding. Thousands of others fled in every direction. Some paused, turned, and gaped in horror once they reached safety. Others kept going without a backward glance.

The tsar and tsarina, escorted by a troop of cavalry, arrived and soon left, stunned. Most of the aristocracy who arrived with the royal couple left with them. A few others stayed on and looked on in shock at the violence before them.

Prince Boris Medved told his coachman to pull out and around the row of carriages in front of him so he could get a better look. His wife, Marina, and son, Ivan, craned their necks, taking in the scene from the carriage window.

"Careful, Ilya, look out for the mob but see if you can get us a little closer." As they drew nearer, a troop of Cossacks passed them at full gallop.

"This is far enough, Ilya. Pull over to the side and stop," Medved said. He sat staring at the carnage, barely aware of the crying little girl in the torn, bloody dress sitting by the side of the road.

Eleven-year-old Ivan shouted, "Papa, look! A little girl. I think she is hurt."

Ivan's mother said, "Ivan, stay where you are. I do *not* want you to get caught up in this." But Ivan was already on the ground and running to the child. Medved followed his son to the edge of the road. "Papa, it is the girl we saw in church," Ivan said.

Ivan's mother looked again at the girl, "Holy Mother, she is the living image of my younger sister who God had claimed by pneumonia in our childhood." She stared for only a moment before her maternal instincts took over. "We must help the poor child," she ordered, alighting from the carriage and hurrying to the side of the little girl. "Who are you, little one? Where are your parents?" The girl only cried harder as Marina took her in her arms, heedless of the blood dripping on her dress.

"Leave her alone," Medved told his wife, "Her troubles are none of our business. I am sure her mother and father will be along any minute."

"Boris, we must not leave her alone until they appear."

They returned to the carriage and waited. They waited until the crowd gradually dispersed, and soldiers, their faces grim, began loading the dead onto carts. Many more lay motionless in the meadow in the grotesque postures of the violently dead. No one came for the girl. The shadows marched across the field as the sun began to set and the afternoon turned chill. In the carriage, the girl lay half asleep in Marina's arms. Weeping.

Boris Medved frequently looked at his watch, his patience ticking away with the minutes.

"Marina, let her go with the other injured. The tsar will send out doctors and others to deal with this and they are better equipped. And look at her. She is dirty and poor, and I do not want some street urchin staying at our house."

"Boris, this child is coming home with us, and that is that. And we should leave now." With that she covered the girl with a blanket and sat back with a look her husband knew well.

Boris sighed to the coachman, "Ilya, home it is."

Marina marshaled the servants to care for the sobbing child. "Nina," she told a maid, "draw a bath and prepare a bedroom." She turned the girl over to two other maids who carefully walked her up the stairs between them as Marina followed. "And Nina, tell the cook to send up broth and fruit."

Tatya wiped the tears out of her eyes with a dirty hand, bewildered at the richness of the scene around her. "Where is my Mama?"

"We will find her, child. What is your name and where do you live?"

"My name is Tatiana Gitina," said the girl. "My mother's name is Olga, like the tsar's daughter, and we live near the factory where my father works, on the other side of the river."

"My son says we have seen you in church. Why do you come so far to worship?"

"If it were up to my father, we would not come at all. But Mama loves church, and we make the long walk there many Sundays when the weather is not too bad. I like the church too, but I am not religious."

"Not religious? Why not?"

"Because Papa says it is all something used to keep the people in line. He does not believe in God. Where is my Mama? When can I go home?"

"Rest, Tatiana," Marina said, "We will send someone to find her."

A maid bathed the girl under Marina's careful supervision, dressed her in a gown belonging to the Medved's daughter Natalya and then put her to bed. "Sleep, child, and God bless you. Everything will be better tomorrow."

Marina left a maid at her door in case the girl needed anything.

After dinner, the children attended to their music lessons. Those finished, Marina issued instructions for the bedding down of her children and then looked in on them before she prepared for that night's soiree.

"Mama," Natalya said," why do we have to keep this dirty little girl in our house and why is she wearing my nightgown?"

"She is only here for tonight and will be gone tomorrow. And you have many nightgowns."

Ivan asked, "Mama, what happened to that girl's mother?"

"I do not know, Ivan. Papa has sent men to find out. We must pray that we find her tomorrow."

"Will God take care of her?"

"I do not know, Ivan, that is why we must pray."

"But does God take care of everyone who is prayed for?"

"I am afraid not, darling, but we must pray anyway."

"But why?"

"Oh, Ivan, I wish I could answer that question."

"If God will not take care of her, Mama, then will the Little Father take care of her?"

"I am sure the tsar will try."

Ivan went to sleep that night with a head full of questions about God and the tsar and Tatiana. The thing he wondered most about was why God did not take care of all His people the way He took care of Medveds. *Maybe when I am grown, I can help the Little Father take care of the poor.* But then he drifted off to sleep thinking of the military and of horses.

Before Marina put her to bed, Tatiana answered Boris's questions about where she lived. When he got as much information as he could he summoned a servant and sent him off to find Tatiana's parents.

As the sun sank toward the horizon, Vladimir Gitin began to worry about his wife and daughter, and he started the long walk to Khodynka Meadow to find them. Moving through Moscow, he heard snatches of conversation about the great tragedy. Thousands dead…trampled. So many wounded. Heart thumping, he quickened his pace. It was nearly dark by the time he approached the meadow.

"You! Where do you think you are going?" shouted a Cossack sergeant.

"To find my wife and daughter."

"No one is on the field but the dead, and we are to keep everyone from them until tomorrow when they can be carried away."

"No one but the dead? But my wife and daughter?"

"I am sorry, but no one can go onto the field until daylight."

Vladimir fell to his knees. For the first time in his life he envied those who believed in God. He sat dazed and shivering until daylight. As the gray dawn pushed the blackness out of the sky, a convoy of ambulance wagons neared the field. Vladimir slipped in behind one of them and followed it past the Cossacks. The drivers and their helpers began the grim task of loading bodies onto the wagons. The reek of the newly dead made breathing a chore. The workers tossed corpses, stiff with rigor mortis, bloody from their wounds, and muddy from the field, into the wagons, one on top of another.

Vladimir ran from wagon to wagon. There were so many dead, so many! Part of a tattered blue dress like the one his wife had worn the day before peeked out from under the corpse of an old man. Ignoring the shouts of the driver, Vladimir shuddered, grasped a cold, waxy arm and pulled the rigid old man to one side for a closer look, and then grabbed the wagon's side to keep from falling. It was Olga! He could hardly believe that this stiff, dirty, open-mouthed, wide-eyed corpse was all that remained of the woman he had loved for many years.

Collapsing, he sat and wept for an interminable time and then regained his feet and began looking for the body of his daughter. There were too many bodies, too many wagons. He ran from one to the other asking if anyone had seen a small girl, nine years old, with curly black hair and eyes and wearing a gray dress. The weary workers either ignored him or shook their heads as they continued their grim work.

Vladimir stumbled home, hardly aware of how he got there. He cursed the tsar, he cursed God and he cursed himself for letting his family go to this affair. He found a partial bottle of vodka and downed it. Then he grabbed the family's food money from a can over the stove.

No one will be needing this money to eat, he thought as he lurched out the door and soon returned with all the liquor his money would buy. He stumbled back into the little hut, latched the door behind him and fell into his bed clutching the bottles. He prayed again and again to a God he did not believe in and drank until blackness came.

CHAPTER 1

FORTY TIMES FORTY CHURCHES

In 1896, Moscow was the city of forty times forty churches; churches whose spire-topped, onion-shaped domes reached toward heaven and animated the skyline of the ancient capital. To Russians, Moscow was the Third Rome, the center of the Orthodox faith and, since the fall of Constantinople to the Ottoman Turks in 1453, the center of the Christian world. On Sundays all classes of people, rich and poor, aristocrat and commoner, worshiped standing shoulder to shoulder for Mass in the Russian tradition and nearly overflowed the churches across the land. The rich came to stand in the presence of God and thank Him for their privileged station, the poor in hopes that God would better their lives, the lame and infirm praying that God would restore their health. Nearly all the faithful prayed that their new ruler, Nicholas II, appointed by God to carry out Heaven's will on Earth, would have a successful reign.

Ivan stood near the altar of the Dormition Cathedral, blinking at the fragrant blue incense that irritated his eyes as it wafted around the shining pillars of Siberian marble. His father, mother, and sister stood nearby amid flickering gaslight that illuminated ancient icons of Russian saints and the golden, bejeweled crucifix that dominated the altar. The heavenly voices of the choir of small boys faded as a priest in jeweled vestments began to intone the Mass, his impressive beard bobbing in time with his words.

How wonderful this church is, Ivan mused, *Our new tsar will be crowned right here in a few days. And someday I will be an officer of a Guards regiment and will be married here.*

Glancing over his shoulder, he frowned at the chatter of the more casual celebrants. There were always those who stationed themselves in the rear and near the doors, carrying on lengthy conversations that had nothing to do with Christianity. They gossiped and concluded business deals constantly coming and going during services. *Why cannot they do those things somewhere else?*. Those who were serious about their religion, like the Medved family, and did not want to be disturbed, stood near the front and watched the liturgy with joy and hope.

As Ivan took in the scene, absorbing the sounds and the smells of holy pageantry, he felt someone jostle into place beside him, but paid no attention. His thoughts had just returned to the altar when a small, sharp voice interrupted his thoughts, "Mama, why do we have to come to church? Papa says it is all superstition."

Ivan looked down at a small girl of eight or nine, at least a few years younger than himself, clad in a ragged woolen dress that gave off a musky odor. A cascade of black ringlets tumbled down her forehead, contrasting with her flawless skin and dimples. Her mother was a plump woman whose concave cheeks and sunken lips bore witness to a mouth sparsely populated with teeth, a woman into whose face a conspiracy of time, hardship, disappointment, and unfulfilled hopes had relentlessly carved deep lines. She looked down at her daughter and was about to admonish her when Ivan whispered, "Shh, you are supposed to be quiet when the priest is saying the Mass."

Undaunted by Ivan's rich clothing and heedless of the ritual before the altar, the girl looked him in the eyes. "What do you know, rich boy? You probably believe all this stuff."

"I believe in God and in paying proper respect in His house," he whispered.

"Well, I do not believe in God," said the girl aloud, her dark eyes flashing in the gloom of the church. Her words echoed though the sanctuary during a pause in the proceedings and turned heads everywhere. The priest's voice lost its rhythm as he scanned the church for the offender. The girl's mother flushed a bright red, clapped a hand over her daughter's mouth, and marched her toward the exit. Ivan glared at them as they left, wondering how anyone could be so disrespectful in one of the holiest sites in Russia. The priest regained his composure and droned through the service without further interruption.

Outside, Ivan and his family stood blinking in the bright May sunshine. The carriages of the wealthy lined up for nearly two blocks, and each in turn rolled up to the front of the church and collected its owners.

The Medveds chatted with friends as they waited. The coronation of the tsar rested on everyone's lips. Ivan's mother gossiped with the other women, exchanging news about who was giving what ball and who was invited.

The Medved children were bored but found no one of their age to talk to, so they kept looking down the row of carriages hoping to see their own. Ivan was anxious to get home to his new horse and Natalya speculated endlessly about what she would wear to a music recital.

"Boris," a voice boomed over the chattering of the crowd. Prince Medved looked up to see the large, bearded, bearlike figure of Sergei Witte, the finance minister, lumbering toward him. Those who knew who he was made way for him. Others looked at him with distaste. After one couple reluctantly moved aside to let him through, the woman whispered, "Who does he think he is? Look at his clothes, wrinkled and stained and disheveled. He looks like someone's stable man dressed in his master's castoffs."

Ivan moved a bit closer to his father to eavesdrop.

"Boris," began Sergei, "have you recently talked with His Majesty about the Far East problem?"

"Just yesterday, Sergei, and to answer your question, yes, he is still pressing the issue of a warm water port on the Pacific, in Port Arthur. We hold it now and are beginning to build a port, but it is clear that the Japanese want it. With China in decline, they seem to think that it is their mission to rule East Asia and they do not want us there. Tsar Nicholas seems to believe that the Japanese will be easy to intimidate, and if war comes, they can be easily beaten. It is not as though he does not have enough to think about, with his coronation this week and the financial state of Russia."

"We have to make him understand," said Sergei, "that the Trans-Siberian Railroad will not support a major war effort in the east. I am sorry that the newspapers celebrated the railroad as Russia's answer to the Suez Canal. The Suez Canal does not travel over thousands of miles of vechnaya merzlota, ground that never fully thaws." He took a deep breath and shook his shaggy head. "I tell you, we have tripled the repair crews and still cannot keep it open all the time. I sent an assistant all the way to the Pacific, the poor fellow. His journey took nearly five weeks each way. The damned train only moved at an average speed of five miles per hour."

"How is the work around Lake Baikal coming?"

"That is another thing. We are a decade or more from completing the tunnels through the mountainous shore and still have to move everything-- men, supplies, equipment, across the surface of the lake. It is a nightmare of a bottleneck."

Ivan saw the Medved's carriage approach, gleaming in the sunshine, the doors lacquered with crimson and emblazoned in gold with the Russian double-headed eagle, a sign that the owner was someone important in the government. The six perfectly matched gray geldings moved comfortable as a team. Their color contrasted beautifully with the dark coach, as they drew it slowly through the city. Six sets of hooves sent small geysers of muddy water in all directions as they high-stepped through the sludge. Two liveried servants rode in front and a footman stood on a step at the rear of the carriage, hanging on with a white-knuckled grip.

"Sorry, Sergei, my carriage is here, and I cannot hold the line up," said Boris. "I will try to talk to the tsar tomorrow. If I do, I'll let you know what he says."

The Medved family quickly boarded and started down muddy Borovskaya Avenue, the carriage swaying side to side on the uneven surface of the street. The prince gazed out the window, breathing deeply of the clean fresh air left by the hard rain of the night before but frowning that it had created ankle deep mud on the many streets that remained unpaved. "So much work to be done," he grumbled. He closed his eyes and tried to clear his mind.

The carriage swerved abruptly to one side of the street to avoid a squadron of mounted Cossacks that galloped past, shouting and whooping, racing as if to battle, lances held high, bearskin hats bobbing and their red pantaloons bright against their dark horses, whose hooves flung even more mud against the sides of the carriage. "Damned Cossacks," the driver muttered under his breath.

"Careful, Grisha," said the diminutive, squint-eyed postilion, "Teodor lost his job, and the prince sent him back to the country for driving into a pothole and breaking an axle."

"Damn you too, Ilya. If you would just do *your* job, we would not have a problem."

"Boris," said Marina, "cannot you do something about those galloping bands of soldiers? There seem to be more and more of them, and they are making the streets unsafe."

Prince Medved opened his eyes. "I will talk to the military governor about them, my dear, but you know how they are...the Cossacks are a boisterous group but good soldiers. They are an independent bunch and hard to control."

Ivan never grew tired of hearing about soldiers, and he prompted his father, "Papa, please tell me what the Cossacks do for us."

Boris smiled at his son's interest in the military.

"Be careful, Ilya," Grisha said, "there is a mess at the next corner. Too many carriages are trying to get through at once and none of them are moving. "Semyon," he yelled to the footman perched on the rear, "get going and straighten this out."

The footman leapt from the carriage and ran forward through the mud, "Give way, give way! This is Prince Medved's carriage. You there, move over to that side, and you, stop where you are..."

In a few minutes Semyon slogged back through the mud and took up his post, and they were underway again.

Boris's explanation about the Cossacks continued as the carriage proceeded through the wide avenues around the Kremlin, past the mansions of the aristocracy that sat side by side with those of wealthy merchants. The horses slowed down as they turned into busy Manege Square.

As they rolled up in front of their house, the footman jumped down into the street before the carriage came to a complete stop, ran forward, put a small stool in place, opened the carriage door, bowed and helped the family down.

Marina paused on the stool and cast a critical eye at her home. "Boris, there appears to be a spot the painters missed at the corner between the third and fourth floors. Please get the workmen to repair it. The town is nearly full with people here for the coronation and we cannot have it looking like that."

Boris sighed but found no reason to answer.

The mansion's front door swung open, the doorman bowing to the family. A maid helped them off with their coats and wraps. "Mama," Ivan called over his shoulder, "I am going to the stable."

"All right, Ivan, but you, Natalya, must practice your piano lesson. Papa and I are going to have tea and we'll be listening." Marina watched as her daughter skipped down the marble-floored hall toward the music room and then she and Boris moved into the parlor.

Prince Medved sat heavily in a red damask-covered chair, pulled a sheath of papers from an inner pocket and began to read. Marina sat erect looking around her, smiling in satisfaction at the perfection of the room. A constellation of light, every color of the rainbow, winked at them through hundreds of prisms clustered in the chandelier overhead. Portraits of Medveds long gone patiently waited in precise formation on two walls, lined up in the order in which they had marched into history. A chain of icons faced them from across the room.

A maid served the Medveds tea, and the couple sat silently for a few minutes as the tea wept a slowly diminishing wisp of steam. Boris Medved contemplated a long afternoon of labor and his wife of other matters.

"Boris," Marina said, "what do you think of this new maid, Nina? She was a bit careless serving the tea just now and I am beginning to think we should have left her in the country."

"I don't know, Marina. Her mother was a maid in the city for a generation and you know how these servants are. She is young. Perhaps she will get better with time."

"I know, but these people seem to think that positions in the households are like royal titles, and they should be passed from generation to generation. Perhaps it is time to change this policy. I have had to chastise Nina twice before, and I wonder if we should not send her back." Marina wrinkled her brow. "Perhaps I could assign her permanently to Natalya. She is only a few years older and perhaps they could learn from each other."

"Marina, I have enough to deal with."

"Of course, but I'll be so glad when the coronation is done and we can go back to St. Petersburg," Marina said. "There is so little to do here, compared with the social events we have in St. Petersburg. Muscovites are so...rustic, and I have fewer friends to talk to."

"I promised that I would send you and the children back right after the coronation, and I will," Boris said. "I'll have to stay in

Moscow. There is much to be done, and the tsar is sure to return to St. Petersburg after the coronation. With him out of the way, I can do more here."

Prince Medved lit a cigar, then blew out a lung full of smoke and watched it drift lazily toward the ceiling, "He will be crowned next week, and I am worried."

"What are you worried about, Boris? You helped him grow up. He told me that you are like an older brother to him."

"I know, my dear, but loving the man personally and having faith that he can rule the country are two different things. I just wish he were older and stronger. His own father thought him too delicate and not smart enough to be the strong tsar that Russia needs." Boris rose and began to pace the room. "If only Alexander had lived another twenty years, or even ten…

"Just the other day, Nicholas told me that did not want to be the tsar, and if it were not God's will that he rule Russia then he would not. 'I do not even know how to talk to the ministers,' he said."

Boris looked intently at the grim, mustachioed portrait of Andrei Ivanovich Medved, a general in Marshall Kutuzov's army, the army that drove Napoleon from Russia in 1812. The Medved family had served the tsars as military advisors or courtiers since the seventeenth century, but their status had greatly improved as a result of the Napoleonic Wars. *Thanks to the Father and the Son, Alexander the First made Andrei Ivanovich, a prince for his service.* Boris thought. *I owe everything to him and will eventually pass this rank on to Ivan. Now it is my turn to serve Russia and serve it I will, whatever it costs me.*

Marina put down her tea and came to stand beside her husband. "Boris, why are you so distressed? Surely— "

"Nothing is sure, Marina." He spoke so harshly that she recoiled in surprise. He softened his tone

"The twentieth century is almost on our heads, and Russia is not ready for it. Perilous finances, unrest among the peasantry, and discontent among the factory workers threaten the country. And then there is the tsar's obsession with the East, with Port Arthur. But most of all, it is his lack of strength that worries me."

"If he cannot be strong then you must give him strong advice."

Boris shook his head, "I try to give him strong advice, Marina, but there is a vast difference between advice and influence. I no sooner leave his presence than he listens to someone else's strong advice and changes his mind. I sometimes think that the only important person in Russia is whomever the tsar is talking to at any given moment."

"If only he did not have that awful Witte advising him, perhaps he would not be so indecisive."

"No, there you are mistaken. Sergei Witte is one of the few sane voices in the court. He and I are the only two who dare tell the tsar that his dreams of Russian military domination in Asia will come to no good. The Japanese are getting stronger each year and mean to have an empire there. Sometimes Nicholas seems to listen to me, for a while at least, but he only pays attention to Witte when it comes to financial matters. All his other advisors, particularly his generals, seem to have just one message: 'Expand, expand, and expand!' This is a message that fascinates him like no other.

"Sergei is disliked by the aristocracy, just as anyone who is close to the tsar is disliked. Many dislike me too. Add to this the fact that he lives to work and shuns most social events, and you have a perfect recipe for a target of malicious gossip. Many call him a belaya vorona, a white crow, a man who cannot fit in. Some think him too outspoken, Marina, but I think he is what the country needs."

CHAPTER 2

THE PASSING OF A SAMURAI, TOKYO 1896

Kenji Dainichi, returning from school, turned down his lane to find two carriages outside his house. The horses snorted and stamped impatiently and one of them emptied his bowels into the muddy street. Two enlisted soldiers leaned against the carriages, chatting, laughing and smoking. One of them glanced in Kenji's direction and said something softly to the other. As the boy approached they quickly crushed out their cigarettes and erased the smiles from their faces.

Kenji raced past them to the doorway and found it crowded with military boots. "Father!" he shouted as he hastily removed his shoes and rushed into the small house.

He recognized his two uncles, but his father was not among the four uniformed men who knelt on the tatami, conversing with his mother in low voices. She knelt motionless, eyes concentrated on the mat, hands clasped before her, silent. A single tear ran down her cheek. Before her on the mat, lay his father's cherished sword.

"Mother, what is wrong? Where is father?"

"He is dead, Kenji. He was killed in service to the emperor in the war against the Chinese."

Kenji bit his knuckles nearly hard enough to break the skin in order to keep from crying. Samurai did not cry and he could not disgrace his father's memory by crying.

The men whispered words of comfort to Kenji and his mother, saying how bravely Colonel Dainichi had died. Their sad duty finished, each bowed in turn to the new widow and her son. Kenji stared at them without returning the bow. His uncle Genichi touched his shoulder and said, "Kenji, we must talk about your future soon." Kenji looked up at him, his eyes glistening. As the delegation departed, Kenji's mother bent forward from her kneeling position and touched her head to the mat between her hands, a solemn gesture of farewell and resignation.

After the door slid shut, Kenji's mother sat up, dried her eyes, and silently stared at nothing. Kenji knelt close to his mother. His head whirled with many things he wanted to say, things he wanted to ask but he knew not how. Finally, his mother rose and busied herself making a simple meal. Mother and son ate sparingly and without conversation, their chopsticks softly tapping the edge of their bowls, their sorrow punctuated by thoughts of what losing the colonel would mean to the small family. Kenji knew his mother worried about money, which was in short supply even with a colonel's pay, and now would be smaller still for his widow. As they finished their meal she poured them both more tea and struggled to look at her son.

"Kenji …Kenji …" she began, breaking off into sobs. Finally, after a pause and several deep breaths, she said, "Kenji, you are my only child, your father's only son, and it is only proper that you become a soldier like your father and your grandfather. Becoming a soldier is the best way to serve His Majesty. You heard your father's last words to me. If something were to happen to him he told me to make sure you followed the family tradition. I never thought I would have to raise you alone, but he is gone and we will never see him again. Therefore, I must do what I can to prepare you for the Academy. Kenji, it is now more important than ever that you become a warrior. Japan is becoming a modern nation and we must be a strong one to keep the western nations from doing to us what they did to China."

Kenji's face fell. "I understand the importance of carrying on the family tradition, Mother, but I am too small and too weak to be a soldier, something that father did not understand. I cannot be a soldier."

"Kenji, you have the blood of great warriors. The gentlemen who visited with the news of your father's death brought his sword back to us. Now it is yours, and I know that someday you will wear it proudly. Look at it. This sword contains the spirit of your father and his father and grandfather before him and on back for more than three hundred years."

Kenji took the ancient sword. He had never been allowed to hold it before and he was surprised at its weight, and he turned it over. Grasping the diamond-patterned grip he drew a few inches of the gleaming blade from the plain black scabbard.

"Be careful, Kenji, this is a sixteenth century *koto*. The blade is sharper than a razor, and if you just touch the edge, it may cut you. Few of this quality are made anymore because the art of making them is all but lost. The blade was heated in the forge and pounded back over itself on an anvil, then flattened and folded again more than a thousand times to achieve the temper that satisfied its maker. It carries the soul of ten generations of Dainichis. What began as a useless piece of steel was transformed into a magnificent weapon for use by a warrior. Although you are small, the Academy will do for you what the sword maker did for this piece of steel." When you are gone you will pass it on to your own son.

Kenji studied the glistening blade, trying to imagine what battles it had been in and the character of his ancestors who had worn it. He gave a small shudder at the vision that came, of bloodshed, violence, *death*. He slid the sword back into its scabbard and with a bow to his mother silently laid it on the tatami.

CHAPTER 3

MOSCOW. THE SOCIAL DIVIDE

Poor neighborhoods ringed central Moscow, expanses of log cabins and two-story barracks that housed the city's clerks and laborers. In one of these neighborhoods the Gitin family talked at the dinner table.

"Why, Olga," Vladimir asked, "do you insist on taking Tatiana to that den of false notions? Nothing, I repeat nothing, has ever come of worshiping something no one has ever seen or ever will and the existence of which cannot be proven."

Olga folded her arms across her chest. "I believe in God, Vladimir, even if you do not, and He offers hope to us all, especially those of us who are poor. Church is the only chance I have to stand among the better classes of people and to show Tatiana that there may be an opportunity in this world, to say nothing of the next, to improve herself. Besides, she likes the music and the beauty of the Dormition Cathedral. And so, do I."

"That is another thing," he replied, waving his arms in frustration. "It is impossible for someone of our class to improve themselves. You should not plant such false hopes in Tatiana's head."

"I do like some parts of church, Papa," Tatiana said. "I just wish I could look around and talk and not be so serious. People are so unhappy there. Today I was so upset by the difference between rich and poor that I could not believe in God. When I said so to this rich boy, Mama made us leave the church. We are poor, but there are some really poor people there, and they are so serious and sad with their prayers. If there is a God, why does he not help the poor?"

Vladimir snorted, "God has never helped them and never will help them. That is one of the reasons I do not believe in him. Prayers are a waste of time. So is going to church. Go if you want, my little dumpling, just shut your mind to all the nonsense about God and enjoy the rest. Also keep in mind that depending on the so-called Little Father to help the poor is as false a notion as depending on God. It is unlikely that the tsar is able to help any of us poor. And it is more unlikely that he wants to."

The yellow light from a smoky oil lamp flickered across the rough plank table, a table that doubled as a bed for Tatiana. The room smelled as though it had been dead for generations. The chill of the evening seeped around the ever-crumbling mixture of clay and straw that caulked the cracks in the wooden plank walls. It was much worse in winter when the family slept in all the clothes they possessed. A small wooden crucifix, the hut's only adornment, hung over the one bed that was curtained off from the remainder of the small dwelling. The roof leaked when it rained hard and they shared the outside toilet with their neighbors. When the weather was really bad, they used a wooden commode, from which the stench of human waste, its surface glazed with ice in winter, filled the small house and stayed no matter how often they emptied it. The price of glass was beyond their means, and the single small window was open to the elements in summer and covered with oil paper in winter. That, the oil lamp and an occasional candle provided their only light. They bathed in a public bath whenever they could, rarely more than once a week and much less often in bad weather.

Despite their poverty, the Gitin family was far better off than many working families. Tatiana's father had ten years of schooling, was literate, and employed as a clerk. Less fortunate workers, the great majority, lived in barracks owned by the factories. They paid up to half of their monthly wage for close, smelly, vermin-filled rooms without windows or sanitation. The workers were invariably greasy, and dirty, and soot-covered and rarely found an opportunity to bathe.

Vladimir Gitin ate his cabbage soup, boiled potatoes, raw onions, and tough pieces of black bread as he talked to his wife and daughter about their day. A thick forelock, mostly gray, fell over his forehead, and his stubble-covered cheeks moved as he talked around the food in his mouth. He was a small, lean man with a briar patch of eyebrows and thick, full mustache, giving him a feral look. Everyone noticed his nearly black, flashing eyes, eyes that he passed along to his daughter.

A man of great passions, quick to anger and slow to forgive except with his small family, he loved his plump, nearly toothless wife and beautiful child as much as anything in the world, and they tempered his anger. His mother wanted him to become a priest, and the monks taught him to read and write in the years he prepared for the seminary. By his late teens he saw much that was wrong with the world and became a confirmed atheist. His mother was heartbroken that he rejected the church, but his father, a sickly man, was happy to have his son working and helping the family with his income. Both of his parents had died in their early forties, as most Russians did, and like most Russian men, Vladimir was the sole support of his family. He and his wife were grateful that they had but one child. They had no idea how they would support two.

Across the city in the Medved mansion a maid announced supper. The children washed and dressed in clean clothes waited behind their chairs. Marina sat first, her chair held by a servant. Boris sat next and then the Natalya and Ivan. The snowy napery and the new electric lights highlighted the silver and china and brightened the room.

As they ate Prince Medved talked with his son about the latest territorial obsession of the court—the acquisition of an all-weather port on the Pacific. Vladivostok was Russia's only port but ice clogged the harbor for six to nine months of the year. The tsar's generals were fixated on the idea of a port farther south, one they could use in all seasons. This sort of father-son topic was common at the Medved dinner table. His wife and daughter shut it out and carried on their own low-key conversation. Boris was used to having an audience of one.

"But Papa," Ivan said, "are not the Japanese just backward little people? You told me that Tsar Nicholas calls them 'monkeys.' Surely, they are not as good as Russians, and we can easily keep them from taking Port Arthur from us."

"Yes, the tsar calls them monkeys, but I wonder ...they have been pushing the Chinese around in their own country for some time now, and it looks like they may take over Korea. I think the tsar still hates them from the time when an assassin nearly killed him when he visited Japan as our crown prince. That scar on his head is a painful memory. I think that assuming we can beat them is dividing the skin of an unskilled bear."

Ivan bounced in his seat, "If we fight them I hope we wait until I am grown and out of the military academy, and then *I* can fight them and I know we will win."

"Enough of this talk of fighting," said his mother, who had briefly tuned in the conversation. "Why is it that men have to always talk about war and violence? Ivan, you have plenty of time to decide how you serve Russia. What did you say to that little girl in church today?"

"She told her mother that she thought that believing in God was superstition, and I told her that she was being disrespectful."

"If she believes religion is superstition, I wonder why her mother brought her to church. There seem to be many like that girl these days, too many if you ask me. But never mind. As soon as we finish supper you and your sister must get to your studies. And do not forget that Madame Charbonneau is coming for your dancing lessons tomorrow. You must practice your steps together."

Ivan rolled his eyes and groaned at the thought of having to dance at all, especially with his sister. Natalya smiled and clapped her hands no doubt imagining herself with a handsome young Guards officer or another member of the aristocracy who would sweep her off her feet and with whom she would fall in love and be happy forever.

For dessert the children ate a chocolate confection. Boris had brandy and his wife more tea.

Boris retired to his study to take up the pile of documents that needed tending. His study was his refuge and his house of labor. Surrounded by thousands of books that gleamed like trophies, and mementoes of the War of 1812, his teak desk stood on an antique Persian carpet. He paused for a moment, his eyes running over the books, wondering where he had found time to read them. A servant quietly entered the study, placed a cup of tea on Boris's desk, added a few logs to the small fire to deal with the evening chill, and silently closed the door behind him. The new wood in the fireplace blazed red and yellow as the fire consumed the bark. The prince's forty-eight-year-old face, lined and weary, creased with far too many wrinkles and framed by silver-gray hair and beard, testified to his exhaustion. His eye sockets were the color of ash. The years had stolen his youth and vitality. He sat down heavily in the chair behind his desk, held his head in his hands for a long moment, sighed, and turned to his work.

Before he could begin, Marina came into the study carrying several sheets of paper. "Boris, before you begin work, could you go over the shopping list I am going to give to Mr. Sobole? He is leaving for his semi-annual trip to Paris tomorrow."

"What? Oh yes, Marina."

He listened with half an ear as his wife read through the list. Four gowns for herself and two for her daughter, four pairs of trousers and a new frock coat each for Boris and Ivan, a hundred pounds of fine loose tobacco, three hundred cigars, twenty pounds of coffee, ten pounds of truffles and on and on. He quickly snapped out of his reverie by her question.

"Do you think that three hundred bottles each of red wine and white wine will be enough; and two hundred bottles of champagne?"

In order to show that he was listening, he said, "Perhaps you should order five hundred of champagne. It becomes more popular every season."

"Thank you, my dear," Marina said as she left the room. "You are quite right."

Prince Medved returned to his work.

CHAPTER 4

THE PEACH GIRL

A few days after Kenji learned of the death of his father, he walked down the street to find his friend Momoko Higashi. Kenji had first met her when they were both little more than infants. Their mothers often took them to a nearby park and began conversing while their children, shyly at first, became acquainted. Neither mother particularly liked the other. Kenji's family came from a line of soldiers, Momoko's from a line of successful merchants. The two classes did not normally mix, but politeness overcame social differences and the two mothers frequently visited in the park where their children played together. Despite each mother's cool attitude toward the other the two children grew fond of each other and had remained friends until they were old enough go to the park without supervision. Most weeks they would meet two or three times at the park, play, and share their dreams.

A maid slid open the door of the Higashi house and then fetched Momoko, who greeted Kenji happily. She held her cat, Snow Cloud. Snow Cloud was a rare animal, pure white with one yellow eye and one green eye. The eye colors were said to represent gold and silver and to be lucky. Momoko's father was fond of both gold and silver and had paid a small fortune for Momoko's pet.

Kenji reached out to scratch its head and said, "Hello, Snow Cloud." The cat wriggled in Momoko's arms, wanting to be let down. He landed on the floor with a thump and disappeared into the rear of the house.

Momoko smiled broadly at the appearance of Kenji, her cheeks as soft and pink as a peach, the fruit for which she was named, her hair a matte black like powdered charcoal. Today she wore a bright pink kimono, patterned with white irises, which set off her complexion. Her small feet were clad in spotless *tabi*, split-toe socks.

"Let's walk down to the park, Momoko. I need to be in the sunshine."

Momoko stepped down into the entrance, slid the door closed behind her and slipped on *geta*, wooden clogs like the ones Kenji wore, that kept her feet an inch above the dirt of the street.

As the two children clopped down the street toward the public gardens, Momoko spied Ogawa-san, the tofu vendor. He shuffled through the neighborhood, shouting out the quality of his wares. Two oblong wooden buckets bobbed at the ends of the long pole he bore across his shoulder, pieces of fried tofu of various flavors resting on the buckets' lids.

"Kenji, let's get some tofu. I have a few sen my mother gave me."

They called out to the vendor, who wore a conical straw hat and a short jacket with the characters for tofu on the back. Ogawa-san's bulging eyes, fearsome wild eyebrows, and naturally scowling expression reminded Kenji of a villain in a Kabuki play. His cheerful disposition shone through his fearsome appearance though and he loved children.

Ogawa-san grinned when he saw the children approach and set his burden on the ground. "Young master, young mistress, which of my delicious wares can I tempt you with today?"

Kenji chose a piece flavored with sesame seeds and Momoko selected one coated with the dried fish that Japanese housewives often used to flavor their food. Ogawa rapidly wrapped the chosen pieces in squares of paper and presented them to the children with a flourish as Momoko dropped the coins into his hand.

He smiled broadly and said, "Enjoy my tofu, and do not forget: tell your mothers that mine is the best and they should buy from me."

Momoko laughed. "This is the same thing you always say Ogawa-san. You know our mothers would never buy from someone else."

They continued toward the park. After a few steps, Momoko said, "Kenji, why do you look so unhappy?"

"Momoko, my father is dead. He has been killed in the war in China."

Momoko's hand flew to her mouth and her eyes widened. "Oh, Kenji. I am so sorry."

"Momoko, I am so sad. I don't know what we will do without him. As long as I can remember he has told me that he expected me to follow him into the army and to serve the emperor like him. I never told him that my secret desire was to go to university and study literature. I am not cut out for the Ichigaya Academy. I am too small and too weak. When my father was alive, I felt that I had no choice, but I thought that with his support I might be able to get through the Academy. But with him gone …I don't think I can make it. Yet my mother and my uncles constantly talk about my going to the military academy and following the path of my father and grandfathers. Momoko, I don't know what to do. If I go to the Academy, I am sure to fail and disgrace the family."

Momoko listened solemnly and murmured her condolences as they knelt on the grass near a pond. From the willows, a shower of green tendrils cascaded toward the water. Near them, nature tested her new palette. Winter's work was finished for the year and had passed the baton to spring. The budding trees fired Kenji's imagination, and for a moment he forgot what troubled him. A partially formed haiku struggled to escape his mind, but the sharp edge of reality aborted the poem in mid-creation and unrecognizable pieces of it littered the ground of his spirit. He slumped and sighed, his misery renewed.

A mother duck led her brood across the grass toward the water. One duckling fell out of ranks and wandered around in circles squawking loudly. Kenji chased it down, gently picked it up, and reunited it with its family just as it went into the water. The ducks hurried across the pond, pulling the long Vs of their wakes behind them, serene in their movements, their bodies gliding peacefully along, their feet paddling furiously out of sight. *How like me they are,* Kenji thought, *calm on the outside but frantic below the surface.*

Kenji dominated Momoko's feelings and thoughts since she could remember but they were not emotions she had ever expressed to anyone. She lovingly and continuously caressed her dreams. She knew that both families had begun to worry about their friendship as they grew older. It was one thing for them to be friends as children, but they were in their early teens now and both families feared that it might lead to some sort of romantic attachment.

Momoko looked softly at her brooding friend and her mind wandered to her own future, what sort of marriage she might make and to what sort of man. Could it be Kenji, or someone like him? Her family were wealthy merchants and although they possessed many times more money than Kenji's family could ever dream of having, they were still only merchants, far below the samurai in social status.

Momoko's four older brothers all worked in the family business. The Higashi family dedicated itself to holding onto and increasing their wealth. They rose early, worked hard, often into the night, and made a religion out of wasting neither time nor money. Momoko's father thought of little else other than expanding his business. Spoiling his daughter was her father's only concession to wealth. He expected that she would marry into another wealthy merchant family or marry a particularly talented young man that the family could put to work in their own business. He kept a watchful eye out for a suitable husband for his treasure. Kenji met none of his qualifications for a son-in-law. Momoko's mother was polite to Kenji but her father, suspicious that there might be a growing attachment between the two youngsters, wore hostility like a suit of armor and was often rude. Momoko knew that her father hoped that Kenji would grow up and go away to military school and leave his daughter to a prosperous future. Kenji's mother was likewise chilly to Momoko. She knew about the family wealth but, even though she must have felt in need of money from time to time, she still looked down on the merchant class.

"Kenji, it will be another four years before you can even go to the military academy, Momoko said, "Much can change by that time."

"Maybe, but I doubt that my mother or my uncles will change their minds. All they ever talk to me about is how important it is that I take my father's place."

With that, the pair stood, brushed the grass from their clothing and slowly walked home. Momoko wondered if she should put her arms around Kenji and comfort him. Unsure of his reaction, she merely reached over and squeezed Kenji's hand at the lane where they parted.

Kenji went home, unrolled a futon and lay on it, staring at the ceiling for a long time.

CHAPTER 5

MOSCOW: TRAGEDY'S AFTERMATH

The day after the tragedy at Khodynka meadow Tsar Nicholas sat in his study with Boris Medved and Sergei Witte. He held his head in his hands, his plain gray tunic and grave mood contrasting with the royal splendor of his surroundings. The light was dim, the corners of the room deep in somnolent shadow.

"It was a riot, Your Majesty," said Boris Medved. "God be praised that it started and was over before Your Highnesses arrived. No telling what would have happened had you been there."

The tsar looked up and spoke slowly. "How many killed and injured, Boris?"

"The dead are over a thousand, maybe as many as three thousand. The wounded could be twice that. I am not sure we will ever get a complete count."

"What an omen of bad luck for my reign! What is to be done? I have told my physician to round up as many doctors as he can find to treat the wounded, and Witte, the treasury is to spend whatever is required to help the families of the killed. Begin with 250,000 rubles. Take it out of my personal funds. I will add more if necessary. Whatever it takes."

"Yes, Your Majesty."

The tsar walked slowly to his private apartments, deep in thought, his eyes fixed on the ground before him, and had walked past the door to his inner sanctum by some twenty paces before for he realized his mistake and turned back. The tsarina, Alexandra, tears streaming down her cheeks, met him at the door and led him to a sofa, where he nearly collapsed into her arms. The royal couple had lain awake most of the night grieving over the event.

"Oh, Sunny," he said to his wife, "what bad luck. What bad luck. Why has God chosen to give me such a burden?"

"Poor Nicky," she said, stroking his head. "God is but testing you. You are the tsar by his will. You must be strong and live up to your mandate."

"I know, Sunny, but sometimes it is so hard. I just do not know what to do at times like this. I have told the finance minister to dispense funds from my personal treasury to help the wounded and console the families of the dead. But how can I replace the dead?" The tsar looked up with tears in his eyes as he said the last. "Such a bad omen! I wonder what will become of us. What will become of Russia?"

The French ambassador, Marquis de Monebello, had scheduled a grand ball for the royal couple that evening. Nicholas and Alexandra, who had spent a long day visiting the injured in hospitals, discussed whether they should attend the ball in the face of such tragedy.

"Nicky, we just cannot go," said Alexandra, "I am afraid that I will cry through the entire thing. Please send our regrets to the

Marquis and tell him that I am too sad. Besides, it will look worse if we go than if we do not."

"I agree, Sunny, I will send a note right away."

As he was dictating a note to his secretary, a maid announced that the tsar's four uncles, the Grand Dukes Vladimir, Boris, Paul, and Alexei were waiting to see him. They had anticipated that their indecisive nephew might decide that he could not attend the ball.

Vladimir, the eldest, spoke for the group. 'Nicholas, you must pull yourself together …" He hammered the young tsar with reason after reason why the ball should go on. The others said little but nodded their heads, murmuring their assent when Vladimir hit the important points. "Canceling the ball would be a scandal," he said, "and an insult to the French. The French government has spent untold thousands of francs shipping massive amounts of silver, rare tapestries, and over ten thousand roses from the south of France especially for the occasion." The arguments overwhelmed the young tsar and he agreed to attend. He broke the news to his wife, who began crying.

That night the royal couple, somberly attired, opened the first dance and exchanged pleasantries with members of the diplomatic corps. Then they sat and watched the other celebrants. They spoke little, each absorbed by the events on Khodynka Meadow. Alexandra dabbed her red eyes throughout the affair, and one observer said it was the saddest ball he had ever seen. Just an hour after the ball began, the tsar could stand it no longer. Alexandra was sobbing into her handkerchief, and he felt himself ready to burst out in tears. He spoke with the Marquis de Monebello and made his excuses. Then he took the tsarina on his arm and they rode back to their Kremlin apartment, where Alexandra collapsed and wept uncontrollably.

Without the tsar and his wife, the ball sputtered to a close within the hour and the guests left in a subdued mood.

The attendance of the royal couple at a ball, as brief as it was, in the wake of such a great tragedy did not go unnoticed by their enemies or by those who were on the border between empathy with, and scorn of, the tsarist system. Revolutionaries, some of whom were imprisoned or in exile, rejoiced at news of the tragedy and of the royal reaction to it. They felt that another spark had been added to help start the flame of revolution. They began calling Nicholas the "Bloody Tsar."

The day after the tragedy on the meadow, Vladimir Gitin lay in a blackout in his bed too unconscious to respond to the pounding on his door. A Medved footman found the factory where Vladimir worked. The manager was reluctant to talk to a footman until his clerk told him that the man was a servant in the household of Prince Medved and reminded him that Medved was one of the most powerful men in Russia. The manager required no further explanation. The Medved servant was ushered into his office, and the manager, an obscenely fat man dressed in a coat spotted with food stains and cigar ash, leapt to his feet, pasted a wide smile on his face and extended a damp and dirty palm.

"Welcome, my dear fellow. Who did you say you are looking for?"

"I am looking for one of your workers, a man named Vladimir Gitin."

"Stepan," the manager asked his clerk, "do we have such an employee?"

"I will check, sir."

The footman obediently waited outside the manager's office for over an hour until Stepan came back with the information.

"Yes, we had a Vladimir Gitin employed here, as a clerk in the shipping department office, but he did not show up for work today, so his supervisor ordered that he be fired."

"Do you know where he lives?"

"Our workers come and go so often that we do not keep that information, but knowing you were looking for him, I asked his supervisor, who asked Gitin's fellow workers. They do not know the exact location, but I have written down a description of what they do know."

Armed with their information, the footman found the depressing block on which the Gitin family lived. After knocking on doors and asking on the street he was directed to a small, unpainted shack. He knocked and knocked, but no one answered the door. He left to question neighbors and came back and knocked again. After spending the better part of a day beating on the Gitins' door and wandering the neighborhood, he gave up, returned to the Medved residence, and reported his failure to Marina.

She talked to Tatiana and confirmed that the house described by the footman was hers. Then Marina asked about where Tatiana's father could have been.

"He rarely goes out, except to work," Tatiana said, "and sometimes he goes to a meeting. But the meetings he goes to are in the evening. He should be at work during the day, so if he's not there, I don't know where he is. I'm sure that he's worried about Mama and me so maybe he is out looking for us."

"What kind of meetings does he go to, Tatiana?"

"I don't know. He won't tell me. I know that my mother asks him to not go. I wouldn't even know he was going to meetings if I hadn't heard him talking to Mama. Please take me home. Where is my Mama? When can I go home?"

"You should not even think about going home until we find your parents. Don't worry, dear, we'll find them."

Eyes hollow from a poor night's sleep, the little girl sat in the large bed looking small and vulnerable. Marina personally spoon-fed her for the rest of the day, and by the next morning Tatiana was able to breakfast with the rest of the family. Marina seated the girl next to herself so she could make sure she ate. The elegant table-ware astounded her, as did the fresh flowers in the center of the enormous table and the rich variety of food before her. This was the first time she had tasted white bread and fresh fruit, but she ate little of anything. Natalya ignored Tatiana and was unhappy about another young girl in the house, and especially about this stranger being clothed in her own dresses, even old ones. The young beauty enchanted Ivan though, and he tried to cheer her up.

"If you come with me, Tatiana, I can show you my horse."

Marina gently nodded her approval.

Tatiana shyly followed him through the back door of the mansion to the stables.

"This is my horse, Svoboda, Freedom," he said. "Here, give her this."

He reached into a bucket hanging on the wall and produced a withered apple.

She had never touched a horse before and recoiled in fear. "Won't she bite me?"

"It is okay, Tatiana, she will not hurt you."

Tatya held out the apple and the mare took it out of her hand with velvet lips, chewed and swallowed it, then fixed its bottomless, melancholy eyes on her expectantly.

"Give her one more and that will be enough," Ivan said.

Tatiana was amazed at the softness of the horse's nose and mouth. She wondered how anyone could be rich enough to have all these things and to live in a house like this and to have one's own horse.

Ivan led her into the house where he showed her all his toys and games. As they encountered servants, Ivan would introduce her. They curtsied or bowed, which made her very uncomfortable. The young maid, Nina, was the exception. She eyed Tatiana critically and merely nodded.

The horror of the meadow clung to her mind, the absence of her parents terrified her, and the stunning luxury in which she suddenly found herself confused her. She cried periodically during the day and often during the night, longing for her mother and father.

On the fifth day after the tragedy, one of the Medved servants came returned to the house to report a success. "I have Tatiana's father in the carriage, but the man is drunk, dirty and incoherent." Boris went outside for a look.

Vladimir Gitin was slumped against the seat. He had a week's stubble on his face and he was filthy from head to foot, and he stank from alcohol and body odors.

"What am I doing here, your honor?" he asked. "Am I under arrest?"

"No, you are not under arrest," said Boris. "We have your daughter and we have been looking for you."

A look of disbelief and then of joy spread across the tattered face. "You have Tatiana? I thought she was dead like her poor mother."

"We did not know about her mother," Boris replied, "and we are sorry, but we do have your daughter. She is emotionally upset but well. In time she will be fine. I suppose you will be taking her right home?"

"Now, Boris," said his wife coming up behind him, "Tatiana is very weak and upset and can stay for a few more days if her father will let her."

"I will take her home where she belongs," said Vladimir. "She no longer has a mother, and I need to tell her that. And all because of the tsar, may he and his reign both be damned."

Boris's face tightened with anger at the insult to his sovereign, but his sense of the man's bereavement kept him from responding.

"I will fetch her," said Marina, "and I will have the maids pack a bag for her."

"Bag? She has no bag and does not need your charity."

"You, sir, are drunk! Do you have money to feed her, to clothe her? It is not charity to help out a poor child who has just lost her mother."

The woman's vehemence silenced Vladimir. He lolled in the carriage until Tatiana was brought to him. He'd thought he had lost her forever, and the sight of her brought tears to his eyes. She cried loudly and hugged her father. She wrinkled her nose at his filthy condition and immediately flushed with shame. The servants loaded a hamper of food and a bag of clothes for Tatiana to the carriage, and Boris thrust a small purse into Vladimir's hand.

"I know, sir, that no amount of money can make up for your loss but the tsa ...that is, those of us who did not lose anyone in the unfortunate incident at the meadow would like to help those who did. Please accept this small amount as a token of our condolences."

Vladimir, his arms still around Tatiana, absently thrust the purse into his pocket as the coach pulled away.

Tatiana could not tear her eyes away from her father's face as the carriage rumbled away. She had never seen him look so ruined. "Tatya, I have the worst possible news about your poor mother" he said, weeping. "She died in the meadow."

"Oh, Papa," she cried, "What will we do without her?" She had never imagined a world without her loving mother. She leaned into her father and sobbed all the way home.

When he got home, Vladimir emptied the purse that Prince Medved had given him onto the rough plank table and found a dozen small gold coins, more money than he normally made in two year's time.

Father and daughter had little to say to each other for the rest of the day. They both had a restless night, tossing fitfully under a pall of sadness and loss. After the soft bed at the Medveds, Tatiana had a difficult night sleeping on her old table.

Before Vladimir turned in, he took a bath for the first time in many days. Then he took the rest of his vodka outside and poured it into the dirt. When he reported for work the next morning, he found his boss was angry with him but did not fire him because Prince Boris Medved had sent someone around to ask that he be kept on.

Tatiana did not leave the house for several days except to shop for food. She had helped her mother but was not able to clean or do the wash as well. She thought she could at least go out to buy black bread, mushrooms, and onions. She had learned a few rudiments of cooking from her mother and knew to boil cabbage and potatoes for soup. Her worries about being responsible for taking over her mother's old chores added to her grief. She made up her mind that she would just have to get things done and that was that. She frequently thought about the few days she had spent at the Medveds' and what she remembered was more like a tear-filled dream than reality. At times she was not at all sure whether she had really experienced a world so different than her own or she had imagined it in some sort of a pink-cloud dream.

For several weeks Ivan looked for Tatiana every Sunday in church but never saw her there. She was different from anyone he had ever met, which made her interesting, and he was curious to know how she was. Finally, he approached the footman who had found Tatiana's father and knew where she lived.

"Will you take me there?" he asked.

"Not without the permission of your father," the man said.

Ivan was reluctant to ask his father but finally got up courage to ask his mother if he could visit her.

"I do not think that is a good idea, my dear." She reflected for a moment, "But what if we go to her house on Saturday and invite her to go to church with us on Sunday? If she would like to go with us, we can pick her up beforehand."

"Mama, that would be wonderful."

The next Saturday Ivan and his mother set out in the family's carriage to find Tatiana's house. The still-jealous Natalya refused to go. Boris reluctantly agreed to the scheme but sent along two of his burliest employees as security.

For the first time in his life, Ivan paid attention to the squalid neighborhood that was common in Moscow. He had passed through them before but never really noticed them. He had never before known a person from this level of society, nor understood that people who lived in such impoverished neighborhoods were real and had genuine problems and bleak futures. When they reached the Gitins' small house, Ivan and his mother remained in the carriage while the footman knocked on the door. Vladimir Gitin answered the door, looking clean and sober and altogether better than when they had last seen him. Standing behind him, trying to see what was going on, was Tatiana. At the footman's invitation they both came out to the carriage to talk with the Medveds.

"Mr. Gitin," said Ivan's mother, "we have come to invite you and your daughter to go to church with us tomorrow."

Vladimir looked around him as if to see who might be watching the exchange. "I do not go to church because I do not believe in God. Sometimes Tatya enjoys it. But I don't know … Sunday is the only day I have to spend with Tatiana, and I would rather be with just her alone."

"Oh Papa, may I go?" Tatiana asked." Church reminds me of Mama, and I would like to pray for her."

Sunday couldn't come soon enough, and Tatiana felt a great sense of comfort as she prayed for her mother in the incense-sweet surroundings of the church. Afterwards the Medveds took her to their home for dinner and she realized how much she had already forgotten about the luxury in which the Medveds lived. For his part, Ivan was happy to see her again and asked if she could stay. Natalya frowned, and the prince rolled his eyes, but Marina once again gave the young girl a wistful look that Tatiana had learned was evoked by her resemblance to Marina's lost sister. She smiled sadly as if they both shared a loss.

It was late afternoon before the carriage pulled up to the Gitins' door. Tatiana alighted with a basket of food from the Medveds' house.

She paused to thank the Medveds as her father came out the door.

Marina asked him, "Who looks after your daughter during the day, now that your wife is, uh …gone?"

"I have to leave her at home alone, but Mrs. Peretsky, a neighbor, looks in on her some days."

"Does she go to school?"

"Sometimes she goes but mostly not. It's a long walk, and we cannot afford the books and such. I have taught her how to read and write a little. And how to do sums."

"What if I send a carriage for her on the days when Mrs. Peretsky cannot look in on her? As for schooling, we have any number of tutors at the house every day, and I am sure that three children cannot be that much more difficult than two for them to teach."

Tatiana's heart leapt at the thought, and she turned her eager gaze to her father.

"I don't know, ma'am, you being the family of a prince, and all, and me just a poor working man. I am not sure it would be good for any of the children, either yours or mine."

"Please think about this, Mr. Gitin. It is an opportunity for her to become educated which is an advantage not many of the working classes have."

Vladimir thought about this for a few moments. He was solidly against polluting his daughter with an association with the privileged. He was an intelligent man, though, and he finally decided that, despite his reservations, Tatiana's future would be better if she were at least literate. Even better, by learning the ways of the aristocracy she might be more useful in overthrowing the old and creating the New Russia that he longed for.

CHAPTER 6

THE EDUCATION OF A SCHOLAR. TOKYO 1901

The military clan that had ruled Japan for two hundred fifty years had been deposed for half a century and Emperor Meiji was restored to the throne. He and his councilors decided that Japan should take her place among the world's most modern and powerful nations by building their own empire in Asia. They knew how the Western powers had forced open and then exploited India, China and lesser nations and were determined to avoid the same fate by adopting a constitution and quickly creating a modern army and navy. They had made tremendous progress by 1901, but the military powers of the West looked upon them with scorn. To them, Japan was a tiny nation, island-bound and insignificant in the real course of things. If anything, the country was just another exploitable Asian nation that one or more of the Western powers would subjugate sooner or later. Someone would get around to it.

Tokyo was the most modern and exciting city in Asia. The government laid tracks for horse-drawn streetcars; rickshaws crowded streets everywhere. Western dress competed with traditional Japanese fashion. Oftentimes the Japanese mixed the two, as when men wore a kimono with a Western-type suit coat over the top half and a Western-style hat, a fedora. The Japanese favored native dress for all traditional functions at court, but white tie and tails and Paris gowns accompanied by precious jewels dominated the scene at social functions.

As Japanese diets changed, they began to eat beef and more pork, a practice nearly abandoned a millennium earlier at the height of the Buddhist period.

Eager to copy their European counterparts, the highborn and the educated learned foreign languages and absorbed Western literature. They read Dickens, Rousseau, de Maupassant, Tolstoy and Dostoevsky.

The new admirals and generals completely reorganized the armed forces along European lines. A conscript army replaced the uneven quality and insufficient quantity of the samurai who had protected the country in the past. Members of the samurai class still dominated the highest levels of the military, but a rising crop of young officers who came from humbler beginnings crowded the lower ranks. The four-class system of samurai, farmers, artisans, and the lowly merchants was officially abolished, though remnants of it influenced the behavior of many.

In the schools, instructors repeatedly enjoined students to "offer yourselves courageously to the state and thus guard and maintain the prosperity of Our Imperial Throne coeval with heaven and earth ...infallible for all ages, and true in all places."

By the turn of the twentieth century the island kingdom had already been training her best military officers with European powers for decades. The Japanese, who had no maritime tradition, began building warships and trained their naval officers with the

British Navy. Their army officers went to Europe and observed the Franco-Prussian War of 1870.

Those who yearned for Japanese expansion on the Asian mainland, and there were many, formed ultra-nationalist groups in secret. The Western powers shattered Chinese and Korean sovereignty, promoted internal strife, and exploited these countries for their own purposes. Japan wanted part of this bounty, and the only power with the potential of thwarting Japanese aims in Asia was Imperial Russia.

One of Kenji's uncles, without fully disclosing his purpose, arranged for him to be tutored by a young member of the Black Ocean Society an organization that envisioned the conquest of all of East Asia.

Kenji was told that Eizo Araki was a devoted scholar of Japanese literature.

Only a few years older than Kenji, Araki was an accomplished poet and calligrapher, and Kenji enjoyed the hours they spent composing haiku and discussing literature. As his lessons progressed Araki began to talk about political matters, matters to which Kenji had given little thought.

"I have exciting news, Kenji. A member of the Black Ocean Society has begun a new movement called the Black Dragon Society. Its founder is Ryohei Uchida. Uchida-san is ahead of his time, Kenji. China and Korea are weak and ripe for the plucking. The Russians mean to expand at their expense, and we mean to stop them. Japan is the land of the rising sun. China's time has passed. It is the land of the setting sun. Mark my words, Kenji, Japan will come to dominate East Asia. We are a country that is rich in spirit but poor in natural resources. We will dominate Korea and China.

The Russians must be stopped. They are a large country but they are weak. We revere our emperor; theirs is barely holding onto power. Uchida-san spent time in Siberia and learned Russian, a difficult language that I am struggling with and one that you should begin."

Kenji said, "Yes, sensei," thinking, *If I learn Russian I can read Russian literature too!*

Under Araki's tutelage, Kenji Dainichi's education proceeded apace. Araki sensei's ideas reflected the philosophy of the new nationalists who envisioned Japan's dominance over the East. He was totally focused on the future of Japan. They would discuss Kenji's future over tea after the lessons.

"It is not enough in today's world to be familiar with Japan's history and literature," Araki said. "Japan has been liberated from the political and social tyranny of the shoguns. Now it must be liberated from the tyranny of our past. Like it or not, Japan is now open to the West. In order to survive we must become modernized. Look at what has happened to India, to China, to the countries of Africa and Latin America.

"Japan now has a constitution. We took Western ideas and adapted them to Japanese values. The emperor will always be supreme. As for the actual running of the country, we need modernists, who understand what is necessary for us to successfully break out of the cocoon of feudalism. These modernists must also be patriots, with the interests of Japan, and only Japan, always in mind.

"We are determined to modernize and join the family of strong nations in the shortest time possible."

"But what does this have to do with me?" Kenji asked. "I want to become a scholar, a professor."

"If you become a professor, you can help Japan by learning of the West through the West's point of view. However, you can do greater things. You are small but very bright and can be one of us, one of the fortunate few who hold the future of Japan in our hands. Learn to read as many foreign languages as you can manage. You must be able read the history and literature of foreigners. It is through studying these subjects that you can get into the mind of those who might threaten us. You must read the military classics. The great Chinese military strategist, Sun Tzu, has been translated into Japanese. The others, the German military philosopher Clausewitz, for example, must be read in other languages for the present. Study hard, Kenji. Whatever career path you set upon, you will be of great service to our emperor."

"Yes, sensei."

Kenji Dainichi rapidly read through the important works in Japanese. He learned enough French to be able to struggle through Balzac and Flaubert. At Araki's urging he concentrated on Russian. He liked it because he could enjoy the rich tales of the writers from the golden age of Russian literature: Pushkin, Tolstoy, Lermontov and others. Araki approved of his interest in Russian because of the teachings of Uchida and the latter's warning about keeping Russia out of Asia. English interested Kenji less but he learned to read and speak a bit. He also devoted a lot of effort on trying to understand the industrial revolution that began in the West over a century before. To this end he read politics and history, particularly the history of warfare.

He was still small for his age and was relatively weak. He hated the martial arts, including judo and especially kendo, mock fencing using bamboo staves instead of swords and wicker armor to protect against serious injury. He would have avoided martial arts altogether if not for the insistence of his uncle Genichi and Araki. He finally gave in to their arguments when they convinced him that the four pillars of kendo were grace, sincerity, dignity, and wisdom.

The first time he tried kendo he stood with other beginners in the dojo, a hall used for the teaching of martial arts. The instructor began with a lecture on the importance of the sword, even in today's army. "The sword carries with it the spirit of bushido, the way of the warrior. Imperial Army officers carry the sword into combat along with other weapons. It is the sword that gives them spiritual power. To use it successfully you must become one with the sword. You must be able to use it without thinking about it. The sword and your mind, your spirit, must be one and the same. Do you understand?"

Few of the students did understand, but they chorused, "Yes, sensei!"

First, two instructors demonstrated how to grip the staves and the basic stances. Then they launched into a series of choreographed moves, simple tactics of basic offense and defense. They demonstrated the kiri, or cut; tsuki, or thrust; and the chiburi, the shaking off of the blood on one's sword.

Kenji understood the theory behind sword fighting but he blanched at the thought of getting out there and failing, of making a fool of himself in front of the others.

After a half hour of demonstration, the instructor paired off the students and told them to don the armor and choose staves. The instructor paired Kenji with a boy much larger than him.

Under the supervision of an instructor, they stood facing each other on the mat. Kenji squinted through the narrow slit in the wicker helmet, struggling to focus on his opponent. The helmet was too big for him, and anytime he moved it shifted enough that he could not see. He began sweating before he even gripped his wooden sword in both hands and attempted to assume the ready position. The sweat ran into Kenji's eyes, further blurring his vision. The instructor led the two combatants through a series of slow-motion parries and thrusts to see if they had the basics down.

When he was satisfied, he told them to stop and face each other three paces apart. Then he shouted, "Hajime!" Before Kenji could even plant his feet solidly and get a good grip on his stave, his opponent was all over him, pummeling him severely about the head and shoulders.

"Stop," the instructor shouted. "Dainichi-san, are you just going to stand there or are you going to fight?"

"I will fight, sensei," came Kenji's muffled reply.

"Well, then do so!"

Once more the two faced off, and the instructor shouted for them to begin. This time was no better than the first. Kenji's opponent had no real skills. He did not need them against such a small, weak man. He simply beat on Kenji until Kenji's head was awhirl and his hands stung from trying to block his opponent's rapid slashes that seemed to come from every direction.

After several more tries during which Kenji only got weaker and more confused by the pummeling, the instructor sent him and his sparring partner to the sideline and called out two more students.

Kenji removed his wicker armor and wiped the sweat from his face with the sleeve of his *gi*. He could hardly catch his breath, his ears rang, and his reddened palms throbbed with pain. Across the circle of students his opponent grinned at him, his eyes telegraphing contempt. Unable to meet his gaze, Kenji looked away, bit his lip in shame, fearing the next time he would have to face him.

He took solace in the words of his instructor: "You will learn by being struck."

In match after match, Kenji slowly improved but still lagged far behind his schoolmates and he was often the first to lose a bout. The other students knew this, and several whom he had befriended always volunteered to compete with him so they could take it easy on him and make him look better than he was. Others were not so kind, taking malicious pleasure in beating him down as quickly and savagely as possible because he was such an easy victory. Over time he discovered that he *was* learning by being struck. Once he got over his nervousness and fear, he began to take note of where he had been hit and how his opponent had scored the blow.

Thinking of his father's spirit and the disappointment of his family if he failed, Kenji vowed to never quit. And he learned to put his quick mind to work to compensate for his physical weaknesses. He carefully watched bouts between the other students. He noted small weakness that could be exploited when he faced them. He noted that most his opponents would glance at the instructors from time to time or at the other students and during these brief inattentions he would strike. After a while, other students were no longer so eager to come up against him.

CHAPTER 7

ZOLUSHKA-THE RUSSIAN CINDERELLA

In the beginning Tatiana stayed an occasional overnight at the Medved mansion; then it was one night a week and then two or more. She did not see her father that much anyway. He worked a ten-hour shift each day and then went out nearly every night. The Medved's coach would deliver her to her father's little house after church on Sunday, the only day he had off. She was also able to get to the house one or two evenings a week to prepare supper for him. With help from the Medveds' servants, she also learned to do the laundry and cleaning for him and acquired some cooking skills. Within a year it became obvious she had surpassed Vladimir in her reading ability, her facility with arithmetic, and a variety of other subjects.

"Intellectuals will be the brains of the movement," he told her, "and the more you know of the world, the more valuable you will be." He constantly cautioned her to not adopt a bourgeois mentality and gradually his objections to her staying with the Medved family tapered off and then ceased altogether.

For the next five years, Boris Medved's business kept him in Moscow more than half the time and during those five years, Tatiana became an unofficial member of the Medved family. When the family was in St. Petersburg, Tatiana would still go to the Medved residence for tutoring and she would make herself useful by helping the reduced household staff, which remained in permanent residence in Moscow. She felt much more comfortable around the servants than around the Medveds' friends. She told the head of the household staff that she wanted to help so she could learn and be of more assistance her father. The staff was reluctant to let her join the household chores, but after a great deal of discussion they reached a compromise. They would let her do some of the household work if she promised not to tell the Medved family.

Only the young maid, Nina, seemed to resent her. *Who was this young poor girl who was given all the things I have wanted my entire life?* Nina thought. *Why do they not do something for me? I am right here in the house, under their noses, and they do not see me. And, Ivan, I am so in love with him and he acts as if I do not exist.* Nina was consistently critical of Tatiana's work and harassed her, unmercifully when the other servants were not around. Tatiana was hurt at first but quickly learned to ignore the maid's jibes.

Tatiana lived in compartmented worlds—her original life with her father; a life of luxury when the Medveds were in residence; and an in-between world in which she lived in luxury but worked long hours assisting the household staff. Nearly every night before she drifted off to sleep, she wondered in which life she truly belonged. She often thought of the tale of Zolushka, the Russian Cinderella.

Ivan spent much of his time with other boys of his age and class, but Tatiana was right there, in the household, and he seemed to find her to be much more interesting than his own sister. He taught Tatiana how to ride, and the three children would often canter through Moscow with an escort from the household staff. In fine weather they would picnic in one of the parks around the city. Natalya overcame her jealousy when she found what a bright, cheerful, and uncompetitive companion Tatiana could be. Before many months passed, they became close friends and confidantes.

As Tatiana became more and more aware of the splendor in which the Medveds lived she became more and more aware of the squalor of her own background and that of the great majority of the Russian people. She pointed out the poverty of the average Russian to Ivan and Natalya who were attentive but uncertain of how to deal with this information. Ivan took her seriously but was unable to come to any conclusions except that this was the way it had always been and always would be. Natalya was self-absorbed and she dismissed the poor as having nothing to do with her own world. Her mother's daughter, she thought of little except social events and what kind of husband she would have. She was trapped in the illusion of love to which women look forever forward and spent every hour of the day thinking about the bright future that had been mapped out before her in the next hour and the next day.

Tatiana blossomed into a beautiful teenager, tall and slender. She let her black hair cascade to her collarbone .and it was a beautiful mass of curls. Tatiana had that special cleanliness that is a gift of beauty. She and Natalya, a blond beauty of another sort, reached puberty at about the same time and were told about the mysteries of the female body by Marina, who also explained some rudimentary things about sex. She repeatedly lectured them on virtue, insisting that women's reputations were more easily bruised than men's. At the same time, Marina fretted over her daughter's growing maturity and blossoming beauty. All her married life, Marina had been one of the most beautiful women at any social gathering. *Soon,* she thought, *more men will be paying attention to Natalya than to me.* The thought made her uncomfortable and fiercely jealous. Tatiana's beauty, on the other hand, did not bother her. She knew that this girl's low social standing would prevent her from being a competitor.

As the three reached their teen years, Ivan and Tatiana began to regard each other as attractive members of the opposite sex. Natalya noticed this. *It is clear that she and Ivan are attracted to each other*, she thought. *The differences in their backgrounds will pull them apart as they get older. And, if she is interested in Ivan, it means that she will not be interested in the young men I am interested in.*

The three youngsters learned to speak French, the social language spoken by Russian society. A dancing master was brought in to teach them ballroom skills. An impoverished French noblewoman helped them polish their French and taught them manners and how to conduct themselves at table. They were all instructed on how to behave around members of the opposite sex.

Tatiana began to fit well into the Medved household but still felt uncomfortable in the social circles of the family. When guests were in attendance, she would put on her best smile and cheerfully go through the introductions, and then try to stay in the background or quietly disappear to her room. Close friends of the Medveds saw her beauty and appreciated her charm but were turned away by her mysterious social status. They frequently asked the Medveds about her and her background but, under Marina's instructions, the family was vague about her origins. Most believed that she was a poor cousin of some sort, brought in from the countryside. After all, if she *were* anyone important, would not she or the Medveds say something about it? Tatiana understood the reason she was often snubbed, but it still hurt and fueled her determination to stay as far as possible from the Medveds' social events.

At those times her poverty fell around her shoulders like a heavy weight. She felt less worthy than those around her. At home with her father, she did not feel poor. Whenever everyone around her was poor, poverty did not seem to be so troublesome. Her real home was with her father, she knew, and when she was with him the luxury of the Medved residence seemed a world away. In reality, she knew, it *was* a world away. It was like living in a foreign country. The dichotomy of her life made her less and less sure of where she belonged. As she grew older and more thoughtful the gulf between the classes expanded in her mind. The people of the poor working class were stuck in the depths of poverty, and ignorance while the people of the upper classes had unlimited opportunity. *I have so little in common with these people. What could a poor girl like me and a rich person talk about? My family? My future?* She felt like a lonely planet adrift in a vast universe.

Tatiana's greatest agony was her growing attachment to Ivan. By the time she reached puberty was sure she loved him, but despaired at the hopelessness of her situation. She would have the same life as her mother. "I will marry a workingman, bear children, live a few impoverished years, and then die young."

Tatiana loved her father more than anyone, but he grew more and more distant. Even when she was there, he often went out at night, sometimes many nights in a row, despite his long days at the factory. When asked where he had been he told her that he had been having a vodka or two and talking with friends. He did not look or act as if he had been drinking, though. Quite the opposite; when he returned, he looked serious and sober, his wolfish look more pronounced.

Russia was in turmoil as it prepared to enter the twentieth century. The peasants, most of whose parents and grandparents had been serfs forty years before, wanted land and bread. The factory workers wanted a wage that gave them enough to feed themselves and their families. They floated helpless and discontented in a gray sea of poverty, drudgery, and broken hopes. One third of all new babies died in their first year. For a member of the working class exceeding the age of forty was considered remarkable. Alcoholism decimated the population. Meanwhile, people like the Medveds lived in unimaginable luxury. The country was the personal property of the tsar, by far the richest man in the world, who was assailed on all sides by greedy relatives and special interests, all constantly vying for more wealth and influence.

Assassination attempts were on the rise. In 1899 a bomb exploded beneath a royal railroad car just as the train entered Moscow. The tsar's coach was completely destroyed but the tsar was not on the train. The car was on its way to the maintenance yard in Moscow. Six months later a man ran out from a crowd and fired a pistol at the tsar's uncle Pavl. The Grand Duke was not injured, but his driver was mortally wounded. The assassin melted back into the crowd and was never identified. At the insistence of family members, the tsar began traveling in armored trains and armored carriages. Some members of the nobility defiantly refused to hide behind armor. Few of the plotters were caught. Exile to Siberia was one of the lighter sentences for those who were. Most were stored away in fetid prisons or publicly hanged.

Vladimir Gitin entered the crowded smoky cellar just in time to hear the chairman begin. "Welcome to a meeting of the Social Democrats. It is pleasure to see our numbers consistently grow. I must warn you again and again to be careful whom you talk to. The

Okhrana are everywhere, and each of us is in danger not only from the tsar's secret police but also from the other groups who struggle to bring about a change in government. There are members of the Social Revolutionaries and the Anarchists who would betray us to eliminate their competition.

"After a secret party congress last week, we had a vote on the direction of our efforts. We won the vote and have decided that we will be known from now on as the Bolsheviks, the majority. Our success is due to Vladimir Ilych Lenin, a great socialist thinker and revolutionary ..."

One day when they were sixteen Natalya said to Tatiana, "In two weeks, Count and Countess Muraviev are having a ball, a *bal blanc*, the kind given for young unmarried women. It will be the first ball I have ever been to as an adult. And yours too, we are all invited, and you must come."

"What do you mean we are *all* invited? Surely that does not include me. I have never even met the Muravievs."

"The invitation *does* include you. Mama said so, explicitly. You are my friend, and whoever is with me will be welcome at the Muravievs. Their son, Pavl, is sure to be there, and he is the handsomest young man in Moscow as far as I am concerned. I am sure that he will ask both of us to dance, so you can see for yourself."

"Will Ivan be going?" Tatiana asked innocently.

"Of course. Nearly every young man in Moscow who amounts to anything will be there, and that certainly includes Ivan. Actually, I think Ivan is more handsome than Pavl, but Ivan is my brother, so he does not count."

"But what will I wear? What will I say to so many wealthy people?"

"Your manners are perfectly acceptable. You are beautiful and are sure to charm any number of young men. And as what you will wear, I have many white dresses, some of which I have scarcely worn. We will get Maria to alter whichever one you would like."

Reluctantly, Tatiana agreed, although as the day approached, she became apprehensive. She and Natalya decided on a gown appropriate for her first ball that hardly had to be altered at all but the tailor lowered the cut of the bodice.

"Natalya, I cannot wear this. It exposes too much of my chest. I would be embarrassed to wear it here, much less at a ball."

"Nonsense, Tatiana, you are going to your first ball as an adult, and you must dress like an adult. Low-cut dresses are the fashion this year, and I know you would like to conform."

Tatiana flushed crimson and shook her head.

"Let us compromise," said Natalya, "I will give you a scarf that covers up the flesh you are so worried about. We will find one that goes well with the dress. And I will lend you some of the jewelry that I have outgrown and I will tell Svetlana to do up your hair."

The evening of the ball, Tatiana looked at herself in the mirror and hardly believed what she was seeing. She scarcely recognized the elegantly clad beauty that looked back at her, and she was grateful for Natalya's influence

Just before the family left for the ball, Tatiana found the serving girl weeping into her arms at a table in the kitchen. "Nina, what is wrong? Why are you crying?" Nina just glowered at her with red-rimmed eyes, put her head down and wept harder. Tatiana shook her head in wonder and left the room.

Tatiana got into the carriage with the family and after a short drive arrived at the door of an elegant mansion that was even more majestic than the Medveds' home. An orchestra played in a brightly lit ballroom with a capacious dance floor. There were people there of every age, but since it was principally an affair for young people, they abounded. Tatiana had had no idea there were so many handsome young men in Moscow though she had seen many of them individually and in small groups. The military cadets and the young officers were resplendent in the uniforms of their regiments.

Natalya explained the various uniforms. "The Curriassers' are wearing white tunics, the Dragoons blue, the Cossacks and Hussars red, and the Life Guard Preobrazhenski officers are in green. This is the regiment that Ivan will join."

A few wore the colors of regiments that Natalya could not identify. All seemed to have an abundance of braid and frogging. Not many of them had any decorations, as the young officers were generally too inexperienced to have been to war. Fewer in number were young men who were not in the military but were sons of rich merchants or of the minor aristocracy. Their plumage was not as brilliant, but they presented a handsome collection, nonetheless. The total was a dazzling array of young, energetic, elegantly attired, hormone-driven males.

Tatiana turned the head of nearly every young man in the room. Their eyes became appreciative and alert when they rested on her. But she drew hostile looks from the many young and jealous women. "Who is she?" they whispered to one another. "Who is her family?" "Is she a poor relative of the Medveds?"

Some of the young men worked hard at solving the mystery. When the music began Tatiana was whisked out onto the dance floor by a succession of young noblemen and military officers, all of whom glared at each other as she changed partners. When asked about her background and family she replied, saying only that she was a guest of the Medveds. Several of the young gentlemen asked if they could call. *Call where?* she thought. *Call on whom? If they knew who I was, not one of them would have anything to do with me.* She politely deflected their inquiries but she had a grand time. The fact that she was evasive made her all the more mysterious and therefore charming to the young men in attendance. They flocked around her in great numbers, vying to gain a little sliver of her heart. Each was disappointed in turn. Tatiana's heart ached with a desire to dance with Ivan. As she caught glimpses of him from time-to-time dancing with one or another of the young women, her heart cried out in despair.

Marina was unhappy. For the first time in her life, she was jealous of Natalya. *I knew this day would come, but I did not expect it to come so soon. I was not finished. Always before, the young men would ask me to dance because of my looks but now only a few of them ask and those seem to be asking out of courtesy and not because they really want to dance with me. Sometimes I wish that I had no daughter.*

Natalya was also keeping score in her head and was pleased that she outshone her mother in the eyes of the young men.

In the small hours of the morning, as guests began to drift away, Tatiana saw Ivan making his way through the crowd.

"My night would not be complete unless I danced with the most beautiful woman in the room. Will you dance with me?"

Her heart skipped a beat, but she quickly recovered as she realized that the remark was the sort of meaningless, flattering politeness that young men of Ivan's class were taught to use. She replied in kind, "Why yes, Ivan. I would be happy to dance with the handsomest man at the ball."

"Did you enjoy yourself, Tatya?" he asked as they glided across the floor.

"Yes, Ivan. I had the most wonderful time ever." *Especially now that I am with you.*

She gazed into his eyes and thought she had never felt better in her life. Then the music ended. And the ball. Tatiana's thoughts tumbled back to Earth as she remembered the social strictures that kept her apart from Ivan. For the first time since the death of her mother, she cried herself to sleep that night.

A week after the ball, the footman who had gone to fetch Tatiana returned with the report that no one had answered his knock. He returned several days in a row without success. He inquired with neighbors and found that neither father nor daughter had been seen.

The day after that Boris Medved came from court and told Marina that the Okhrana, the secret police, had uncovered a new plot to assassinate the tsar. "Several conspirators have been arrested and several more are being looked for. A member of the group betrayed them and gave the Okhrana a list of names of other members of the group. The list included Vladimir Gitin. Luckily for the Gitins, the people on the list were scattered around the city and it took the police several days to get to the Gitins' neighborhood."

"Oh, Boris, how could they do such a thing? After all we have done for Tatiana!"

Marina's heart was less distressed than she let on. A dark part of her rejoiced whenever one of the young and beautiful women of society, a society that she had dazzled with her youth and beauty, fell by the wayside. Her own glory days were long past, and she was jealous of anyone who still enjoyed the fullest flower of their youth.

Tatiana and her father had gotten away from their home just in time. The neighbors knew who belonged in the neighborhood and who did not and had seen several suspicious strangers skulking around at all hours of day and night. Most of the neighbors wanted to stay out of any police affairs. They hated the Okhrana but feared them even more. One night, when a knock came at the door, Vladimir rolled out of his bed and told the sleepy Tatiana that it had to be the Okhrana; no one else knocked on the door at two in the morning.

"Tatiana, that is the police. I will admit guilt to whatever they charge me with in order to deflect it away from you. When they question you, say you know nothing about my activities."

"But father, I truly don't know anything about your activities," Tatiana said, suddenly alarmed at how naïve she had been.

Vladimir took a deep breath and opened the door. Rather than two men in greatcoats, there stood their neighbor, Mrs. Peretsky. She was breathing heavily and looked shocked and afraid. "Vladimir," she whispered, "you must get out and go somewhere else. There were Okhrana spies asking about you yesterday. They will probably come for you tomorrow night. I must go. The other neighbors did not tell you because they were afraid, but I have known you since Tatiana was a baby and I just had to warn you." With that, she disappeared into the night.

Vladimir and Tatiana packed their meager belongings and left before dawn. They trudged across the city to the home of a comrade who offered to take them in for a few days so they could obtain new papers and move on.

Another week after the Gitins disappeared, a ragged young boy showed up at the Medveds' with a note for Ivan. It was written in pencil on a small piece of cheap paper that had been folded over twice. Ivan gave the boy a few kopeks and took it inside. To his shock and distress the note said, "Ivan, we had to leave Moscow. Please do not tell anyone that we are gone. Thank you for all you and your family did for me over these years. I love you and always will. Tatya"

CHAPTER 8

TOKYO: DUTY VS DESIRE

Hardly a day passed without Kenji getting together with his best friend, Momoko Higashi. While Kenji was in school, Momoko was enrolled in classes designed to make her a more acceptable wife, a woman who would be welcome in another wealthy family. She studied calligraphy; ikebana or flower arranging; how to play the stringed instrument, the koto, and she practiced origami, the paper-folding art.

Most important was the ancient and intricate ceremony known as chado or chanoyu, the way of tea. Under the guidance of a Master of Tea, Momoko practiced endlessly in the small family teahouse her father built for her. For her graduation ceremony, she invited not only her own mother and father, but Kenji and his mother as well. Kenji's mother was still skeptical of Momoko's worth as a potential daughter-in-law, but her family was wealthy, and money was getting to be a problem. Momoko's father resisted inviting Kenji and his mother, but he gave in to Momoko's pleas. He balanced this by inviting the Shimada family, which owned the bank with which the Higashi clan did their financial business. Momoko's four brothers did not attend. There was always work to be done, and her father would not waste their time.

The guests gathered outside the teahouse where Mr. Higashi made the introductions. "Mrs. Dainichi and Kenji-san, this is Kenzo Shimada-san, the family's banker, his wife, and his son Kozo." Both parties bowed. Kenji's bow was deep. His mother gritted her teeth and then bowed after a moment's hesitation. Her hesitation did not go unnoticed by the other two families. The Shimada family took in Kenji's clothing and their bows were hardly bows at all. The Shimadas were, after all, important bankers, and this boy and his mother were obviously of no consequence. The father and son quickly turned their backs on the Dainichi family and began chatting with the Higashis. Kenji could see that his mother was outraged at the snub; in the old days it would be the merchants and bankers who bowed the lowest to the samurai. She fixed a defiant stare on Mrs. Shimada, who wrinkled her nose in a gesture of contempt before she too turned away.

The teahouse door slid open. Momoko bowed deeply and invited her guests to enter the small structure and then knelt on the mat facing them, the implements for the ceremony before her. Momoko looked beautiful in a blue and white brocaded kimono, her face powdered white in the old style and her coal-black hair done up in the oshidori style of a teenager and tied, as tradition demanded, with silk floss. She tucked the edges of her kimono under her legs and with another deep bow toward her guests she began. Momoko performed the many steps flawlessly, seemingly without effort, through the many steps, making each movement with grace and fluidity. Finally, she whisked the tea to a pale-green froth, and poured, and handed the delicate cups to her guests. Momoko gave them another solemn bow. Kenji's mother seemed impressed.

The Higashi and the Shimada families set off to a restaurant for a celebratory meal right after the tea ceremony. Momoko's father had extended a reluctant invitation of the Dainichis to join them, but Kenji's mother declined for them both. She felt uneasy in the company of merchants, was angry at their snub and wanted to take her son home to eat.

On the way home, she put aside the way the Shimadas had treated her and confessed to her son, "Kenji, I must say that I was amazed at the quality of the tea ceremony. Momoko's grace and abilities are a result of a great deal of study and effort. She is not like the children of so many of the rich merchants but has an elegance that is like those of a daughter of samurai."

"Mother, she is also taking a course to teach her how to be a good daughter-in-law."

His mother seemed to file this information away with an inner smile and presumably on the plus side of the mental ledger she kept on the value of Momoko. It was the custom in Japanese households for a widowed woman to move into her eldest son's house after their marriage. The mother-in-law would rule the roost, dictate cleaning and cooking chores, control the money and the like. The mother-in-law was called the *hera-mochi*, the one who had the right to hold the spoon that was used to serve the rice. Most mothers-in-law wielded the spoon like an imperial scepter. Mothers-in-law traditionally transferred all the irksome household duties to the new bride. The bride was required to brush out her new mother-in-law's hair and massage her whenever she demanded. Most Japanese women prayed for a son so that someday they would be a mother-in-law themselves. If Momoko *were* to marry Kenji she would not only bring money but an elegant hand at tea and in other duties around the house. For a merchant's daughter, she might do.

The Higashi party entered the restaurant and was shown to a private room. As they knelt at the table, Momoko was introduced to Kenzo's son Kozo, whom she had barely noticed during the tea ceremony. He was rail-thin and had several nervous habits; blinking his eyes rapidly when he spoke was one, pulling on his earlobes was another. He did it so often that she wondered how his ears stayed on his head. He also regularly strip-mined his nose with his thumb. Kozo's most irritating characteristic, though, was a high-pitched, wheezing laugh that seemed to come forth at the most inappropriate moments. When he laughed, he seemed to be choking on something or having a seizure, and his whole body shook.

Momoko's father and the elder Shimada talked business, the two wives discussed social matters, and Momoko mostly stared at the mat and was silent. Kozo mostly stared at Momoko. He, too, was silent. Momoko had no intention of becoming friendly with this young man, and Kozo was so bereft of social graces that apparently he knew not what to say. Both youngsters sighed with relief when the lengthy meal came to an end and the families parted.

Shinkichi Higashi had other plans for his daughter's future than marrying into the honorable but impoverished Dainichi family. He was always looking for ways to improve his business and increase his wealth, and several days after the tea ceremony he was approached by Kenzo Shimada, who suggested to him that he might be able to offer better financial terms and services than his present arrangement. While sharing *sake* with the banker, Kenzo outlined a plan.

"With my access to money, Higashi-san, and your expertise in dry goods, there is much we could do together. We can expand beyond Tokyo, from Sapporo in the north to Kyoto in the south. Here is how: You would not only sell cloth and make clothing, but you can also begin to buy up mills for the weaving of cloth and then get into the exploding import-export business. We modern samurai of industry can make enormous fortunes. All we need is our partnership and courage. What do you think?"

Kenzo reminded him that his son had been introduced to Momoko and he hinted that they might see each other again. a marriage between Kozo to Momoko would form an alliance of family as well as business. Kozo seemed a rather fatuous young man, which worried Mr. Higashi a bit, but on the other hand, there was the talk from Kozo's father about merging the business with the bank and using the bank's money to benefit both.

He began to talk to his wife about the wisdom of betrothing Momoko to Kenzo. Momoko was sixteen and Kozo eighteen, so they could marry at any time. When Momoko's mother told her daughter that her father was thinking of arranging a marriage between her and Kozo the girl was horrified. "What could father be thinking of?" she asked, "Kozo is repellant. Plus, he is the sort of man who will sit in his home every evening and pay homage to his own self-regard. Please, Mother, tell Father no!"

At sixteen, Kenji still held out hope that he would be permitted to go to university. These hopes turned to ash when his mother arranged a conference with her brothers and Kenji's uncles from his father's side. After conferring they called him before them. His uncle Genichi, his father's younger brother and a war hero in his own right, began the conversation. He knelt on the tatami facing Kenji in his best uniform with its decorations.

"Kenji, your mother and we have discussed your future. We are happy to see that you have done so well in your studies and have passed the exams for the university. But we are a family of warriors.

We have always been warriors. I know it will be hard for you, but we have talked it over and unanimously agree that you should give up your ambitions to be a scholar and to join the family tradition of service to His Majesty. Although anyone, even a commoner, can become an officer these days, the officer corps needs samurai blood to make sure the traditions of Japan, particularly *bushido*, the way of the warrior, are preserved. You owe it to the memory of your father and even more so to His Imperial Majesty to serve. Accordingly, we have arranged for you to begin at the military academy in the next class."

"But Uncle Genichi," Kenji said, "will I not have something to say about this? I do not want to dishonor the memory of my father and grandfather, but I am not good at the military arts. Would it not be worse if I went to the academy and then failed? Failing there would be a much greater disappointment to the family. It is my heart's desire to study and teach languages and literature to others. That is something I know I can do and do well. Can I not serve the emperor by helping to raise a generation of scholars in the traditions and literature of Japan? Since we have opened our doors to the West, I am afraid that we will gradually lose the qualities that make Japan unique."

"The best way to preserve Japanese values is to protect them from outside influence," replied his uncle. "If the history of the European conquest of other countries over last few hundred years is not to repeat itself in Japan, we must be able to protect ourselves militarily. Troubled times lie ahead. The Russians are trying to push into East Asia, and we must not permit this. It is Japan's destiny to rule East Asia, and beyond. To do so, we will need every true warrior we have. Kenji, please understand this—you have the blood of the samurai. There is no way you can fail if you devote yourself to the army. It is not easy overcome the difficulties of becoming an army officer but if it were easy we would not have a good army. If you do your best you will be a credit to your ancestors and help create the new, modern Japan."

"The men in our family have been warriors for well over five hundred years. We were samurai two hundred years before the first Tokugawa shogun came to power. We supported the shogunate through the early civil wars, and later we fought to restore the emperor to his rightful place on the throne. The changes Japan has made are necessary if we are to emerge into the modern world and escape the exploitation of our country by foreigners. True, we have a conscript army from all classes, but it is best if officers in whose veins the blood of the samurai flow lead them. You are one of these men, and you must serve. History, unwritten, awaits you."

His elders appealed to his family history, the memory of his father, the needs of his country and his love for his mother. None of it was new to Kenji. He already knew it all by heart. In the end, it was just too much for him.

After the uncles left, Kenji ran down the street to find Momoko and tell her what had happened. They walked toward the public park.

"Oh, Kenji, I am so sorry that it has come to this. I had so hoped that your mother would let you go to university and study what you wanted. I have bad news too. My father is determined that I be promised in marriage to Kozo Shimada, that awful son of the banker he wants to do business with. If I have to marry him, I think I will just die. My mother is on my side and thinks that Kozo is a disgusting young man too. But I do not know how I will resist my father's pressure. Especially if you are gone away and are not here to talk to. I support you in all your dreams for your future and I know you support me in mine. Each of us is being pressured by our family to do something we do not want to do, but something that will shape the rest of our lives." Tears formed in her eyes as her cheeks turned bright red with embarrassment and woe. "Kenji, I have never said this to you, but *you* are the one I love. If I get married, I want to marry *you*. I am so confused…"

Stunned by Momoko's proclamation of love. Kenji gazed at her intently as if seeing her for the first time. Momoko had become a beautiful young woman. She had a lovely slender figure and still retained the soft, colorful cheeks that set off her dark eyes and brilliant teeth. He was amazed at the discovery of what had been growing unnoticed before his eyes.

"Momoko, I do not know if I love you or not. Maybe I do. We have been friends for our entire lives and while it is true that we are both unhappy, our unhappiness comes for different reasons. I suppose whatever will happen, will happen. The thing you must do is to prevent your family from making you marry Kozo. If you can do that, then if you can wait a few years, we will see if we have a future together. Whether we do or not, my fate is sealed. I cannot avoid going to the academy and becoming an army officer."

Her dark eyes swam with tears, adoration, and hope. He felt deeply moved but was not sure what his feelings meant. She was his best friend and his confidante, and he knew he would miss her very much.

On their way home, Kenji and Momoko encountered a one-man street theater. The man's right half was dressed as a woman and the left half dressed as a man. A few coins glittered in the small box at his feet. He had drawn a small crowd that watched as the man acted out a potboiler about thwarted love and *giri* versus *ninjo*, obligation versus emotion. Both Kenji and Momoko thought about how true it was, how true that life was a struggle between duty and desire. Momoko dropped a copper coin into his box as they departed.

Kenji and Momoko spent as much time together as they could in the few weeks remaining before the academy class started. They strolled through parks in late-summer Tokyo admiring nature. On the few nights they stayed beyond dusk, they would sit quietly and contemplate the glow of the abundant fireflies whose blinking on and off like tiny flying lighthouses inspired the pair to compose poems about them.

The last time they met Kenji looked at them for a minute or so, sighed, and then quickly spoke:

"The lonely firefly

Gone from my life forever

We both blink farewell"

The poem saddened both of them.

That evening Kenji walked Momoko to the door of her house and looked long into her eyes until they began to fill with tears. Then he quickly squeezed her hand, turned, and strode away.

What is love? he wondered. If love was missing someone, then he was in love because he missed Momoko already. He was heartbroken at the thought of a future without going to university and a future without Momoko. He would have to abandon his thoughts of university and maybe abandon his friendship with Momoko too. He had taken her for granted, and now the thought of coming back from the academy and finding her married to someone else overwhelmed his emotions. He was afraid to tell Momoko of these new and unexpected feelings because he was afraid it would make her anguish much worse. And his.

His uncle Genichi took Kenji to Yasukuni Shrine dedicated to the spirits of all Japanese who died in the service of their country. It was one of the most sacred places in all of Japan. The shrine itself was a solemn and physically impressive structure. The two passed under the Shinto gate and down the walkway, past thousands of paper lanterns on either side, each bearing the name of a fallen warrior. The shrine had been built and dedicated in the unique native religion of Japan, Shinto. In addition to the warrior ethic, Shinto was also a religion of ancestor worship and was dedicated to fertility, family, and rice wine. The Japanese believed that the spirits of the dead remain eternally on earth and protect their descendants. The warrior ethos was emphasized in slogans written everywhere. Loyalty to one's lord came before loyalty to one's family. The slogans dictated sobriety and frugality and deplored extravagance, whether in dress, emotion or expenditure.

"The Emperor Meiji gave the shrine the name Yasukuni," Genichi told Kenji. "It represents his wishes for that the Japanese nation could enter the modern world in peace. This, Kenji, is why you must be a soldier. Your father is one of the thousands of spirits immortalized here. There is a saying that no doubt you have heard from him, 'If you die in battle, you will return to Yasukuni.'"

The two slowly walked across the near-empty courtyard up to the shrine itself. There they bowed and each offered silent prayers. Kenji had given little thought to his prayers before this, but he was overcome with emotion and prayed fervently to his father, his grandfather, and his other ancestors to give him strength during his coming trials at the military academy.

After prayers for the dead they set out for the Academy, located at Ichigaya, not far from Tokyo. Uncle Genichi took Kenji to the entrance, where the sentry on duty stood rigidly at attention and saluted him while Genichi said farewell to his nephew.

CHAPTER 9

FLIGHT TO ST. PETERSBURG

Bundled in heavy winter coats with high collars, scarves, and with hats pulled low over their foreheads, Tatiana and her father stood impatiently in the Moscow train depot waiting for the train to St. Petersburg. The train finally huffed into the station and screeched to a stop amid a great clattering of the cars and an enormous cloud of steam. Vladimir whispered to his daughter, "Board quickly and act as if we are strangers. If the police search this train, I do not want them to connect us. We must not sit side by side but on different sides of the aisle, and not too far away."

Vladimir had obtained forged internal passports for himself and Tatiana. They kept their given names but the family name had been changed to Smirnov. He also had papers saying that he had been accepted for a job in the Putilov factory in St. Petersburg. Although his new name was false, the job was a real one, obtained along with the papers from comrades in the movement. The Putilov factory had been founded over a hundred years earlier to make cannonballs for the Russian army. Unknown to the Okhrana, it was also becoming a hotbed of revolutionary thought.

Their third-class compartment was hot and smoky when the woodstove was working and freezing cold when it was not. Tatiana and her father crowded into seats on the wooden benches inside, apart but not too far, and held their bags on their laps. All around them people huddled in their woolens and sheepskins. Some smoked foul cigars, some chewed on black bread, and still others nipped from bottles of vodka. Most just stared out the windows at the blackness of the night or at the floor. The car was full of the poor and defeated, and the poor and the hopeful. Hot or cold, the packed mass of human beings gave off a ripe odor.

It was Tatiana's first time on a train, and she fought motion sickness and struggled in vain to find some fresh air to clear her head and quell her queasy stomach. An older man sitting next to her ogled her openly and made repeated attempts to engage her in conversation, his breath rank with the awful combination of tobacco, vodka, and raw onions. She had to breathe through her mouth to keep the foul odor from making her sicker.

"Are you going all the way to St. Petersburg, young lady? It is a beautiful city. I have been in Moscow to see my new grandson. What a beautiful boy he is. Of course, he looks just like me. I am from Novgorod myself and will be getting off there. You should get off too, and I can show you around. Novgorod is the most Russian of cities, and our cathedral of St. Sophia the most beautiful in the land..." The man prattled on but did not seem to expect any real conversation in return, so Tatiana kept up with nods and "How nice," in order to keep him talking. She was afraid to say anything because she had no idea what to say that would not make the man suspicious of her fugitive status. She girded herself for the seventeen-hour trip.

The train shuddered to a stop in a small town outside of Novgorod. A few passengers got off the train and others just as tired and just as dirty took their places. As the train sat and sat, the wood stove blazed away and smoke gathered thick in the compartment, adding to Tatiana's discomfort. Finally, following a wave of murmurs that began at one end of the car, two men made their way down the aisle. They wore greatcoats bearing the insignia of the Okhrana, the tsar's secret police. Tatiana saw her father stiffen. He had been warned by his party contacts that his documents would only pass a cursory inspection. Simple possession of false documents was proof that their possessor was a subversive, an illegal immigrant from the hinterland, or both, and he would be summarily banished to Siberia or worse.

As the police moved through the car they randomly demanded papers from various passengers.

Then, just three seats away from Tatiana, one of the Okhrana looked long and hard at the papers proffered by a young man only a little older than she. He began questioning the man sharply and then ordered him off the train for further interrogation. The man stood, glanced in the direction the policeman was pointing, and suddenly pushed the nearest guard into the one furthest away and bolted for the door in the opposite direction. Just then the train lurched as a preliminary for getting under way, and both guards were thrown off their feet. In the confusion, the young man fought his way to the exit and leapt to the ground.

The two police rapidly recovered and bolted after him, one blowing vigorously on his whistle, the other shouting. They too jumped from the train and pointed at the fleeing man, who was trying to gain the top of an embankment. A soldier standing nearby saw the pursuit, calmly raised his rifle, sighted on the man, and fired. The man tumbled and rolled gently through the snow, leaving a trail of blood behind him, down to the bottom of the hill, where he lay in a heap next to the tracks. The last thing that Tatiana saw as their train picked up speed and left the station was the man lying on the ground with the police standing over him.

The train finally reached St. Petersburg. The pair stepped down into the cavernous station and Tatiana's father looked around. A tall, unkempt young man stood lazing against a lamppost and smoking. The man surveyed the crowd carefully from under the bill of his leather cap. When he and Vladimir locked eyes, the young man flung down the remains of his cigarette and sauntered over.

"Citizen Smirnov?"

"Yes, and you are…?"

"Pyotr Bolkonsky. My instructions are to meet you and take you to a room near the Putilov plant. No one said anything about a woman. Who are you?"

"This is my daughter, Tatiana," said Vladimir.

Tatiana gave the young man the sort of uncertain, shy smile that dimpled her cheeks and made her eyes sparkle. The noblewoman who had tutored her and Natalya in how to act around men had coached her in smiling like that and she brought it off without thinking about it. She suddenly realized where she was and switched to a stern look.

Pyotr apparently fancied himself a ladies' man and he met her gaze, put on his own best smile, and made a slight bow. "But of course. There is always room in St. Petersburg for another beautiful young woman."

Tatiana caught the gleam in his eye and her first thought was that he would not pass muster in Moscow society. Then she felt ashamed at the thought. She had to bring her mind up short, dismiss what she had learned at the Medveds' and relearn to live like what she was, a poor woman.

Pyotr swept up the canvas bag that contained all of Tatiana's belongings and indicated that they should follow. Outside the train station he flagged down a one-horse carriage and they all boarded. He gave directions to the driver, and they clopped off into the night.

Pyotr had found them a room in a workers' apartment building not far from the plant. The room was small, barely ten by twelve feet, and they had to share the kitchen down the hall with all the other residents of the floor. But there was a common bath in the building so they would not have to go somewhere else to bathe. The toilet was outside. The furnishings consisted of two rough chairs, a plank table, and a single bed, more like a shelf, built into the wall. The place smelled of unwashed bodies, tobacco, and stale food, and was coated with grime everywhere. After Pyotr left, Vladimir and Tatiana decided that he would use the bed and she would make do on the table, just as she had at home, with a couple of spare blankets they had brought with them from Moscow.

The next morning Pyotr came to the house to take Vladimir to his new job. Tatiana was left in charge of their meager funds and told to find food. The first thing she did was to borrow a pail and scrub brush from the communal kitchen and scrub the room down, floors, walls, and shelves. She pushed the table around so she could stand on it and wash the ceiling. Then she asked directions to the market, where she bought cabbage and a few potatoes, black bread, and a small piece of sausage for their dinner. The vegetables and sausage went into a soup that she had hot and ready to eat by the time her father came home.

He was tired from his first day at work but happy to have a job and aglow with the few words he and Pyotr had exchanged about the movement. He finished his soup, wiped the bowl with the last scrap of bread and told Tatiana he had to go out to a meeting. Tatiana wondered how he had found a meeting to go to already. They had just arrived in St. Petersburg. She anxiously watched him go out the door. *I wish he would stop going to these meetings,* she thought, *It is the reason we had to leave Moscow and if we are chased out of St. Petersburg, where would we go?* It was late into the night before she heard him return.

This became their routine. Vladimir left for work, came home, ate, went out several nights a week, and came back home, and slept. Lacking the papers to obtain a regular job, Tatiana cooked for her father, cleaned, and was able to supplement their income with a few kopecks she earned by taking care of a half-dozen children in the building whose parents worked. The children loved her. She had read a lot in the Medveds' home and remembered what she read but here she had no books. She turned stories she remembered into children's tales and embellished them. Drawing on her experiences with luxury, she spun fantasies of princes and princesses and the wonderful world in which they lived. She recovered two books from a trash heap and tried to teach the children how to read. But the books were for adults, and the children squirmed and focused their attention elsewhere, then begged her to continue with her stories. After a few attempts at lessons, she gave up and returned to the fairy tales. A favorite was the story of Zalushka. The children could never get enough of her stories and were reluctant to leave when their mothers came to collect them.

Pyotr came by from time to time. He seemed to show up when her father was not there, and he always wanted to come in. After she had turned down several requests to enter, he began to ask her to go out for tea. She accepted his invitations, just to have something to do and get out of the small house. He took her to "safe" little teashops where they could talk politics with a relative degree of security.

His message was the same as her father's. The working classes were starving and mistreated. The ruling classes lived in luxury, oppressed the poor, and stole the benefits of the labor of the workingman. He told her about the teachings of Karl Marx and of the writings of this fellow Lenin. On one occasion he brought her a copy of Lenin's newspaper, *Iskra*, or Spark. "You must be careful and not show it to anyone. If the wrong people know you have it, mere possession is enough to get you thrown into jail."

She took it home and read it with interest. The style was colorless and cramped and the message was always the same. That is, about how the workers of the world were exploited and kept in poverty by the rich so that the latter could continue to live in luxury. It also predicted that soon, very soon, the working classes of the industrial nations, Germany and England, would rise up against their capitalist masters. After the industrial nations revolted, Lenin argued, Russia would soon follow. Together the worker and the farmer, the wielders of the hammer and the wielders of the sickle, would rule a workers' paradise. Though the repetition of the message bored her, she realized its importance.

Iskra was passed from hand-to-hand among the revolutionaries. Those who could read, read it to those who could not. It went from hand to hand until it was falling apart and the print was smudged beyond recognition, and then the paper was carefully burned and the ashes scattered.

Tatiana had never seen any exploitation of anyone in the Medved household. They paid their servants well and rarely abused them. But there was no denying the abundance of poverty and suffering elsewhere. As soon as he thought he could, Pyotr began to take Tatiana to secret revolutionary meetings. They went only when her father was at other meetings but not let him know.

"No, Tatiana," her father said, "I will not take you to the meetings. It is dangerous, and you are too young. I will take you when I think you are ready. In the meantime, I want you to think about how Russia is and how much better it can be. You have seen luxury, and I hope you have learned from it that people of our class are in the grip of eternal poverty. Our people go hungry, are ragged, and receive no medical attention. Those like the Medveds have everything. Their futures are assured, not because of their abilities but according to their birth. You can never be a part of that class.

"The tsar's army is a good example. Men from society automatically serve as officers. Our people are drafted as privates and cannot rise above sergeant, no matter our qualifications. Did you know that the draftees have to serve twenty-five years? When they are drafted, their families hold funerals for them because they know they will never return to their villages. Those who do not die in combat will be carried off by disease or a life of hardship. In some villages the entire population of young men are drafted, leaving no one to till the fields."

Over the next year, Tatiana and Pyotr became friends. It was then a small step for them to become lovers. Pyotr was experienced sexually, and after a time he encouraged her to occasionally have sex with other young men, and even women in order to broaden her view. She reluctantly did this at first, but then grew to like the variety. “Monogamy,” scornfully declared Pyotr many times over, “is the province of the bourgeois.”

One day Tatiana confronted her father about her feelings toward revolutionary activities.

“Father, you know I have been spending lots of time with Pyotr?”

“Yes, of course I know. I see him several times a week. He is a fine young man with the true revolutionary spirit. He confided in me that he has been seeing you. Have you become lovers?”

Tatiana blushed at the thought that her father knew, or had guessed, what was going on. It was one thing to take a lover. It was another to admit the same to one’s own father. She could not look him in the eyes when she replied, “Yes, father, we have.”

Vladimir looked at her, his face a mask of sadness. His daughter was now a woman and he mourned the passing of her childhood. “It is okay. I am glad that you told me. Things were different when your poor mother and I got together. In those days, young couples were expected to marry. But now… so much is changing. Anyway, Pyotr is a fine young man and I am sure you will be good for each other.”

“Father, it is not our relationship I want to talk to you about. It is about the movement. I am seventeen now, an adult. I was afraid to tell you, but Pyotr has been taking me to a few meetings. The bickering is mind-numbing, but the overall message is not. I believe in what you are trying to do and I want to be a part of it. My father is active in the movement and so is my lover. Don’t you think it is about time that I contributed something too?”

Vladimir’s sad expression deepened. “I had wanted to keep you out of this. You could get hurt very badly. You are my only child, the best thing I have left from your mother. I do not know what I would do if I lost you too."

"But if the police arrest either you or Pyotr, they are sure to come for me anyway. What difference would it make to them? They would never believe that I am just your daughter or just his lover. No, Father, I am already in danger, and I am comfortable with the idea. Now, what can I do?"

That night Vladimir took her to one of his own meetings. The two wandered through the back streets of St. Petersburg, changing direction several times, going completely around blocks and checking who was behind them to make sure no one followed. At last they came upon a darkened building. A man crouched in the shadows next to a cellar entrance. He jerked his chin at Vladimir and whispered, "Who is she?"

"This is my daughter, Tatiana," replied Vladimir. "She wants to contribute to the movement and this will be her first meeting."

"You are just in time. The meeting will start in a few minutes."

Tatiana followed her father down some stairs and came to a door where he knocked softly. When the door opened a crack, Vladimir whispered, "It is me, Vladimir Smirnov."

The door swung back, and the pair walked down a pitch-dark hallway, opened another door, and entered a large room. The room flickered with the yellow light of kerosene lanterns and was foul with the smell of Russian tobacco and body odors. About twenty people stood in the room. Vladimir took his daughter around and introduced her to everyone. The group was mostly male although there were four other women present. All of the participants had a hard, starved, determined look. All worked at the Putilov plant, so they called themselves the Putilov Soviet, the Putilov Council.

This group provided leadership for the growing numbers of revolutionary-minded workers at the factory.

They sat around a table or on benches against the wall. A man who appeared to be a chairman stood. "I have news from abroad. Comrade Lenin, who is, as you know, in exile in Zurich, Switzerland, sends his greetings." He flourished a sheaf of papers and slowly read the contents to the group. Lenin's message differed little from previous ones or from the columns he regularly penned for *Iskra*, but Tatiana listened attentively. The attendees at the meeting discussed these issues exhaustively and exhaustingly. It seemed to Tatiana that they easily became distracted by minutiae and poured a lot of passion into rather insignificant points.

She found Lenin's message and the discussion to be in one sense discouraging, due to his belief that revolution would begin in the industrialized countries. Russia would have a long wait. How long? she wondered. Would revolution even come to Mother Russia in her own lifetime? She would ask her father about this later.

Near the end of the meeting, Vladimir stood and told the group that his daughter wanted to become active in the movement and wanted something to do. A number of suggestions floated about, and the majority finally decided that because of her education she could serve best by helping to edit and produce the St. Petersburg underground newspaper. This involved more than a little bit of risk, since the Okhrana relentlessly stamped out all voices of reform and revolution and made a particular effort to target any disseminators of seditious literature. If the Okhrana caught her she could expect no mercy. An exile to Siberia would be sure to follow, or the hangman's noose.

Tatiana took to her new assignment enthusiastically. She rapidly learned the issues that most concerned the movement and the phrases of encouragement that Lenin and others constantly used to motivate the masses. Most Russians could not read, so it was the responsibility of the leaders of the movement to repeat again and again the reasons that the tsarist system must be overthrown and replaced by a government of the people. She was to translate the news from abroad and decisions of the Putilov Soviet into simple, plain language, words that all Russians would understand.

Her job exposed her to much more risk than if she only attended meetings and wrote articles. The group had but one printing press, and messengers had to take the handwritten articles all the way across St. Petersburg. Often, when there was no one else available to carry the material to the press, Tatiana carried it herself. The ubiquitous presence of the militia and Okhrana with its many informants made this very dangerous. Even more perilous was the picking up of the printed material and then distributing it. One could never come up with a convincing explanation as to why one had not one but several copies of seditious material in one's possession.

One day she delivered the material to be printed in the next issue and picked up the copies that had just come off the press. No sooner had she left the underground print shop with about two dozen copies of the printed newspaper under her skirts then a pair of policemen stopped her.

"Your papers," one demanded.

Tatiana gave the man her best smile, reached into the pocket of her dress, and pulled out a ragged and worn set of papers. As she handed them to the policeman, she kept her smile in place and threw her chest out, emphasizing her breasts. Before the policeman could carefully examine her papers she casually raised her skirt a few inches and exposed some leg, something a proper young Russian girl would not do.

"She is nothing but a whore," the other policeman said.

"Perhaps that is the reason she has forged papers," said the first. "Should we let her go or should we take her in?"

"We should let her go. She is far younger and better looking than most, and she will give us a special price for letting her go. Eh?"

Oh, yes," Tatiana said, "Anytime for half price. How about I meet you tonight just after dark?"

"Half price," said the policeman, handing her back her papers. "We'll see you right here at dark. Do not be late."

When Tatiana reached her home, she took off her skirt and removed the papers tied to her thighs. She discovered that her legs had sweated so much during her conversation with the police that streaks of ink had run down past her knees.

From that day forward, she had to choose a wide and circuitous route to the press and back. She needed to avoid those two policemen at all costs. They would not be fooled a second time. She told neither her father nor Pyotr of her close call. She knew that they would forbid her to continue her courier duties.

CHAPTER 10

THE ICHIGAYA MILITARY ACADEMY

Kenji hesitantly walked down the street between two rows of large buildings until he found the parade ground, where a hundred or more newcomers in civilian clothes milled about, in small groups of three or four, nervously talking among themselves. A few of them rapidly burned through cigarettes. A few more stood alone, away from the small groups, staring at the ground or into space as if wondering what they had gotten themselves into. Kenji was among them.

One of the newcomers spotted a young man in uniform striding over the parade ground toward them. This cadet nudged his fellows and whispered. Word quickly passed, and a hush fell over the group.

As he approached the newcomers the man in uniform shouted, "I am Senior Cadet Goto. Line up in three lines. Hurry and remain silent."

The cadets quickly formed themselves up in ragged ranks as Goto shouted at them. Senior Cadet Goto walked down the lines, stopping before each new man to make sarcastic remarks and give instructions. Having been berated and instructed, each cadet, in turn peeled off the formation, picked up his bag, and ran in the direction of the barracks.

Goto's eyes lit up and he grinned as he stopped in front of Kenji, the shortest and slightest of the new group.

"Are they sending us midgets now? Children? What is your name, cadet?"

"K-kenji Dainichi," he stammered.

"At this school you will answer 'sir' to all senior cadets and officers. Do you understand?"

"Yes, sir!"

"You will be in Barracks Five, on the south side of the parade field. Pick up your things and go find an empty bunk in a room."

"Yes, sir!" replied Kenji. He hoisted his bag and struggled to the other side of the parade field.

In Barracks Five, he looked in one room and then another and still another. Each room had four bunks and four cadets. Finally, at the end of the hall he came to a room with four bunks and just three new cadets. "May I come in here?" he asked, bowing deeply.

The three young occupants of the room looked him up and down and one said, "Sure come on in. You are small enough to fit." The others laughed, and Kenji turned red with embarrassment.

Kenji pitched his bag onto one of the bunks and introduced himself. The other three boys all had the muscled bodies and tanned faces of farmers. They introduced themselves as Taro, Hiroshi, and Yukio.

The trio regarded him with polite curiosity. "Why do you want to be a soldier? Are you not awfully small for this?" Yukio asked.

"My ancestors have always been soldiers. My father died honorably in the war with China and my mother and uncles made me come to military school. I really hoped to go to the Imperial University, though, and become a scholar."

"A scholar?" the three chorused.

"But what better way to serve the emperor than as a soldier?" asked Taro.

Kenji had no reply to that because he did not want to dishonor his father's memory or to offend his new roommates.

An hour later Senior Cadet Goto came through the barracks blowing a whistle and shouting for them to fall outside and line up again. Then he marched the poorly formed group to the supply department, where they formed a single line and filed into a large building that smelled of mold and wool. A supply sergeant looked at Kenji, shrugged, shook his head, and tossed some uniforms on the counter. Kenji bowed and thanked him, picked up the uniforms, and then ran outside to once again fall into formation. After each cadet had received his uniforms, they staggered back to the barracks under the burden of a mountain of musty-smelling new clothing.

The uniform issue had taken most of the afternoon, so Senior Cadet Goto had them drop their uniforms on their bunks and then fall in again outside. Their next stop was the mess hall for their evening meal of soup, rice, and fish. Then he marched them back to the barracks and instructed them to bathe and fall out the next morning dressed in their uniforms. Before he dismissed them, he shouted, "Pay attention to this, I am only going to show you one time." Then he removed his leg wrappings, puttees, and demonstrated how to neatly wind them around ones' leg. With that, he dismissed the cadets for the day.

When Kenji tried on his uniform he found it much too big. The pant legs had to be rolled up so he would not trip on them, and he rolled up the sleeves so he could use his hands. His cap fell over his eyes, so he had to stuff paper around the inside of the band to secure it. Only his boots fit properly. He looked like a little boy playing soldier. Wrapping his puttees proved an impossible task. The cloth covering had to be wound around his legs from the top of his short boots and over his trousers to just short of the knee. He could neither wrap them tightly or uniformly enough to appear to be the slightest bit military. He wrapped and unwrapped them several times, hoping for help from his roommates, but their own concerns dominated their thoughts.

The following morning, they fell out for breakfast and then marched to the armory, where the armorer issued them Arisaka-35 bolt-action rifles. Each weighed ten pounds and was fifty inches long. To Kenji, the weapon was heavy and seemed to be nearly as tall as he. When they marched on the parade field to learn the rudiments of drill, Kenji got off to a bad beginning with his marching instructor. He started off on the wrong foot the first few times, turned one way when the instructor commanded them to go another, and had a hard time holding onto, much less shifting, his rifle properly in response to commands. Then the end of one of his puttees came loose and he tripped over it, falling on his face and dropping his rifle. The instructor stood over him and rewarded him with screams.

"Cadet Dainichi, how are you ever going to make a soldier if you keep falling down? Dropping your rifle, any weapon, is an unforgiveable offense unless you are shot dead. Without a weapon you are useless. Do you understand?"

"Yes, sir,"

It was Kenji's misfortune that his instructor, Captain Shoji, was a member of the new army, the army formed after it began accepting commoners rather than just members of samurai families to fill its officer ranks. He loved to pick on those who came from the old warrior class, especially one who presented as easy a target as Kenji. The captain selected Kenji to be made an example of and continuously berated him.

That afternoon, right after the noon meal, they spent in the classroom reviewing the military history of Japan and the bushido, the way of the warrior. None of this was new to Kenji. Since he came from a military family his father owned many books on military subjects, including some by foreign authors that had been translated into Japanese. Others he had borrowed from Araki sensei and read in the original German, French, and Russian.

After the classroom an instructor led them through muscle-building exercises until Kenji almost dropped of exhaustion. Senior Cadet Goto then sent them off to hot baths and an evening meal. At their last formation of the day Goto read off the study assignments for the next day. "Read all night long if you have to, but be prepared to discuss the material tomorrow afternoon."

Kenji was so tired he could not even open his books that night but fell right to sleep after supper. The other cadets read into the night.

The second day was more of the same. Exhausting drill in the morning followed by a classroom session after lunch. The unaccustomed exercise and the sleepiness that set in after a midday meal fogged many of their minds. The classroom instructor, Captain Murata, began by questioning the students on the lessons of the previous day and on the reading assignments.

He addressed Kenji's roommate, Yukio, "Cadet Nishi, please review for me the role the of western clans in the restoration of the emperor to the throne." Yukio stood, turned red, and stammered out a partial answer.

"Unsatisfactory answer, Cadet Nishi, sit down! Cadet Shibata?"

"I do not remember, sir."

"You do not remember the events leading up to the restoration to power of our sacred emperor?

"Well not exactly, sir."

"Cadet Togo?"

"No sir."

"Cadet Dainichi?"

"Yes, sir," replied Kenji. He stood and in a wavering voice gave a long and detailed answer about how the western clans, particularly those from the provinces of Satsuma and Choshu, led the Restoration movement.

Captain Murata, who had witnessed Kenji's difficulties on the drill field, gave him a long, serious look. Then he smiled and said, "Very good, Cadet Dainichi. That was an excellent answer. The rest of you need to study as hard as Cadet Dainichi if you expect to graduate from this academy and become officers in His Majesty's army."

Back in the barracks, his roommates gathered around him. "Kenji," Taro said, "you did not even study last night. You fell asleep immediately after supper. How did you do that?"

"I don't know, except that I have never had trouble learning anything out of a book, and the assignment covered things that I already knew about."

"I am not very good with book learning, Kenji, and I do not think the others here are, either. Will you help us with our studies?"

"I will, Taro, if the three of you will help me with the rest."

The bargain was struck. Kenji would tutor the others in military history, tactics, strategy, and other intellectual subjects. In return, they promised to help him over the more physical aspects of the training.

Kenji and his roommates exchanged information about their families and their upbringing.

"My father is a silk grower," Taro said. "We have a small grove of mulberry trees and cultivate the worms fairly successfully. But it is a small business and able to support only one small family. I am the second son, so my older brother will inherit the business."

"Do you wear silk clothes?" Kenji asked.

"No, we wear cotton. We need the income from every last bit of silk to feed our family and keep the business going."

"And Yukio, what does your family do?"

"We are poor farmers. My father had to sell my older sister into prostitution when she was sixteen. I found her two years ago; she was working in a brothel in the Yoshiwara district in Tokyo. But I did not see her. The maid at the door said that she was too shamed to ever see any of her family again and she refused to see me."

Yoshi was the son of a coastal sailor. His father had a flat-bottom boat that was built for rowing but had one sail, made of woven hemp, to assist it going downwind. Yoshi's father expected him to join the navy, but Yoshi had had enough of the ocean and decided on the army.

While Kenji spent his spare time with his treasured books on history, languages and literature, his roommates read for their lessons and then read for pleasure. They especially liked books made with woodblock prints. These common, poorly printed books told tales of superheroes who rescued their samurai masters from their enemies. Or they were spooky tales involving ghosts, malevolent badgers, and foxes.

In the classroom, instructors drilled the cadets on tactics, map reading, how to use artillery, signals, and lesson after lesson about bushido. Out of the classroom other instructors put them through their paces with physical training, drill on the parade ground, and the martial arts.

Map-reading proficiency eluded most cadets.

"How do I understand what I see around me from the lines on a map?" asked Taro.

Kenji slowly and patiently explained how to pick out prominent terrain features, how to understand contour lines, and how to orient one's map to terrain features on the ground. After several days of late-night sessions, all of his roommates finally grasped the principles of map-reading and land navigation and they all passed the examination.

In judo, Kenji's performance was surprisingly good. Judo was more than just a contest of strength. If one were nimble enough and a quick thinker, one could use the opponent's own strength against him. Kenji could do this. He was nearly at the top of his class in judo and did well in kendo. He hated them both.

Dealing with firearms was another serious shortcoming. After a few weeks, he got used to carrying his rifle and could execute the manual of arms. He had no problem learning the parts of several different weapons and was skilled in taking any one of them apart, cleaning it, and quickly putting it back together. But when he got to the rifle range for marksmanship practice he did poorly. His first day was a disaster. With an instructor standing behind him he inserted his first round into the chamber and closed the bolt. His hands shook while he was trying to sight in on the target and he was prepared to flinch at the sound of the shot going off so near to his ear. And flinch he did. His first shots missed the target by a wide margin. After three days of practice, he was able to get most of his rounds somewhere on the target but usually not anywhere near the center except by accident. His roommates had no such problems. The instructors constantly praised Taro as the best shot among all the first-year cadets.

Kenji's roommates drilled him after hours on the proper way to hold his rifle, how to breathe properly and how to sight in on the target. They kept him up late dry firing without ammunition.

In order to graduate from the academy each cadet had achieve a minimum score of 200 out of a possible 250 on the rifle range. In the days leading up to the final one when the scores would count, Kenji's best day was only 178 points. Most days he scored far below that. The day before he was to fire for record Captain Shoji called him into his office.

"Well, young Dainichi, I think we will be seeing the last of you soon. You know that tomorrow you must either qualify with the required score with the rifle or be sent home, do you not?"

"Yes, sir."

That night Kenji told his roommates about Captain Shoji. All offered their advice and worried about his performance the next day.

More than just losing him as a tutor, they had grown to like him. The last thing they wanted was for him to wash out of the academy

Kenji awoke that morning with a feeling of dread. He knew he had little hope of getting a high enough score to pass.

The cadets fired in relays of twenty-five men each. When the turn for his relay came, Kenji stepped up to the hundred-meter line and, along with twenty-four other cadets, loaded his rifle. He sighted in on his target and slowly fired his twenty rounds, one shot after another, trying to remember what his roommates had told him. He did better than expected. Five points were awarded for hitting the center of the target and a lesser number for hitting it elsewhere. He scored eighty-seven points out of a possible one hundred. That was his best score ever but the hundred-meter line was where he always got his highest score and he did not expect to improve on it. He knew that when he got farther from the target his scores always dropped.

The cadets moved back to the two-hundred-meter line, where they could fire while sitting, rather than from the standing position. For most cadets, this was an advantage that permitted them to shoot from a steadier platform, but Kenji's small size worked against him. The weight and length of the rifle was difficult for a small man to handle. He sat, leaned forward, and rested his elbows on his knees, and told himself to relax. Before each shot he took a deep breath, sighted in and fired. He shot the allotted twenty rounds, hoping against hope that he could improve his scores. After he expended his ammunition and tallied his score, he found that he had only scored another seventy-nine points. His total was but one hundred sixty-six points and he would only be allowed to fire ten rounds on the 300-meter line. His best score at this distance was only twenty-five points and he found no hope that he would improve upon it. When all the cadets had finished firing and moved back to the 300-meter line, Taro, who shot next to him in the same relay said, "Kenji, how are you doing?"

"Oh, Taro, it is terrible. I need thirty-four points at the 300-meter line, and the best I have ever fired from that distance is twenty-five. Usually my score is somewhere between fifteen and twenty."

"Kenji, just do what I told you. Breathe in before each shot. Let part of it out. Make sure your sights are lined up and that the blade of your front sight is resting just under the target. Then slowly squeeze the trigger. Do not jerk it."

"I will try Taro."

He fired his first shot and waited for it to be scored. When no score came he called to the instructor and asked why they had not scored the shot. "It was obviously a miss," the instructor replied. Five points completely gone! Kenji despaired of ever even hitting the target. He took a couple of deep breaths and fired a second shot. Miraculously, it hit just outside the bull's eye and was scored a four. He still needed thirty points to reach the magic score of 200 and only could fire a maximum of forty if he put them *all* in the bull's eye.

Under the shadow of certain failure, he was not confident of even hitting the target. Resigned to his fate, he decided to go ahead and expend the remainder of his bullets without worrying about it. He was going to fail, and there was no sense delaying the agony. He casually pointed his weapon down range, sighed heavily and fired. It came up marked a five. A bull's eye. The next one was also a five, just at the edge of the bull's eye. Amazed, he fired off his remaining ammunition and when he was through he had accumulated thirty-four points, just the number of points he needed to pass.

After the cadets exhausted their ammunition and cleared their weapons, Taro, who was in the position to his right said, "Kenji, how did you finish?"

"Taro, I passed! I passed! How about you?"

"You know me, Kenji, I always do well at this sort of thing."

That night the marksmanship instructor posted the official scores on the bulletin board in the barracks. Kenji rapidly ran down the list to see his name, in writing, among those who had passed. After he found his own name he looked for his comrades. They, too, had all passed the rifle range. He noticed that Taro, usually the best shot in the group, had had a bad day. He only scored 202 points. Normally he scored 230 or more. And his score on the 300-meter line was far lower than what it normally was. Kenji thought about that for a long time, but when he asked Taro about it, the latter gave him an evasive look and said that it had been a bad day for him and he was not feeling particularly well. "But do not worry, Kenji, we all passed."

During the second half of the year the cadets attended twice-weekly lectures by Major Hiro Minobe from Imperial Army Headquarters in Tokyo. Major Minobe repeated much of the same message that Kenji had gotten from Araki, his tutor, and his uncle Genichi about Japan's future in East Asia. "Japan is destined to rule," the major said over and over again, "and we must keep the western powers, particularly Russia, out. The Russians are trying to encroach on East Asia by building a base at Port Arthur. Let them do that and there is no telling what they will do next. Japan must stop them. Russia is a failed empire and will not last. It is corrupt. Its people do not revere their emperor the way we revere ours and they weaken by the day."

In June, Kenji returned to Tokyo for a three-month vacation from the school. His mother happily greeted him, and his uncles all waited at his house to congratulate him on completion of his first year at the academy. When his uncles had gone, Kenji went to see Momoko, eager to tell her about his survival at the academy. A serving girl met him at the front door.

"I am sorry, sir. Miss Momoko knows you are back but does not want to see you."

"Does not want to see me! But why?"

"I do not know, sir, I just know what she told me to say to you."

Kenji walked home crestfallen, kicking up clods of dirt along the way. When he got home he lay on a futon and tried to think pleasant thoughts, but his mind returned again and again to Momoko. *What is going on?* he wondered. *Is she engaged to Kozo Shimada? Is she sick?* A thousand thoughts raced through his mind. He made up his mind to keep going to her house until he got an answer. But after making four trips and receiving the same reply from several different maids, he was at a loss about what to do. He decided to make just one more effort, and if that failed, he would accept that Momoko really did not want to see him and give up.

When he knocked on the door, Momoko happened to be standing near the entrance and slid it open herself. Right behind her stood one of the servant girls who had turned Kenji away.

"Kenji," she said. "You are back! How long have you been back? Why have you not been to see me?"

"I have been to see you, Momoko. But this girl told me that you did not wish to see me."

Momoko turned to the servant girl. "Is this true? I said no such thing."

"I know, mistress," she said, "but your father ordered us to say you did not want to see Dainichi-san. He said you are to be betrothed to Kozo Shimada and you are not to see Kenji any longer."

Momoko's face turned pale with anger. "Well, I will just have to talk to my father about that. And I am *not* betrothed to Kozo Shimada and never will be! Kenji, please come and see me tomorrow. I will speak with my father."

Momoko kept her word and Kenji was able to visit the next day, but her father placed a restriction on their visits. They could no longer see each other alone. They could only meet at Momoko's house or with a chaperone.

Away from the academy, Kenji had much time to reflect on his life and his future. Despite his successful completion of his first year at the academy. he did not like the military life, mostly because it was a dress rehearsal for violence and violence went against his nature. His heart yearned to be a poet, a scholar, a writer, and a man of peace. No matter that his family had spent generations, centuries, in military service, he did not feel comfortable with it. He had other worries as well. *What will happen*, he thought, *if I actually have to go to war? Will I be able to perform? To do my duty. Or will I be overcome by fear and my natural tendencies toward peace? It is a mistake for me to become an army officer. If I go into combat I will surely let down not only my family but the emperor as well.*

He spent most of his holiday trying, and failing, to expunge such thoughts from his mind. His suffering over the worries for his future, combined with his agony over Momoko's father's attitude toward him, made his thoughts nearly unbearable.

The summer quickly passed. He saw Momoko at every opportunity but the sharp gaze and alert ears of a chaperone cast a pall over their meetings. They could not have a private conversation without the chaperone hearing and reporting back to Momoko's father. On the day before he returned to the academy he bade Momoko farewell. "Do not worry about things, Kenji," she whispered," especially about my father betrothing me to Kozo. It will not happen."

CHAPTER 11

TATIANA: FOUND AND LOST AGAIN

As expected, Ivan enrolled in the Imperial Nicholas Military Academy in St. Petersburg, named after the "Iron Tsar" Nicholas I, who ruled Russia from 1825 until 1855, and was the namesake of the current ruler. Nearly all the cadets came from the aristocracy; some were relatives of the tsar. Others belonged to once-prominent families whose fortunes had declined and for them the military was the only future for them other than the church or a life of poverty. Still others were second or third sons whose elder brothers inherited the family estate. Most of the remainder were sons, grandsons, or nephews of former military officers and had been raised in the Russian military tradition. A few sons of wealthy, influential merchants rounded out the mix. These young men hoped to find their way into the aristocracy by heroic service.

Ivan did well at the academy. His lifelong admiration of the feats of his great-grandfather motivated him to read many books on military subjects in his father's library. Moreover, he excelled at horsemanship and, thanks to the tutors his father had hired, was a good fencer, though a mediocre pistol shot.

Ivan wanted to excel at military service. He regarded it as the most glorious of occupations and certainly more appealing than the dull life his father led as a bureaucrat. And a connection with the tsar could not hurt his career. He expected to inherit his father's title some day and thought about how it would be wonderful to be one of the tsar's generals as well. His ambitious dreams dominated his imagination.

Both his parents expressed delight that Ivan had chosen a military career. His mother had specific ideas about his future. "Ivan, you are assured a job at court and will not even have to go to war," she told him. "As a member of one of the Guards regiments your place will be at court. When the time comes, you will be an advisor to the tsar like your father. Then you will leave the army and become a government minister." His mother's idea of a good career for him did not match his dreams but Ivan held his tongue.

He got along well with his classmates, although he did not participate in their drunken parties nor in their wenching. Alcoholism was the bane of Russia, even among its upper classes, and he was determined to stay away from it as much as possible. And, using his parents' marriage as a model, he wanted to devote himself to the woman who would be his wife. His classmates liked him but considered him a prude.

Ivan usually spent summers with his family in St. Petersburg, where the tsar resided for the season and kept Ivan's father busy with government matters. One summer day Ivan was strolling through an open-air market, looking for the military memorabilia he collected, when he saw a young woman about his age in the crowd. She had a mass of dark curls and wore simple, working-class garb. She obviously had a good figure. Could it be her?

"Tatiana," he called out, "Tatiana Gitina."

She looked to see who had cried out. On spotting Ivan, her eyes widened and she immediately turned and took off running. But her skirt slowed her down, and Ivan was fast on his feet. He caught up with her and grabbed her by the arm.

"Tatiana Gitina, it is you! How have you been? After all this time! Why did you leave so suddenly? I have been so sad, and so worried. Why have I not heard from you?" The questions tumbled out of him in a torrent as Tatiana struggled to get out of his grasp.

"Shhh," she whispered as she scanned the crowd to see who might be listening, "I go by the last name of Smirnov now. Tatiana Gitina is dead forever."

"But, why?" he asked.

"Surely you know that my father had to leave Moscow because the police falsely blamed him in a plot against the tsar."

"Please, let's talk. Can we go to a restaurant for a meal, or just some tea?"

"Well, perhaps some tea, but only if I choose the place," she replied, and she led him to an out-of-the-way and inexpensive teahouse. She carefully eyed the customers before choosing a seat close to the back door, where she could watch the front. The owner and the other customers stared at the well-dressed young man with the beautiful, young, poorly dressed woman. When Ivan stared back at them, they quickly averted their eyes.

Over tea Tatiana related how she had spent the past year. Her father worked at the Putilov plant under their assumed name. She had papers but not very good ones, so she dared not try to find a real job. She worked part-time caring for the five children of a minor merchant who was not meticulous about papers and who had no connections within the ranks of the upper levels of society like those known to the Medveds. One of the reasons that the merchant was not careful about her papers was that he suspected that she was living in St. Petersburg illegally so he could take advantage of her, paying her less than normal. The man also frequently tried to grope her and get her alone. So far, she had fended him off, but it was a constant struggle. She knew that if she told the lady of the house of her husband's advances, she would immediately be fired and would be reported to the police. Her father's friends had gotten them new internal passports that gave them new names and, for him, better papers, but they would not bear close inspection.

She asked about Ivan's family and smiled when Ivan told her that his sister had a wide range of young men interested in her and that his parents enjoyed good health.

"Is there a young lady in your life, Ivan?"

"Not yet, Tatya. It is too early in my life to think about romance. I am at the military academy and am concentrating on my career in the army. There are several young women of whom I am fond and am glad to see at social affairs. My family will be happy to know that I have found you."

Tatiana's eyes widened, "No, you must tell no one! You do not realize how many enemies we have and how serious they are."

Ivan pulled out his watch, then said, "Tatiana, I have to go. My mother is entertaining, and these days she depends on me to play the host for her since my father is so busy with the government and left yesterday for Moscow. Can we meet again soon?"

Her face contorted as she struggled over the answer. "All right, but you have got to promise me that this will be a secret. And we cannot meet too often. You are obviously rich and I am obviously poor, and I cannot afford to draw attention to myself. Please wear something a little plainer. You look like just what you are, a member of the aristocracy."

That evening one of Ivan's mother's friends remarked that he looked pale and distracted. He was not rude but did not seem to feel his usual charming self.

Why, he could not help wondering, *do these people here have little to worry about except their social status, when people like Tatiana fear for their lives? She may come from a poor family but she is proof that even poor people can become as educated and refined as any of our family friends. Why must she hide from the police and live the life of a fugitive? She has become so beautiful.* He wished that he could introduce her to society as an equal.

In the time since he had last seen Tatiana, Ivan's sister, Natalya, had become his best friend. They had often discussed Tatya and wondered what had become of her. Despite his promise, he just had to tell Natalya that he had found her. He did so, swearing her to absolute secrecy beforehand.

"Oh, Ivan, how wonderful. You must take me to see her."

"I cannot, Natalya, I am not even supposed to tell you that I've her. I am meeting her tomorrow; I will ask."

The next day he met Tatiana again. Halfway into their second cup of tea he said, "Tatya, I know I promised you that I would tell no one, but I broke that promise and told Natalya. She knows how much I missed you after you left Moscow, and she is happy that I have found you. She is good at keeping secrets and she wants to see you again."

Tatiana's dark eyes turned nearly black. "Ivan, how could you? You promised."

"Yes, I know, but she has such wonderful memories of the time we spent together, as do you and I. I swore her to absolute secrecy, and I know that she will tell no one."

"She only tolerated me at first, and then only because she knew I could not compete with her for any of the young men around because of my social class. But you are right. We became good friends, and I would like to see her. But Ivan, I beg you, we must be careful. I dare not tell my father that I have seen you. And for God's sake, do not tell your parents. It could result in jail or worse for me and my father if the Okhrana found out."

The three met the next day and sporadically after that and talked as if they had been together for years. Tatiana chose where they met and sometimes was late or did not show up at all because she did not like the looks of some of the people in the area where they were to meet. Sometimes, when Ivan was busy with other matters, just the two girls met. Natalya being very much her mother's daughter, always had much social gossip to pass on. She mentioned this person and that, people whom Tatiana had met, and who was in love with whom and who was invited to the best parties. But, as Natalya would report back to Ivan, Tatiana seemed constantly fearful and kept her part of the conversation focused on memories of her years with the Medveds and on Natalya's interests.

On a day when summer drew near its end and Ivan was about to go back to the academy, and Natalya was busy with other matters so Ivan and Tatiana met alone. She asked if he could come to her house the next day. This surprised Ivan, as Tatiana had refused to even let him know which neighborhood she lived in.

He approached her house with some caution. It was in a rough neighborhood, and although she had lived in a similar environment in Moscow, there a servant always accompanied him. Now he nervously walked through the neighborhood alone, and even though he had dressed plainly he still stood out from the others in this neighborhood. He wished he had borrowed clothing from one of the household servants and dressed even poorer. When he finally found the house, he looked around him, gathered his courage, stepped up to the door, and knocked. Tatiana immediately opened it.

"Come in quickly, Ivan," she said as she grasped his arm and pulled him through the door. She immediately shut and bolted it behind him. Ivan took in the rude structure with its bed against the wall, a small table with two benches and a small stove used for cooking and heat. The house was neatly kept and clean. Tatiana wore a pretty but threadbare dress. She looked freshly scrubbed and her hair shone. She smelled wonderful, like soap and femininity.

She led him to a table in the center of the room. and "Tea, or perhaps you would like a little vodka?"

Ivan normally did not drink alcohol, but to settle his nerves he said, "A small vodka would be nice."

Tatiana grunted and poured a generous measure into two wooden cups. and sat on the bench right next to him. She threw her vodka back with a practiced toss, huffed out her breath, and turned to Ivan. He tried to do the same but choked on the burning fluid before he got it all down. He spilled the remainder when she patted him on the back. She got up to get him some water from a pitcher and then sat beside him once more. It took a few moments for Ivan's breathing to return to normal and he felt a bit lightheaded from the small amount of vodka.

They met each other's eyes, hers dark, his a light shade of blue. She smiled, her dimples forming in both cheeks, then reached around to the back of his head and pulled him toward her. Her lips touched his, tentatively at first and then fully. Ivan gasped, startled. He had never kissed a woman with passion in his entire life, although since puberty he had often imagined such an event. He kept his eyes wide open as he kissed her and noticed with amazement that she closed hers. He closed his too. They parted, and his breath came short. His tunic suddenly seemed several sizes too small, and he felt himself becoming erect. She began to unbutton the tunic and then the shirt beneath. All the time she bared his chest she kept kissing him. He was becoming embarrassingly aroused and he crossed his legs, afraid she would notice. She began kissing his chest, then took one of his hands and drew it under her shirt, and slid it over her breast. The softness, the luscious weight almost drove him crazy.

"Come," she said as she stood and pulled him in the direction of the bed against the wall.

An hour later Ivan lay nearly speechless. "Tatiana, I do not know what to say. That was the most wonderful thing that has ever happened to me. I love you."

"Love? We cannot love. You are from a princely family, and the police are looking for my father. Our two worlds shall never come together."

"I will ask my father. He knows who you are and liked having you in our household all those years. He knows how beautiful you are and, and how well mannered. I am sure that someday he will let me marry you."

"Marry me? Do not be silly, Ivan. None of your family will ever let you marry me. We can have all the sex you like, but that is as far as it can go."

Ivan returned home that afternoon with his head awhirl. For two days, he struggled over what to do and finally decided to talk to his father about marrying Tatiana after he graduated from the academy.

"Marry whom?" Boris Medved nearly shouted. "You are too young to marry anyone. And no son of mine will ever be permitted to marry a commoner of that sort. Her father is probably a subversive, for the sake of God! How can I possibly maintain a position at court while my son is involved with a woman whose father wants to overthrow the tsar? Impossible! You must not ever see her again. If you do, I will have the police follow you and find out where she lives. If we arrest her father, then where will you be? Maybe they will arrest her too. Do you understand?"

"Yes, Papa," came the meek reply.

After Ivan left the room, Boris sat down at his desk, thought for a minute, and then slowly penned a note to the Minister of the Interior.

Ivan could not bear the thought of not seeing Tatiana again and they met several times during the remaining two weeks of the summer. On what he knew would be their last meeting he stopped in a jewelry shop and bought her a gold locket. In it he placed a small photograph of themselves that they had had taken several weeks before.

After hey made love the last time that year, he presented it to her and said, "Tatya, please take this to remember me. To remember us. It will be next summer before I see you, and I love and will miss you."

"Oh, Ivan, it is so beautiful, and I will wear it always."

When Ivan returned to the academy, he received letters from both Tatiana and his sister Natalya. Then, just before the holidays, three weeks passed during which Ivan had not had a letter from Tatiana. Finally, he received a note from Natalya. "Ivan," it began, "I do not know how to tell you this, but I have not seen Tatiana for several weeks. I have gone to her house looking for her but no one answers the door. I do not know what else to tell you. We can both go look for her during the holidays."

Ivan arrived in St. Petersburg for the holidays in hopeful spirits. The next day he set out for Tatiana's house. No one answered his knock, but a neighbor woman told him Tatiana and her father had moved. "She said you would be around and I was to give you this." She handed him a small parcel wrapped in plain paper and string. Ivan opened it on the way home and found that it contained the locket he had given Tatiana. With it was a note.

"Dearest Ivan, I stopped writing to you because someone set the dogs of the Okhrana on us. Thankfully, our neighbors saw them sneaking around the neighborhood and warned us. They began watching the house within a week of your departure. We have been forced to move several times, and my father has had to find another job. I think the secret police dared not move on us until you returned to the academy.

"Now the times are more dangerous for us than ever. Love between us can never be. Neither your family nor mine will permit us to marry. They are right. Your family supports the tsar and mine thinks that the tsarist system is what is wrong with Russia and what must be changed. And as I get older and see more, I realize the uselessness of the church. In this my father is right. He is also right about the tsar and the oppression caused by our system of government.

"I have joined the cause to rid Russia of both of these evils. I have also taken a lover. He will never take your place in my heart, but he is a man as dedicated to the cause as I am and is working hard to bring about change in Russia. Good change. Positive change. Pyotr and I are going to dedicate our lives to this change for better or for worse. Take care, my love. In a perfect world, we could be lovers forever. Please burn this note after you have read it. Tatiana."

With tears in his eyes, Ivan carefully burned the note and crumbled up and scattered the ashes. He slipped the locket into his pocket.

CHAPTER 12

BIRTH OF A WARRIOR

Captain Shoji, his tormentor, was busy with new first year cadets and Kenji rarely saw him. Although Kenji easily outstripped his contemporaries in academic subjects, he remained far behind them in the military arts. He was afraid of and hated horses and was a poor rider. He retained his dislike of kendo, and judo, and all other physical training. Yet, he managed to improve and he passed these subjects, some of them just barely. He had his uniforms tailored so that they fit better, and he filled them out with muscle. He got hats that fit, and he learned to wrap his puttees to perfection. Whenever he saw a first-year cadet having difficulty with them, he would stop and help.

Kenji could easily solve tactical problems on the blackboard in the classroom, and in the field, he could stand on a hill and meticulously plan its defenses or could plan an attack on a far position. Once maneuvers began, his talents really shone. His classmates learned to rely on him in planning a mock battle, for he invariably had the best solution, and to rely on him once the battle was joined, because his mind could process multiple thoughts simultaneously. He could rapidly sort through the fluid conditions of a mock battle, conditions that confused and baffled others, and find solutions.

The lessons he absorbed in kendo, learn by being struck, served him well. The senior members of the faculty were quick to notice his abilities.

Because of his mental agility, cadets who were larger and physically stronger than himself looked up to him for his ability to lead. He kept the same roommates, Taro, Yukio and Hiroshi and they continued to protect him, although he no longer required much protection. Besides leading his comrades, Kenji helped school them, by patiently explaining every step of the reasoning behind his solutions to complex military problems. The instructors tested him by giving him larger and larger bodies of cadets to command.

In the final exercise of the year the instructor gave Kenji command of his entire class of second-year cadets, in a maneuver against the senior class, the class that was to be graduated and commissioned as officers in the summer. This was an annual exercise, which the senior class always won. The instructors thought that inevitable loss would help the younger cadets by teaching them character, and how to sacrifice themselves and how to endure hardship when they met a superior foe.

The exercise was to last three days and it took place in a remote, hilly region to the north of Tokyo. Spring had come to the Kanto Plain area around Tokyo, but the morning the exercise commenced turned cold, and a few snowflakes fell that afternoon, when they disembarked from the wagons that had carried them north.

The exercise was simple in conception. The White Forces, the seniors, held a small hill in front of a river. The instructor ordered the Blue Forces, under Kenji's command, to advance on the position, outmaneuver the defenders, and to take their position by force or reduce it by siege. Each group numbered about three hundred cadets, with a sprinkling of instructors to grade the cadets and keep the sides honest. The instructors gave the White Forces an extra day head start to move into the objective area and fortify it, or dispose their forces around it as best they could. They did not permit Kenji and his "staff" to study maps of the area until just before they reached the debarkation point from which they began.

Kenji used the extra day to appoint his subordinate commanders and select his staff. In each case, he selected those he considered to be most qualified and played no favorites. After his cadets had reached the debarkation point, he gathered his commanders and staff, issued maps, explained the situation to them, and asked for comments. The approximate enemy position was marked on the map. Just as they had heard, it sat on a small hill with a river at its back. The map also showed them that on either side of their hill lay two steep draws, containing rocky streambeds, which ran past the position and into the river. After some study, all sorts of suggestions came his way. Some favored a frontal assault up the slope that led to the enemy position. This was the easiest solution, and it was one the students had almost always attempted in the past. Kenji thought that in a real battle it would cause entirely too many casualties and would fail. Many of the cadets and not a few of the officer-instructors favored this approach because it would result in the largest number of casualties. This was, they reasoned, the true spirit of bushido, which called for sacrifice, the honorable ultimate sacrifice, for the emperor. Better to learn it here, and become familiar with it, than to hesitate over using it on the battlefield. Kenji understood the importance of bushido but reasoned that bushido combined with victory would be the best way to serve His Majesty.

The other commonly used solution was to divide the attacking force into thirds. A force of about a hundred men would attack up each of the streambeds that bordered the hill. The remaining third, in the center, would lay down an imaginary base of fire and the White Forces' position would be attacked on two sides in a double envelopment. This solution, too, had been tried in the past with no success. The current White Force attempted this earlier when they had been the Blue Force. They could be depended on to prepare for both contingencies.

Kenji knew that he must do something different, something bold and unexpected but he had no idea what. The first order of the day was to make a reconnaissance. He put his troops in tactical marching formation and they moved slowly over the ground the four miles to the objective area. While on the march Taro saw a dove on the ground that gave him a thought that he passed to Kenji.

"Kenji," he said, "do you see that dove that is limping away from us?"

"Yes, Taro, but what of it?"

"It is trying to deceive us. These birds, Kenji, have a habit of doing that when they think their nest is threatened, of pretending to be wounded in order to get us to follow it away from the nest and its young ones. If we chase it, it will lead us off track and then suddenly recover and fly away. Maybe you can think of a way to use this to deceive our enemy."

Kenji thought about this for a moment and filed it away.

He halted his forces when his scouts reported that the enemy position could be seen over the next long rise. He took his maps, his operations officer, his subordinate commanders, and his binoculars, and crawled up to the crest of the hill. The map was accurate as far as he could tell. He watched the enemy troops digging fighting holes and trenches on the position. He carefully examined the draws through which the streambeds on either side of the objective ran, and as much as he could see of the river behind the position. Then he crawled back down the hill.

"I can see why the old solutions failed. There is nothing to either one of them worthy of consideration," he said. What we must do is something so different and so unexpected that it will overwhelm the enemy. The frontal attack may be in accordance with bushido but it will fail to win which is the reason I reject it."

"But what should we do?" his chief of staff asked.

"I have a plan," he said. "It will not be easy. It will require a lot of careful preparation, timing, hard work, and risk, but if we pull it off, we have a chance of becoming the first Blue Force to ever win this thing." In an effort to lighten the mood, he said, "Maybe we should pretend they are Russians and will give up easily." This drew a laugh from the others.

Looking around at the expectant faces of his subordinates, he continued. "What we must do is find a way to ford the river."

"But, Kenji," said another cadet, "there is a ford directly behind the enemy's position. But it makes no sense to try to cross over there under their guns. We would just cross the river twice for no reason. The nearest other ford is nearly twenty miles upriver. If we try to cross between here and there, the river is too swift and too deep."

"Besides," came another objection, "it is true that their defenses are oriented toward the front. But if they discover us, and they probably will, how long will it take them to turn around and pin us against the river? Not long at all!"

"First," said Kenji," we must make that march to the farthest ford. It will be difficult, but war is difficult, and this is nothing to what we will be facing on the battlefield. We just must make up our minds that we can do the forty-mile round-trip in twenty-four hours. It will be twenty miles to the ford and twenty miles back to the position. We will re-cross the river directly behind the position just after dark and take them from the rear in a night attack. As far as them turning their defenses around, we will create a diversion. I got the idea from a dove that Taro pointed out while on the way here. We will use a combination of deception and an attack in an unexpected manner. We must fix their attention and make them think that our entire force is still arrayed in front of them or they may grow suspicious about what we are up to. Secondly, we must try to convince them that our force is weak and disorganized and try to draw out a part of their force from their position just as we attack them from the rear. We can do that if we make them think we have gotten ourselves in trouble, and are crippled like that dove we saw, and they rush out to finish us off."

The instructors who accompanied Kenji's force listened impassively. Kenji impressed them. Here, at last, was a cadet who had the courage and imagination to try something different. Whether it would succeed or not was another matter.

"I am dividing our force into two groups," Kenji said. I will take two thirds of you up the river, cross, and come back in the dark. I am appointing Taro the commander of the other third. He will remain behind to create the diversion."

He spent a couple of hours carefully briefing his subordinate commanders and staff and listening to their suggestions and going over the maps with them.

"Taro, use the remaining daylight to send a couple of scouting parties to let the White Force know that we are active. The rest of you commanders must brief your men and prepare them for a long and difficult march. We leave an hour after sunset."

Darkness fell, and Kenji marched his men east along the river in tactical formation. To misdirect the attention of the White Forces, Taro sent patrols up the draws on either side of their position. The patrols made more noise than necessary; Taro hoped that they would keep the enemy from sending out patrols of their own. He need not have worried. The senior cadets felt safe and were confident and lazy. They expected to wait a day or so until their enemy attacked and then to wipe them out. This was the way it had always been. Whether it was a frontal assault or a double envelopment up the draws did not matter to them. They prepared for both.

The terrain was rugged, and Kenji's men had little time for rest if they were to make their schedule. They stumbled along, following the river all night and when daylight came, they had still not reached the ford. As the sun rose, they picked up the pace and Kenji thought they would reach their objective on schedule although they had been without sleep for over twenty-four hours. A few cadets could not keep up and fell out of the formation. Kenji left them behind. He cautioned them to not return to the main position because the enemy might see them and give the game away.

An hour after sunrise, a scout came racing back to the column to say that he had found the ford. But he also had bad news.

"Kenji, the ford is swollen with the spring rains, and it is faster and deeper than you thought. It is narrower there, though, so we will not have so much distance to cross."

"Well, we are committed now," said Kenji. "It is either this or failure. We must pick up the pace so we will have more time to figure out how to get across." With that, Kenji drove his formation harder and an hour later they reached the ford.

The water ran nearly chest high for most of the men, and for Kenji it would be shoulder height. He looked down at the racing water and wondered if they could get across, or whether his whole plan would blow up and he would be humiliated. There was a hand-pulled ferry at the ford. It would only bear six passengers at a time and the ferryman pulled the boat across hand over hand on a rope strung across the river.

The ferryman was napping on his boat when Kenji's men arrived. Once the ferryman overcame his surprise at seeing so many uniformed young men at his place of business, his eyes widened at the prospect of so many customers, and he became friendly. He quoted Kenji a price for ferrying all his men across the river.

"I doubt that we have that amount of money among all of us," Kenji said, "Even if I could afford that, it would not do. At a pace of six at a time, it will take several days to get across. Let us see what we can come up with." He turned to his men,

"Okay, cadets, search your pockets and see how much money you have and you are willing to give."

A quick count showed that they had enough to pay for a few men. Kenji quickly made a decision. He needed to be at the other crossing behind the enemy position just after dark.

"How, many of you are non-swimmers or weak swimmers?" he asked. A few hands shot up. "We have enough money to ferry you across. How many of you are strong swimmers?" Again, a few cadets raised hands, Yoshi's among them. "Yoshi, you are in charge of this group. Half of you strong swimmers will swim across the river, act as scouts and, if needed, assist any of us who have trouble getting across. We have a few ropes that we will tie together and one of you will carry an end of it across. The other half of you strong swimmers will remain on this bank, to help any of us who have difficulty near this side. Once the rest of us are across, you will follow us."

The strong swimmers conferred among themselves and four of them detached from the rest of the group and immediately began swimming for the far shore. One of them had the rope tied around his waist and one of the swimmers on the near shore paid it out. After the scout-swimmers reached the far shore, they tied both ends of the rope to a tree. The remainder stationed themselves on the near shore ready to act immediately if needed. The ferryman got ready to take the non-swimmers across six at a time. The instructors had no intention of getting wet and the ferryman agreed to take them across too.

The ferry started across with the first six men. The rest of the men lined up at the rope and began to cross on foot. When they entered the water, the cold took their breath away. Kenji was not a strong swimmer, but he wanted to lead by example and cross in the water with the majority of his men. He stepped into the river and thought he was going into shock as the freezing water moved up his body. His rifle slung over his shoulder and his other field equipment weighted him down. As he moved toward the center of the river the current was so strong that the only way he could keep his head out of the water and breathe was to kick himself off the bottom every step, grasping the rope hand over hand. The strong current, the weight of his body and equipment and the cold worked against him.

Kenji lost his grip with one hand where the current ran the strongest. He struggled to regain it but the current pushed him sideways. Despite all his effort his other hand gave way. Down he went.

Down into the water and downstream. The cadets on either side of him cried out in alarm, but were unable to help because they, too, fought the river and could just hang on. The scouts on the far shore were standing and shivering as they wrung the water out their uniforms. They heard the cries and saw Kenji go down. Two immediately dove in after him.

Kenji bumped along the bottom, badly needing to breathe. He dropped some of his field equipment and kicked at the elusive bottom, trying to get his head above water and draw a breath. As he raced over a relatively shallow spot, his kick gained him the surface, and he sucked in a mouthful of air. Then he went under again, trying to reach the life-giving surface once more, and involuntarily breathing in a bit of water. He was sure he would drown when a strong hand grabbed a strap on his pack and started to tug. Another grasped him under the arm. The three cadets cleared the surface and Kenji's two rescuers swam for the far bank keeping Kenji between them. They got him to the edge where others reached out and pulled him to safety. They rolled Kenji over on his stomach and began pounding his back. He choked and vomited water and had a hard time catching his breath but after a few minutes he could sit upright and was greeted by the sight of nearly all his men standing on the bank and wringing out their clothing. They cheered when they saw him sit up.

The senior instructor who accompanied Kenji's force said, "Cadet Dainichi, you must retire from the field. You are in no shape to carry on. Please choose which of your men you would like to command in your place."

Without the slightest hesitation he said, "No, sir, I began leading this group and I will finish leading it."

Kenji told his men to take a two-hour break. This would put them behind schedule but they wore their fatigue like part of a uniform and he hoped to make up lost time on the march with a refreshed force. Some built fires during the break to try and dry out their sodden clothing, but with little success.

By late morning, they resumed the march, still weary but refreshed by their rest. Drawing on unexpected physical resources, the cadets did not complain because Kenji had nearly drowned, and he drove himself as hard as they. It was a cold day but the activity of marching hard made it hot. Steam rose from their wet clothing and boots chafed and added to the discomfort. Many of them got blisters on their feet but gamely limped along with their comrades. A few dropped out and Kenji once more decided to leave the stragglers behind. If this was a mock battle it should resemble as nearly as possible real combat, and in real combat sacrifices like this would have to be made.

As the afternoon shadows lengthened, Kenji halted his column an easy hour's march from his objective. At dusk, he sent scouts ahead to take a look and admonished them to be careful. If the enemy spotted them, the whole effort would come to failure. They came back with the report that they could see little of the enemy force and what they did see faced the south, away from the river. Also, they reported, the river did not appear to be as swift nor as deep here. It was wider but shallow enough to permit an easy crossing.

Kenji gathered his subordinate commanders and briefed them. "As soon as it is fully dark we will cross the river. After we get across we will assume an attack formation and wait. Precisely three hours after the disk of the sun disappears from the horizon, we will attack. Taro will begin his activity two and a half hours after sundown to try and draw out the enemy. We will begin our assault a few minutes after we hear his assault. When we attack we will do so in a line. I am going to commit all my troops, and not have a reserve. Before the attack and under the cover of darkness, the scouts will carefully crawl to the top of the hill and lay down white pieces of cloth to mark the direction of the attack and help the attackers find their way. Are there any questions?" The cadets looked at each other with confident expressions. They knew they were part of something special and, win or lose, they would be remembered for having a part in it.

On the other side of the enemy position, Taro issued his own orders. "Tonight, we will create a diversion and hope to draw out some of the enemy and ambush them. We will send noisy patrols up the draws just after sundown to let them know we are active. When the patrols are fired upon I will withdraw them back to this position and a couple of hours later we will light small fires, like campfires."

"But, Taro," one cadet said, "Is not that against discipline? Should we really be lighting fires where the enemy can see them?"

"That is just the point. We must make them think we are poorly disciplined and see if we can draw some of them out to attack us. Once we light the fires, we will leave no men with them, but will withdraw them to the flanks, and if they come out to attack what they think are men sitting around the campfires, we will attack them from both sides. If we do this right it should coincide with Kenji's attack on their rear."

On the hill, the White Force commander wondered what was going on. He was a bull of a man, selected for his physical prowess rather than his intellect. His name was Kato Oshiro, and he was one who had taken delight in beating Kenji down with kendo staves. He looked forward to beating him in a mock battle.

"What could they be doing?" Oshiro asked his staff, when the Blue Force lit the first of the fires. None of them knew for sure. Such a thing had no precedent in their experience. They came to a consensus that little Kenji had lost control of his men and they were breaking discipline by lighting campfires. Well, come tomorrow, Kenji's force would attack them in one of the two usual maneuvers and be declared the loser by the instructors.

"Kato," one of his men said, "Why do not we attack them while they sit around their campfires? It may not be enough to get the instructors to declare us the winners, but it should ruin their morale and make them easier to defeat tomorrow."

"I like that idea, Hideki, we can show the instructors that I am just not sitting around waiting for an attack but that I am taking the initiative. Here is what we will do: Hideki, since you thought of this idea, I will let you take half the men and make the attack. I am the overall commander and will remain here. Do not fool around with them. Creep up as close as you can and then assault them frontally. Surely they will scatter like chickens and the instructors will designate some of them as dead. Have you got that?"

Taro's men were ready. They propped up their packs and equipment, everything but their weapons, around the campfires in hopes the enemy would think they were warming themselves next to the fires. Then they deployed to either side of the fires in the draws. They were on line and ready to go.

Kenji's men were also in place. They had a relatively easy river crossing and shivered from the cold but they had made it without incident. The scouts had laid down the white cloth for guidance, and the subordinate commanders knew what to do and were ready.

At the appointed time, they heard shouting and the firing of blank cartridges on the other side of the hill. Kenji's men started to rise but he passed the word along for them to remain prone.

The White troops assaulted the campfires and then stood around in bewilderment wondering where their enemy had gone. Suddenly they were attacked from both flanks. The White Forces outnumbered the Blue but Taro's men had the element of surprise. The instructors moved among the combatants, telling this man and that man that they were dead for the purpose of the exercise and could no longer participate. Kato Oshiro peered through the darkness trying to find out what was going on when Kenji's forces attacked his rear. Kenji and his men quickly overran the hill and the instructors marked the majority of defenders as dead.

As soon as the battle ended the instructors conferred but briefly, assembled all the men and told them that the junior force, the attackers, had won for the first time in the history of the school.

"This battle was won because of the brilliance and determination of Kenji Dainichi," the senior instructor said. "His ability to think of innovative tactics is something you should all learn."

Kenji's men cheered and cheered and treated him like a hero. Kato Oshiro's men hated him.

A few weeks later General Maresuke Nogi visited the academy and the cadets turned out for his review. The superintendent, Colonel Inouye, told General Nogi, "We have a most promising cadet at the academy, general, the best I have seen in my years as superintendent. He is small in stature and unimpressive in appearance but he has a first-rate mind and is a brilliant tactician. He is also an outstanding leader and the other cadets would follow him anywhere. Moreover, he is well-read, and is familiar with not only our own classics but those of Europe as well. It is said that his true love is really literature and not the army. Finally, he is of samurai stock. I would be grateful if you would say a few words to him. His family has countless generations of service to Japan and to our emperor. He is the only cadet who has ever defeated the White Forces in the mock battle that we have conducted for a generation."

"That *is* impressive. I remember that exercise well from my cadet years. You must point him out to me. We have a great need for young officers who have the potential to move us into the modern age. So many of them these days seem to be farm boys, who are dedicated enough but not particularly talented. Most of them will make good junior officers but few will have what it takes to move up the ranks. As you know, war is the most complicated activity known to man, and few really understand it, even military men. I am also happy that this cadet is interested in Japan's unique arts. I, too, am a devotee of our literature and intellectual and religious traditions. I considered becoming a scholar but decided that Japan's greatest need after the Restoration was to strengthen our country."

The cadets stood in their best uniforms, lined up in perfect formation. The general and the superintendent took the report from the commander of cadets and proceeded down the ranks. General Nogi paused at random to say a few words to cadets in the ranks. He nearly passed by the small, unimpressive man who was dwarfed by the cadets on either side of him when the colonel spoke up.

"General Nogi, this is cadet Dainichi, whom I mentioned before."

The general looked down in surprise. The superintendent had told him that this cadet was small but he was still astounded at Kenji's short stature. "Cadet Dainichi, the colonel here tells me that you are the first one to ever solve the decades-old problem of attacking the White Force in the defense. You have my most sincere congratulations. Like all others before and after, my own class failed in its attempt to take the position. You have a great future in the army. Sooner or later war will come and when it does we will need young officers with your skills." Kenji could only blush and murmur his thanks.

After the formation, word quickly spread about the general's compliments to Kenji. His roommates, and even cadets he did not know, came up to him and congratulated him on his recognition by the general. The cadets who had served with Kato Oshiro with the White Forces in the exercise felt doubly humiliated by the general's words to Kenji. They shunned him and spread rumors that the only reason he was singled out for this honor was because of his family's samurai background.

CHAPTER 13
KENJI TO MOSCOW

In March of 1903 Kenji was surprised by a visit of an orderly from the office of the academy superintendent who told him that the superintendent wanted him to report immediately. *What have I done wrong?* Kenji wondered, as he approached the office.

Bid entry, Kenji walked smartly into the office, stopped at attention in front of the superintendent's desk, bowed, saluted and said, "Cadet Dainichi reporting as ordered, sir!"

The superintendent looked up from a file he was reading and said, "Sit down, Dainichi, I have something for you."

He sat at attention on the edge of a chair facing the superintendent, wondering if there was bad news about his mother.

"Dainichi, you have an unusual record here. You got off to a rather rough start and you never have really mastered many of the physical skills we require of officers-to-be. But you have the reputation of being one of the most brilliant cadets we have seen here in a generation."

The colonel paused for breath. Kenji did not know if he was supposed to reply so he remained silent.

"It says here you speak Russian?"

"Yes, sir, I do. I read it fairly well and I suppose I speak it, at least a little."

"Any facility with that language is rare for a Japanese and soon will be much needed. You will be leaving the academy immediately and going to Russia."

"But what about graduating? What about my commission?"

"You need not worry about that, Dainichi. Unusual times call for unusual measures. You will be promoted to commissioned rank immediately and unofficially graduated. Your graduation will be legitimate but will not be made public until your classmates graduate. You will go to Russia where you will report to Colonel Motojiro Akashi in our embassy and you will lend your language skills and sharp mind to his work there."

"What sort of work does Colonel Akashi do, sir?"

"Let us just say that there is reason to believe that war between Japan and Russia may be coming and your skills are needed there. Tell no one about this. I will think of a reason to tell your fellow cadets why you are no longer here."

"What may I tell my family?"

"You may tell them that you have been selected for a special assignment in Europe and will be commissioned early, and no more."

On a warm spring day, just when the sakura, the cherry blossoms, gloried at the height of their beauty, Kenji boarded ship in Tokyo. He was to travel on a civilian merchant ship, one that sailed under a British flag, and his orders were to wear civilian clothes so as to not attract undue attention. His mother and his uncle Genichi and Momoko rode with him in a carriage to the docks to see him off. As they passed a magnificent cherry tree, Uncle Genichi said,

"The sakura are just like warriors. They bloom to perfection and then die at the very apex of their beauty."

Kenji's mother and Momoko did not care for the analogy.

Neither Momoko's father nor Kenji's uncles approved of her going to see Kenji off, but all decided that Kenji's absence from Japan for a long period of time would wither the relationship.

On the dock, Uncle Genichi was just finishing his instructions about Kenji's duty to the emperor when the ship's whistle blew and drowned out his last few words. Kenji was relieved that he did not have to hear them yet another time. The whistle blew once more ,and the stewards shouted that it was time to board the ship. Kenji bowed respectfully to his mother, then to his uncle Genichi and then took Momoko's hand. He said nothing. Momoko tried to smile but her chin trembled and her black eyes pooled with tears. "Write often, Kenji," was all she could manage to say. He merely nodded, squeezed her hand a little harder, bowed to all three of them again, picked up his bags and walked up the gangplank. He did not look back until he got to the top. When he turned for a final look, he saw Momoko sobbing into a handkerchief as his mother tried to comfort her. Uncle Genichi stood stoically by and pretended he did not know the two women.

The ship steamed out of Tokyo Bay and headed a bit east and then south. In the days that followed, it skirted China and then the French colonies of Indochina. Kenji had never even been in a fishing boat much less on a ship at sea. By the second day he became violently seasick. He rushed from his cabin to the deck to get some fresh air. A crewmember told him to move to the rail on the leeward side so the wind would be blowing from behind him if he got sick. "Otherwis you will be wearing your breakfast." He barely reached the rail in time. Nearby crewmembers had a hard time restraining their laughter.

Seasickness was one of the worst things he had ever experienced but seasickness has no lasting effects and four days later he had completely recovered and wondered that he had been sick at all. He learned to roll with the ship when he walked without even thinking about it. And he could go to the dining room and eat solid food.

The weather was alternately fair and foul. On the fair days, the ship moved through placid royal blue seas under great pillows of clouds moving gently across the sky. The nights were particularly fascinating. When the moon was down and the night was clear, Kenji lay on the foredeck with a telescope borrowed from a ship's officer and looked at the sky. The stars had never seemed so bright and clear. Even the River of Heaven, what Westerners called the Milky Way, was clearer and he could see that it was made up of countless individual stars. He did not do so well in rough weather; the ship rose and fell with the onset of waves that seemed huge to a landsman. He did not get seasick again but felt uncomfortable and he found it difficult to stay in his bunk at night and to chase the food around on his plate in the dining room. This was his first experience using knives and forks, and in the beginning he ate slowly as he watched how others used theirs. He quickly mastered the proper techniques but missed using chopsticks.

The ship stopped in the British city of Singapore at the tip of the Malaysian peninsula for four days to take on provisions and coal. There, Kenji got his first taste of an exotic country. People of all colors, nationalities and religions crowded the streets. There were East Asians like himself although most were Chinese and a few Vietnamese. There were Polynesian islanders; there were tribesmen from the Malaysian peninsula who carried knives and spears. There were Caucasians from every country in Europe. There were black people from the islands of Melanesia. Kenji explored the temples and shopping bazaars and looked for mementos to buy for his mother and for Momoko. He tasted a wide variety of non-Japanese Asian food for the first time in his life, sampling curries, strange vegetables, and unusual-looking sea creatures.

Several European men boarded the ship in Singapore. Among them was an odd-looking little Englishman. He was short for a Caucasian, only a few inches taller than Kenji. He wore a bowler hat and a long but lightweight overcoat everywhere he went, even on the hottest days, and he was always scribbling on a pad of paper.

Then the passengers boarded ship again. They sailed northwest through the Straits of Malacca and headed nearly due west across the Indian Ocean.

One evening after dinner Kenji was leaning on the rail of the afterdeck and watching the long line of phosphorescence that marked the ship's wake and thinking of home and Momoko. He felt someone come up beside him and turned to find that it was the Englishman.

He was surprised when the man asked him in Japanese, "What is a young Japanese fellow like you doing on a ship to London? Are you to study there?"

"Who are you?" Kenji asked.

"Excuse me, I did not introduce myself. My name is Alfred Addington and I write for the London *Times*. We English are interested in Japan. After all, our navy trained your navy and I have been in Tokyo for two years writing on the modernization of Japan. I stopped in Singapore for a month to look at how our British colony is getting along. Your fellow countrymen were kind to me and I would like to repay the favor by showing you around London."

"I am part of the diplomatic mission from the Imperial Court of Japan to the Imperial Court of Russia. And my name is Kenji Dainichi," he said with a bow. "I am grateful for your kind offer, but I will be in England only long enough for the ship to replenish its stores."

Addington questioned him closely about exactly what he expected to do in Russia. He seemed to be interested in the Japanese military and what Kenji thought about a possible conflict between Japan and Russia. Kenji, suspicious of Addington's motives, was careful to answer the man's questions in only the most general way. He was determined to not spend any time with Addington when the ship laid over for a few days in London.

For five days the vessel raced the sun across a flat sea until it reached Cape Town, South Africa. There the ship re-provisioned and refueled again and once more Kenji went ashore to look at the local wonders. He stared at the black tribesmen who came in from the bush to buy provisions, sampled still odder food and was awash in thoughts about how big the world really was. He took a two-day trip into the bush and saw elephants, giraffes, zebras, and other wondrous animals he had only read about. He would have plenty to tell his family and Momoko when he returned to Japan.

Once more he went aboard and the ship headed north, around the west coast of Africa, past the Straits of Gibraltar and then past the Iberian Peninsula. Then it docked in England where Alfred Addington said his farewells and departed.

Kenji managed to visit a few sights: the Tower of London, the British Museum and other of London's wonders. Most of the

British, who were accustomed to having foreigners from their vast global empire in London, treated him politely. Kenji also practiced speaking English.

As he boarded ship to resume his voyage, he heard voices speaking Russian. Cautiously looking around, he saw two men, clothed in civilian garb but with the unmistakable bearing of soldiers, speaking with an attractive young woman.

He tried to avoid them but one night the dining room was nearly full and the only seat available was at their table. He approached the table bowed, pulled out a chair and sat without saying a word. They spoke to him in Russian, which he pretended to not understand and then in English, a language in which he was limited. Finally, the woman tried French. Kenji admitted he could speak a little and began a conversation with the woman, who translated into Russian for her comrades. She asked if he were Chinese to which he replied yes. He immediately regretted this when the woman translated the exchange into Russian and one of the men began jabbering at him in Chinese, a language he could read but could not speak at all. After the barrage of Chinese, Kenji continued speaking to the woman in French, and asked her to tell her companion, that he had been raised in Indochina where he had learned French and only spoke a dialect of Chinese that was localized. The woman translated this and one of the men, looking at Kenji skeptically, replied to her in Russian, "At least he is not a God-cursed Jap. Or is he?" He studied Kenji's eyes as he said this but Kenji showed no emotion. He ate about half of his supper, excused himself by saying that he felt a touch of seasickness and left the table. From then on, he entered the dining room slowly, pausing at the door, in order to choose a table other than where the Russians sat. When they saw him, they nodded in greeting but, to his great relief, made no effort to approach him.

CHAPTER 14

JAPANESE EMBASSY IN RUSSIA

Kenji's ship turned east and entered the Baltic Sea and then the Gulf of Finland.

Finally, the ship sailed past the Russian naval fortress of Petropavlovsk and came to rest alongside a pier in St. Petersburg. The Russians were the first down the gangplank and a tall thin man in a black overcoat and fur cap who carried a briefcase, greeted them.

Eager for his new assignment, Kenji had packed his bags the night before and could have been one of the first passengers down the ashore, but he held back until the Russians were out of sight. When they were gone, he descended to the pier and looked all around for someone who might be waiting for him. At the same time, he looked in wonder at the Russians who crowded the pier. He tried to understand what they were saying to one another but there were so many of them talking rapidly that he could only pick out bits and pieces of conversation. He stood and stood and stood and finally, after about an hour found a spot next to a building that shielded him from the chill wind and sat on one of his bags. He kept busy by speculating about the passersby and wondering what his new assignment would entail. After another interminable wait another Japanese man approached, bowed, and said, "Dainichi-san, I am Tanaka from the Japanese Consulate here in St. Petersburg. I apologize for tardiness but we did not receive word that the ship had docked until a half hour ago. Let me help you with your bags." He took Kenji to a waiting carriage and the two men drove through the busy streets of St. Petersburg.

The sights amazed him. There seemed to be churches everywhere. Dozens of military men in colorful uniforms moved through the streets on horseback, in carriages, and on foot. The vast majority of the population seemed to be white, but here and there fierce-looking, swarthy Asians carrying both guns and swords moved through the crowds in small groups. Kenji thought they must be Mongols.

The Consulate, a modest building, sat on a quiet street in an out-of-the-way neighborhood. The sight of the Rising Sun flag brought a bit of homesickness into Kenji's heart. He disembarked the carriage and a Japanese Army enlisted man ran up, bowed, and picked up his bags. He followed the man into the consulate and down a hallway to a room where he was told to change into his uniform, and then shown where to report to Colonel Motojiro Akashi, the Japanese military attaché. Kenji knocked softly and a voice commanded him to enter. He found himself in a stuffy room facing a Japanese Army colonel who sat behind a desk covered with papers. A photograph of the Emperor Meiji looked benignly down at them.

"Lieutenant Dainichi reporting as ordered, sir," he said as he bowed. This was the first time he had met a senior officer, other than his father and uncles, outside the military academy.

"Sit down, lieutenant, we have much to talk about. You have been sent here because I am told that you speak Russian. Is that so?"

"Yes, sir."

"So do I and we have a great deal of work ahead of us. The tsar spends much of his time here in St. Petersburg but we get most of our intelligence from social and diplomatic circles in Moscow. We leave for our embassy there tomorrow morning.

"War with Russia will come very soon, and our job is to study and report on the internal conditions in the country of our future enemy. A good deal of what we learn comes from talking to Russian officials and military officers. They are so confident in their superiority vis-à-vis Japan that they openly talk of military matters at social functions where their tongues are loosened with wine and vodka."

"I am happy to serve His Majesty in any way I can," said Kenji, "and I hope my language skills will be up to the task. Russian society is alien to me and I wonder how I will fit in."

"Your language skills will rapidly improve and your unfamiliarity with their society is a bonus. It will add to their perception that we are just a backward and weak country. They are more likely to be careless in their talk."

The Colonel was right and once Kenji picked up the tone and rhythm of spoken Russian his vocabulary blossomed. He soon became confident that he could converse intelligently with the Russians.

Colonel Akashi and Kenji accepted every invitation they received.

At one such affair Kenji accompanied Colonel Akashi to a soirée given by Countess Androv, an ancient fat woman who affected red wigs and disgustingly low-cut gowns for a woman of her years. Time had confiscated her teeth, and her breasts wobbled like uncertain moons, tentatively held in place by the gravity of her planet of a body. Kenji thought she looked like she belonged in a museum. She had a high-pitched giggle that grated on everyone around her. As if she were not spectacle enough, she unsuccessfully affected the litheness of a cat. But she was one of the arbiters of society in Moscow and had been for two decades. Her rich husband had died young and she reportedly had affairs with many men in Moscow and St. Petersburg over the years. A popular rumor had it that she had once had a lengthy liaison with one of the Grand Dukes, an uncle of the tsar. This was a rumor she did nothing to discourage.

Kenji paid his respects to the countess and tried to engage several senior officers in conversation, but they did not indulge a junior officer's company for long, especially a Japanese junior officer. They would slowly tighten the little circle in which they stood, and gradually squeeze him out. Kenji took the hint and looked around for someone who might talk to him. As he surveyed the room, Kenji found a man in the uniform of the Okhrana staring at him. As the two men locked eyes, Kenji realized that it was one of the Russians that he had met on the ship. Kenji quickly looked away. Seeing that Colonel Akashi was talking to several Russian civilians Kenji did not know what to do with himself and edged his way across the room to a table where an abundance of food and drink was artfully arranged. He nibbled on a cake that he judged was too sweet and accepted a cup of Russian tea that was too strong. As he was deciding what to do next, a pair of men entered the room. The elder, was a distinguished looking man with a full beard, and clad in civilian clothes adorned with a couple of elaborate decorations that shone like sunbursts against his coat. The younger was a slender, tall blond young man wearing the uniform of a junior officer. The other guests parted, making way for them as they entered, and several called out a greeting to the pair.

"Who is that?" Kenji asked a servant.

"Oh, that is Prince Boris Medved, an important advisor to the tsar, and his son Ivan."

Kenji stood in place as he watched the two men make their way around the room, extending greetings, handshakes for the men and double kisses on the cheeks for the women. As the prince and his son grew near, a pair of Russian generals stopped the elder Medved and engaged him in conversation. His son continued on to the refreshment's table and poured himself a glass of punch. There was no one to introduce them so Kenji bowed and then held out his hand and said in Russian, "My name is Kenji Dainichi."

Surprised that an Asian could speak passable Russian, Ivan took the hand and gave his name.

Both knew that they might soon be enemies, and their discussion was wary and discreet. Each was curious about the other, and after they unsuccessfully probed each other with questions about the military, they wandered into a discussion of family, society and traditions.

Ivan soon changed the subject to horses, something that Kenji knew or cared little about, but he hid his distaste behind a mask of indifference and let the young Russian do most of the talking. "You must let me show you our stables and our horses. Tomorrow is Saturday, would you like to ride with me?" Ivan asked. Kenji did not like horses and was a poor rider. It was another of the physical skills at which he was deficient. He considered declining the invitation, but duty won out. So he agreed, and Ivan said he would send a carriage for Kenji the next day.

Later, in the Medved household, while father and son shared a bedtime brandy, Boris asked, "Tell me about that small Japanese lieutenant you were talking to, Ivan. One of our police officials told me that they saw him on the ship from London and he passed himself off as Chinese?"

"His name is Kenji Dainichi, and he is some sort of junior attaché to Colonel Akashi. That means that he is a spy of some sort although he does not look like one. He is an interesting fellow for a Japanese, brighter than I ever expected any of them to be and speaks several languages, too. His Russian is sometimes grammatically incorrect, but he has no trouble making himself understood or understanding what I said. Did you notice how small he is? If most Japanese are that size, we should have no problem routing them out of China. Who do they think they are, anyway? They were still in a feudal society sixty years ago."

"Yes, and forty-five years ago we still had serfs. And we are still the most backward nation in Europe and are making no real effort to catch up. Our industry is a joke, the masses are seething and our ruler is weak. Don't make the mistake of underestimating the Japanese. They have thrown off the bonds of feudalism and are working hard, harder than we are, to become a modern nation. We may be a more western nation than them but they are on their way to becoming a more modern nation than us. It is not the physical size of their soldiers that will matter if a conflict comes but the spirit behind them and, most importantly, the quality of their arms and their generalship. They have completely reorganized their army along European lines and, while the samurai class still dominates, they put a great deal of emphasis on merit rather than birthright and their generals have all earned their rank. I fear our best generals are too old. Many of the rest are friends of the court, which is no qualification for success on the battlefield."

"I have invited him to go riding with me tomorrow morning," said Ivan. "I will take a closer look and see if there is any hint of what you say about the character of modern Japan."

A carriage from the Medveds appeared at Kenji's quarters the next morning to fetch him. Ivan was not in the carriage. Instead, there were two young Russian women. The better dressed of the two introduced herself as Natalya, Ivan's sister.

"Ivan sends his regrets," she said, "for not being able to pick you up but he has a music lesson first thing on Saturday mornings, and he thought that we would be better company for you anyway."

She indicated the other woman, who was pretty but hard-eyed "This is Nina who works for us. Mother sent her along to act as chaperone." Nina looked Kenji in the eyes with a cold smile that she seldom bothered to remove. Natalya was excited to be talking to a man, and a real Japanese too, and chattered about social events and moved from one subject to another scarcely pausing for breath. The other woman said nothing and continued to stare at Kenji. Kenji was happy to just listen.

When they drove up to the Medved mansion and alighted from the carriage, another servant met them and led Kenji around to the stables. Ivan was there, critically watching as a groom saddled two horses.

The number of stalls for the horses amazed Kenji. The stable held at least two-dozen horses and all, even to Kenji's inexperienced eye, were fine ones.

Rows of gleaming harnesses, saddles and other tack lined the walls; at one end of the building stood a forge and equipment for a farrier to work.

Kenji's horse was a beautiful bay gelding, Ivan's a magnificent black stallion.

"Kenji, good of you to come. I gathered from our talk last night that you are not all that keen on horses. Not to worry. We have chosen a gentle one for you," he said with just a trace of condescension. Like most Japanese, Kenji was attuned to the subtlest nuances of speech and behavior and Ivan's words embarrassed him. He certainly did not want a potential enemy to think him a coward or weakling.

They mounted their horses, Kenji with the help of a groom who held a stool for him. Since he was so short and the horse fairly tall he could not reach the stirrups by himself. Once again he felt humiliated.

Ivan and Kenji rode, through the streets of Moscow and into the countryside at a gentle pace. Once again, probing questions got nowhere and they got around to things in general and, each finding it easier to talk about personal matters to a stranger than to a friend.

Ivan told of his frustration at being in love with a commoner that his family would never permit him to marry. Kenji told Ivan about Momoko and said that he wanted to marry her but there was opposition within both families and he believed that marriages should only be carried out with one's parents' permission. Nearly all marriages in his country were arranged, he explained. Kenji told Ivan that he understood his frustration and they were both astonished to find an unexpected bond between them.

They talked and rode at a slow pace while Kenji told of his desire to be a scholar rather than a warrior. Ivan was surprised and pleased that his new friend was passionate about Russian literature and the two of them quoted verse from Pushkin. Kenji tried to explain the mysteries of haiku, the seventeen-syllable Japanese poem, to Ivan but Ivan had difficulty grasping the Zen concept that less was more and that part of the mental slate was to be left empty to permit one's imagination to fill in the blanks.

Ivan pointed out the sights. They gradually came in sight of the large, walled misshapen triangle of the Kremlin that stood on the banks of the Moscow River and dominated the city.

"The Kremlin gets its name from the word *kreml*, or fort," Ivan explained. "This site has been occupied since before there was a Russia, over two thousand years. It has four palaces, royal apartments, barracks, prisons, cemeteries, chapels and four cathedrals. It is the official seat of our government although most of our tsars since Peter's time have spent the majority of their time in St. Petersburg."

"Here, Kenji," Ivan said as they rode into Red Square, "is the most dramatic of all Russian churches, St. Basil's Cathedral. Ivan the Terrible commissioned St. Basil's in the 16thCentury to celebrate a military victory over the Mongols. After construction was complete, Ivan had the architect blinded so he could never create another church that might compete with the dramatic beauty of this one."

The cathedral's central spire soared toward the Christian paradise, surrounded by onion-shaped domes painted in a dazzling array of colors. Some were adorned with vivid checkerboard designs, some with a swirl of spiraling stripes and still others with more intricate patterns.

The two were talking religion as they re-crossed the Moscow River near where they had begun their ride and they saw the carriage of Grand Duke Alexander Mikhailovich, the tsar's cousin. Ivan told Kenji who it was and as they paused to salute the passing carriage a figure ran out from behind a low building and rolled something under it. A bomb! The carriage safely passed over it before it exploded. The blast hurt no one but the roar rang ears for a city block. The Grand Duke's horses could just barely be contained by the driver and Ivan's stallion reared and it took a few seconds to get him under control. Kenji's gelding rolled his eyes and took off back toward the bridge over the Moscow River. Kenji lost one of his stirrups and almost his seat as the horse rounded the corner and onto the bridge proper. In the confusion, Kenji forgot what little he knew about horses and he concentrated on just hanging on. Ivan gave chase on his horse and at a full gallop managed to lean over in the saddle and grab the reins from Kenji's hands. He brought his own horse to a controlled stop but the gelding, uncertain of what was required of him, stopped as suddenly as if he had run into a wall. Kenji found himself pitch-poled over the horse's neck and head and onto the cobblestones where he landed flat on his back. The wind was knocked out of him, his uniform was torn and he had a scrape and a bump on the head. He lay there desperately trying to suck air into his lungs. Ivan quickly dismounted and peered down at him, a concerned look on his face. "Stay there for just a moment. Get your breath." Once Kenji was breathing normally, Ivan helped him to his feet. The only thing that was really damaged was Kenji's self-esteem. He felt just like he did in his first year at the academy when the other cadets made fun of him. Ivan was solicitous and helpful but he wondered to himself how a junior military officer could hope to succeed if he could not even ride a horse.

When they appeared back at the Medved mansion Ivan carefully related the story of the accident in terms that left Kenji with dignity. Regardless of what might or might not have happened to him physically, Kenji was grateful to Ivan for this. Nonetheless, the experience humiliated him and he did not want to repeat it.

Since they were both dirty and out of sorts Ivan suggested that they go to the banya and cleanse themselves.

"A banya is a Russian bath, Kenji. It gives us an opportunity to purge ourselves of dirt internally as externally. Most Russians have to go to a public banya but we have our own."

"In Japan we have our public baths, too. First, we sit in a steam bath to get all the dirt out of our pores through sweating. Then we scrub ourselves and after that soak in a furu, a tub filled with water that is so hot one can hardly stand it. After that, sometimes we get a massage to further relax us and keep our muscles toned and our joints flexible."

"You must try a Russian bath. It is different but I think that you will find it just as cleansing."

The two young men went to the back of the house, entered the bath and stripped off their clothing. Kenji looked even smaller when naked, was as hairless as a young boy, and Ivan once again wondered about his suitability as a military officer. The amount of chest, arm and leg hair on his host amazed Kenji. He had heard Westerners called "hairy barbarians" and now he knew why.

They entered a small room full of steam and sat on benches. A bundle of thin, young tree branches lay on the floor. Ivan picked one up.

"These are branches from young birch trees. We must beat each other with them. The leaves are known to have great medicinal value. The purpose of the beating is to improve the circulation of our blood and to remove impure thoughts from one's mind."

Kenji thought his was a barbaric custom but deferred to his host and went along with it. He discovered that the branches were applied in a moderate fashion and hardly stung at all.

After Ivan judged them to have been purified, they moved into another small room and again sat on benches. A servant entered with buckets of water, made very cold by ice from the family icehouse, and poured the water over Kenji and Ivan. It was so cold, compared with the heat of the banya that Kenji thought his heart was going to stop. Ivan told him that in winter Russians would often go outside after the steaming and roll in the snow.

Kenji dined with the Medveds that day but he concentrated on his manners and his use of knives and forks and was quiet during the meal. The discussion revolved around social matters with which he was unfamiliar. Prince Medved was faultlessly polite and the three men made casual conversation about life in Japan and Russia. Marina and her daughter said little but carefully watched the young Japanese officer, curious about his table manners. After the dinner Kenji sat in Prince Medved's study and had a brandy with him and his son before being taken back to the embassy.

Kenji said, "Prince Medved, you have a marvelous library. I have never seen so many books in one room. You have more than even my sensei, Araki-san."

"You are welcome to borrow any of them, Kenji. For my part, it is interesting to see a young officer from Asia so interested in Russia. Ivan tells me that you have read some of the authors from our golden age of literature. Here is a volume of short stories from this fellow Anton Chekov who has become the most admired writer in modern Russia. It is an extra copy, and you may keep it."

"You are too kind, Prince Medved. I shall treasure it."

Upon his return to the embassy, he immediately reported to Colonel Akashi but had little to relate. He had learned nothing of military interest, he reported, the meeting was entirely social in nature.

Kenji and Ivan saw each other at social gatherings after that but Kenji politely resisted further invitations to visit the Medveds. When they did meet Ivan carefully avoided the subject of riding and horses.

Kenji and Colonel Akashi amassed much intelligence of strategic value. Their biggest discovery was the fragility of the Trans-Siberian Railroad. The Japanese had for some time sensed that it was a tenuous lifeline for any war effort in the Russian Far East but now they had confirmation. Russian officers and bureaucrats talked freely about the problems of moving across the vast reaches of Siberia on a wobbly one-track railroad that had a serious bottleneck at Lake Baikal.

"Logistics are their Achilles Heel, Kenji. I sent one of our men across Russia on this railroad of theirs and he confirmed what we already suspected that the rail line is insufficient to support a major war effort in East Asia. This is further confirmed by our spies in Port Arthur who keep count of the war materials coming into that city from the railway. The Russians might fight at first but we can cripple them if we can cut the railway somewhere in the short distance where it runs through China before it reaches Port Arthur. We can also hamper Russian shipping on the sea lanes. The Japanese army has yet to be tested against a European power and we may not be able to win the war against Russia through raw military force but we can win the war logistically."

The intelligence the Japanese collected was not limited to logistics. They also collected order-of-battle information about their potential enemy. They compiled a detailed list of the Russian units in Port Arthur and those that were earmarked for the journey across the steppes. Remembering Napoleon's dictum that there were no bad regiments just bad colonels, they took a hard look at the Russian commanders. Many, they judged, were either too old or too incompetent, or both, to be commanding troops in the field. In the tsarist system, where everything depended on the whim of the autocrat, it was hardly surprising that many Russian generals had achieved and held onto their positions only because of their connections in court. A few genuine heroes stood out among the incompetent and infirm, mostly officers who served with distinction in the Turkish Wars. Too many of the rest were either, too old, were fools, or were drunks.

Colonel Akashi sent summaries of his most important reports to Tokyo in coded telegraph messages. Akashi's clerk coded the bulky ones and sent them by rail to major European ports and then by ship to Japan.

After Kenji had been in Moscow for a little more than six months, an invitation came for both him and Colonel Akashi to attend a ball to be given by the Medveds. Akashi insisted that they both go. They appeared in their full-dress uniforms, Akashi's with campaign medals from the China war and Kenji's the understated plain tunic of a junior military officer. Ivan was there in the resplendent uniform of his new regiment, the elite Preobrazhensky Guards.

Natalya was gorgeous in a pink gown sewn from a Parisian pattern and turned heads everywhere. Kenji stumbled through a dance with her once, awkwardly but out of a sense of duty. All the Russian women towered over him as they danced and with some his face was about even with vast expanses of sweaty, quivering, and powdered breast flesh. Most of them smelled extremely bad to his Japanese nose.

He tried champagne for the first time and two glasses made his head swim. He saw the other guests as a kaleidoscope of faces, old, young, fresh and wrinkled, fat and thin. He stepped out onto the wide veranda to get some air. From the other side of a partition, he heard some women chattering. At first, he paid no attention but then he picked up the words Japan and Japanese.

A male voice inserted itself into the conversation. "Russia needs a warm water port on the Pacific Ocean if we are to be a world power. The Japanese took Port Arthur from the Chinese in 1895 but international pressure made them give it back. Now we have it and the Japanese would be foolish to act against us. I do hope they try, I really hope they try. I would like nothing better to be blooded in combat against them."

"I think the tsar is right," said one of the female voices, "they are nothing but little monkeys. Surely if we go to war, we can beat these Japanese."

A man replied, "Did you see the two here tonight. The older one is ugly, so ugly that he should be an orderly in a home for the blind and the younger is no bigger than a monkey." His audience laughed.

Kenji flushed with anger, but he stood silently in the shadows until the conversation staggered to a halt and the voices moved back inside. Then he rejoined the party but not for long. He looked around to find his hosts and Colonel Akashi. Once he had spotted them he made excuses of not feeling well and left.

The next day Ivan sent a note hoping that his health was okay and that they could meet again soon

CHAPTER 15
RETURN TO JAPAN

A few days after the ball, Kenji went to see Colonel Akashi and requested that he be sent home. He thought that the Japanese would soon to go to war with Russia and he knew that his family, especially his uncles, would not approve of him staying in Europe if a war started in Asia. He told Colonel Akashi that he thought his duty lay with the army. Colonel Akashi told Kenji that their mission in Russia was almost done anyway and gave him permission to catch the next ship back to Japan.

"I will leave Russia myself before long, Kenji. Hostilities could begin at any time. I have set up a network of spies here, and will decamp to either Sweden or to Berlin to keep an eye on things from afar."

Kenji was elated. He was going to go home to Japan and to Momoko. He was also troubled at the prospect of going to war with his hosts, the Russians. They were no longer a faceless enemy about whom he knew nothing. His conversations with Ivan convinced him that Russians had the same hopes, fears, and wishes for the future as did Japanese.

Kenji's return trip to Japan seemed much longer than his trip westward. He had little taste for leaving the ship and seeing more of the world of foreigners. His voyage to Russia and the time he had spent there satisfied his curiosity. He spent much of his time on deck. He was often there when the sky ahead of him turned from dark to the silvery gray of dawn. He was there when the sun passed overhead and was there when it sank behind him. Thoughts of Momoko, his family, and above all of the coming war with Russia consumed his consciousness. He was confident in his tactical knowledge, and his ability to lead other soldiers, but he fretted over his courage and physical ability. "Will I be brave enough to not disgrace myself? Will I have the physical stamina to carry out my duties?"

While Kenji was sailing back to Japan, General Maresuke Nogi, his wife, and his two sons, Katsuske and Yasuske, both lieutenants in the Japanese Army, had a farewell family dinner prior to the three men departing for China.

Nogi looked at his wife and said, "This is likely to be a difficult war. I will be occupied, and you will not hear from me until the war is won."

She replied, "Oh, can't you be in a cheerful mood just once? It is the last time the family will be together for a while."

The general said, "A father and two sons are going to war. No one knows who will be killed first. Promise me there will be no funeral until all three of us are returned in coffins."

To this she merely bowed her head.

Nogi was an unusual officer. In an age when all army officers dedicated themselves to the emperor, he was more devoted than most. He had not wanted to be a warrior but a farmer and a poet. His father talked him into becoming a soldier. As a young officer, he was reprimanded for drinking and carousing in the red-lantern districts. As he matured he settled down to serious soldiering and served with distinction. With the exception of losing his banner in the war against the rebels in 1877, his record was exemplary, and he rose quickly through the army ranks. Aritomo Yamagata, the head of the Japanese Army, ordered Nogi to commit suicide for losing his banner. The emperor himself, who knew and admired the young officer, personally intervened and told Nogi, "As long as I am alive, you must stay alive to serve me."

When the war with the Chinese began in 1895, the emperor asked him to assume a role in the war against them. As a colonel, he took Port Arthur with a single regiment. Now he was a general and the emperor had once again called on him to serve. It looked like he would fight again over familiar ground, this time as the general commanding all Japanese troops.

When Kenji's ship docked in Tokyo, he found his mother and uncle Genichi waiting for him. His uncle had used his influence to find out the time and date of arrival that the ship's captain had sent ahead over the wireless. When it was Kenji's turn to come down the gangplank he bowed to his uncle and then to his mother.

"Mother, Momoko is not here. Did she not know I was coming?"

"Kenji, I left a note with one of their maids that you were arriving today but received no reply."

The next morning, he reported to army headquarters and received his assignment. That afternoon, Kenji walked down the street to Momoko's house. He was able to talk only briefly to her. He explained that he was to go to China and join the Japanese 3rd Army that was camped near Port Arthur.

"Kenji," she told him, "my father has become even more strict about me seeing you. He agreed to this one time and one time only so I could tell you this. He is still determined to have me marry that moron Kozo, and I am just as determined not to. I can only hope that eventually he will give up. In the meantime, I am not permitted to see you again. Oh, Kenji, I will pray for you when you are gone."

CHAPTER 16
FIRST COMMAND

On the appointed day, Kenji put on his father's sword for the first time and reported for duty. He had secretly hoped that he would be assigned to an intelligence staff where he could put his knowledge of languages and history to good advantage. His heart told him that he would not be able to perform in an honorable manner if he were assigned to a leadership position in a combat unit.

"Lieutenant Dainichi reporting, sir" he told the captain at army headquarters.

The captain looked at the diminutive Kenji with skepticism. "Well, lieutenant, I am glad to see you. We are short of infantry officers, no pun intended, and I am assigning you to a battalion where you will be further assigned as a platoon leader. How does that sound?"

It did not sound good at all, but Kenji bowed and replied, "I am happy to be assigned wherever it will best serve the emperor."

The interview over, Kenji picked up his bag and went to his assigned unit. While waiting outside the battalion headquarters he looked over the rosters that were posted on the bulletin board outside the battalion office and was delighted to see that his old friend

Taro was assigned to the 3rd Company of the same battalion. He also noted that one of General Nogi's sons was on the roster of the 2nd Company.

When he talked to the battalion personnel officer, he requested to be assigned to the same company as Taro.

"I understand your wishes, Lieutenant Dainichi, but we have a full complement of officers in that company. I am going to have to assign you to the 2nd Company. Lieutenant Nogi, the general's son, is in that company and is an interesting and capable young officer. I am sure that you will enjoy serving with him."

On his way across the parade field to the company office, he saw Taro drilling troops. He stopped and waited until he could catch his friend's eye.

Taro halted his men, dismissed them, and ran over to where Kenji was standing with a big smile on his face. They bowed to one another, and then shook hands, and then clapped each other on the back, delighted to renew an old friendship.

After exchanging news for a few minutes, Kenji excused himself and hurried to company headquarters. His new commanding officer, Captain Kawamoto, greeted him with a smile. Kawamoto had been a tactics instructor at the academy and remembered Kenji.

"Lieutenant Dainichi, how good it is that you have been assigned to my company. I remember you well. Your platoon is in the field under the command of the senior sergeant and will return tomorrow morning. Take the time to get settled in your quarters and prepare to meet your men tomorrow. Is that a koto you are wearing?" he said, pointing to Kenji's sword.

"Yes, sir, it is. It belonged to my father, my grandfather."

"Those are beautiful and deadly works of art, Dainichi. I am sure that the spirit within it will carry you successfully along the dark paths of warfare. I envy the inspiration it will give you."

Kenji was up the next morning between the dawn and the day and was waiting in front of the barracks as his platoon returned. It was a cold, cold day and the platoon had been training in the field for six days. They were tired and dirty but still looked like soldiers. The senior sergeant spotted the young lieutenant standing in front of the barracks, figured that he was his new officer, and halted the men a few paces in front of Kenji. He aligned the ranks and then walked up to Kenji, bowed and then saluted and said, "Sergeant Iwao, reporting the lieutenant's platoon, sir."

"I would like to inspect the men, sergeant."

"Sir, they are just returned from the field and are dirty and worn. Perhaps an inspection would be better after they are prepared."

"No, Sergeant Iwao, I want to look at them after they have been under stress. Please introduce me to each man as we go down the ranks."

"Yes, sir," he replied.

"Men, this is Lieutenant Dainichi, your new platoon commander. He wishes to inspect you."

The men shifted uncomfortably and drew themselves to attention. Kenji started down the ranks with Sergeant Iwao trailing behind.

Kenji stopped before each man, asked him his name and where he was from. The questions startled the men. They had never been asked personal details before, but it pleased them. One thing they all noticed was that their new officer had to look up at them. None of them dared look down for fear of showing disrespect but kept their eyes fixed on a space above his head. Sergeant Iwao was not so sure about the qualities of his new boss. But Iwao was a combat-experienced NCO from the war in China a decade before, and he knew that part of his job was to act as mentor for the young lieutenant. He was also willing to learn, even from such a young, small, and inexperienced officer as this.

Kenji was pleased by what he found. The men, though dirty and tired, had obviously been well trained to take care of themselves and their equipment. Each was shaved, and their hair was cut to the scalp. Their puttees were properly wrapped, their bayonets clean and sharp, their bolt-action rifles in good order, and their packs were squared and blanket rolls were draped over them in an inverted U. Every other man had a small shovel with which the troops could dig foxholes or trenches. Each man's tunic was properly buttoned, and his cap was squarely on his head.

"Excellent, Sergeant Iwao, you may dismiss them."

With that, Kenji strode to the edge of the field, turned and watched to see how the men reacted upon dismissal. As they walked to their barracks, they chattered excitedly. Most were impressed by the interest their new lieutenant showed in them personally. Some of the older soldiers were more cynical and warned that they had been disappointed before by an officer who appeared to be interested them and turned out to be more interested in promoting his own career than in their welfare.

In the weeks that followed, Kenji drilled the men on the parade field and put them through their paces on maneuvers. He impressed Sergeant Iwao and the lower-ranking enlisted men with his tactical knowledge and his ability to take apart a field problem in his head and then put it together in a fashion to solve it. He was careful to explained to the men why he made certain decisions.

"If I fall in battle, and if Sergeant Iwao also falls, some of you will have to take over and lead the platoon to its objective. I expect each man in my unit to be able to make the correct decision without guidance from me or your sergeant. The accomplishment of the mission is the most important consideration. You must carry it out, regardless of how many of the rest of us fall."

The soldiers also noted Kenji's stamina and determination in the face of some of the more strenuous exercises. Although he showed strain and sometimes exhaustion, he managed to carry out his duties. Kenji's senior officers also thought that his abilities were remarkable and took note of his efforts. A few thought he would go on to bigger things.

Two months after Kenji's arrival, they received orders to prepare to board ship for transit to China, as reinforcement for those units that were already in place. Several days later, they silently filed aboard ship, each man lost in the thoughts of the family he was leaving, and the future he was entering. Kenji's mother and his uncle saw him off. Momoko did not.

The ship steamed northeast, and through the strait dividing the northernmost Japanese islands of Honshu and Hokkaido. It then turned southwest. The Strait of Tsushima, the narrowest point between Japan and Korea was rough, but apart from a great deal of seasickness among the men, the ship transited the strait without incident. Upon arriving in China, they moved into a camp that was a three-day march from the Russian held town of Nanshan, a key point that controlled the short portion of the Trans-Siberian Railroad that ran through China. They began a rigorous training program and they thought about war.

CHAPTER 17
IVAN VOLUNTEERS

In the autumn of 1903 Ivan resigned from the Preobrazhensky Guards Regiment in order to seek his fortunes among the troubles brewing in the Far East. He wanted to get away from the scene of his loss of Tatiana, and he wanted to be a real soldier and not just a member of an elite guard. His mother was unhappy about his decision.

"Ivan," she said, "you can have a brilliant career right here at home. Eventually you will inherit your father's title and there is a good chance that you will be an influence in the court. The tsar is in need of officers to advise him on military matters. As far as promotion, you can advance just as fast here as you can by going off to Asia and fight a war. Maybe even faster."

"I know I can have a good career here, Mother. But think of our family history. We might not be anything at all had it not been for my great-grandfather's service to Alexander I in the war against Napoleon. If I am to really carry on our family's legacy, I must prove myself by fighting in at least one of the tsar's wars. Otherwise, I will be just another member of the court with no real military experience. Father has said many times, that one of Russia's problems today is that too many of its senior army officers hold their rank because of family connections, and not because of their experience in combat. I do not mean to be one of these men. I promise that if I see war this time, then I will come back to St. Petersburg and serve here for the rest of my career. I will have upheld the family's honor, gained some experience in warfare and will be better prepared to advise the tsar. I may not need to go to war again. Besides," he added, "if we do go to war with the Japanese everyone knows that we will achieve a quick victory."

"Oh, Ivan, I wish you would change your mind."

In his heart of hearts, since he was a small boy, Ivan always wanted to be a hero, just like his great-grandfather had been in the war against the French. He fancied himself on a magnificent stallion, leading great numbers of fearsome soldiers that swept the enemy before them in glorious charges. He pictured himself coming home victorious in the war against the Japanese and being awarded the Cross of St. George by the tsar himself. His portrait, in a uniform covered with medals, would adorn the walls of the Medved mansions and be an inspiration to generations to come. He was, he thought with certainty, made of the right stuff, the stuff that gives birth to heroes. Did he not excel at horsemanship? Was he not the most dedicated to military strategy in his class at the Imperial Military Academy? What else would he need to be to be successful? He would show his comrades and his family how brave he could be.

As a Guards officer, Ivan had seen the tsar many times but had never met him. Despite the fact that his father had known the tsar for the tsar's entire life, Ivan had never been presented to His Majesty.

A few days before Ivan left for the Far East his father brought him to court. Ivan walked beside his father as they entered the Winter Palace. An officer of the Imperial Guards Regiment greeted them and acted as escort. The beauty and elegance of the royal surroundings fascinated Iván. His family's own two mansions looked positively shabby compared to the royal palace. The two Medveds trod down a marble hallway, took a turn into a shorter corridor where another officer greeted them outside the tsar's study.

The officer knocked and a voice commanded him to enter. "Prince Medved and his son to see His Majesty."

"Yes, of course, please show them in."

The tsar, clad in a plain gray tunic, sat at a desk studying some papers when they entered. He immediately rose, walked around his desk, smiling with greeting. He shook hands with Boris first and kissed him on both cheeks. Then he shook hands with Ivan. Ivan, who had never seen his sovereign except on horseback or in a carriage, was amazed at how short His Majesty was—no more than five feet seven or so. At age thirty-four he was an extremely handsome man in the full vigor of his manhood. Many women thought him the handsomest man in Europe.

The study was plain; floor to ceiling bookshelves lined all four walls. There were no paintings or other distractions. The tsar had them removed upon ascending to the throne because he thought they might interfere with his concentration in the business of running his vast empire.

"So, young Medved, you have volunteered to leave one of my elite regiments in St. Petersburg in order to go to Port Arthur?" the tsar asked.

"Yes, Your Majesty."

"I wish all of our young officers were as eager to serve as you. All most of them can think of is how well they can advance themselves if they stay around the capital and curry favor with me and my generals. The empress and I are proud of you and wish you the best in helping us obtain our rights in China. We not only need a warm-water port in the Pacific but we need something else as well. As you may know, there are many dissident elements abroad these days. They seem to come from the ranks of the so-called intellectuals and the lower reaches of the merchant class and they like nothing better than stirring up the workers. What do they want anyway? There is talk of creating a parliament. What nonsense! This is Russia, not England. God has given me the responsibility to rule it as my forefathers did and not turn it over to the rabble of a parliament. Unfortunately, the rantings of these dissident voices are spreading among my people. I need something to make them forget their ideas of western democracy and realize that the present system is the best for Mother Russia. What we need is … a short victorious war, one that will unify the population, silence the critics and give the people something to be thankful for. Do you not agree?"

Hardly knowing how to respond, Ivan merely murmured, "Yes, Your Majesty."

"I will wire our commanding general at Port Arthur, General Petrov and ask him to take good care of you. Your father has performed valuable service to me for many years and I will ask the good general to find a place for you on his staff."

Ivan, who wanted to serve with a combat unit, hid his disappointment and said, "Thank you, your Majesty. You are very kind."

The tsar, clearly pleased by his decision to take care of the young Medved, said "The empress and I will pray for you, Ivan. May

God bless you. Thank you, Boris, for bringing this fine young man to see me. And thank you, Ivan, for coming. Boris, please remain behind for a moment. There is a matter I wish to discuss with you."

Recognizing that this meant dismissal, Ivan bowed and turned and left the study. He waited in the corridor and chatted with a Guards officer whom he recognized as having been two years ahead of him at the Imperial Military Academy.

"Medved, how good to see you. Why were you in to see His Majesty?"

"I am leaving for Port Arthur and my father brought me in to see the tsar before I left," Ivan said.

"Port Arthur? Did you do something wrong?"

"I chose to go," Ivan responded.

"You can have it. There is no way I will volunteer to serve on the other side of Siberia, where no one at court will remember me."

Ivan was about to answer when the door to the tsar's study opened, and Boris joined his son. The Medved pair reversed the procedure of their entry, and soon found themselves out on the street where their carriage awaited them.

"Father, I really want to get into a combat unit. How will I ever be able to explain to my academy classmates and later to the children that I am bound to have that I spent the war as a general's aide?"

"Take heart, Ivan, do a good job for the general and you can ask him for transfer at a later date."

Ivan's family, swathed in layers of furs, drove him to the train station. They rode through a cold, gray day. A dusting of snow covered the city and the sky promised more. The world looked as if an inverted gray bowl covered it. Natalya held her brother's hand the entire way and Marina, eyes red and filled with tears, could hardly keep from sobbing aloud. Prince Medved tried to put a good face on it and distract them with small talk but the women were having none of it. Boris's youngest brother, Mikhail, Ivan's uncle, sat next to Boris in his priestly garments, ready to give blessing to Ivan and the rest of the Russians.

The station hummed with activity. Uniformed men bearing arms stood in formation all around. There appeared to be over a thousand of them. Hundreds of horses whinnied and nickered as their handlers restrained them and then moved them up the ramps into the waiting cars. The smells of horses, manure and urine, sweating bodies, gun oil, musty wool and burning coal filled the air.

Officers and NCOs strode down the lines of Russian infantrymen, inspecting them to ensure that each man was properly dressed, and had the required clothing and equipment. Each infantryman wore a fur cap and a long overcoat that reached down past the tops of his high boots. A tightly rolled blanket looped over his left shoulder and tied under his right arm near the waist. His leather belt, fastened on the outside of his coat, held a cartridge box on the front left where his right hand could easily reach it and each soldier carried a knapsack on his back. They were armed with Mouzin bolt-action rifles tipped with eighteen-inch bayonets, a favorite weapon of the Russian infantry. There was no scabbard. It was always fixed on the rifle. The enlisted men were conscripts from every corner of the Russian empire. There were pale Europeans, darker skinned men from the southern reaches of Russia's Central Asian borders and short, black-haired Mongols from the Russian east. Most had not seen their families in years and did not expect to ever see them again. There was no one to bid them farewell.

Once the inspections were complete, their officers gave the men leave to relax but not to stray from their position. Most stood; others sat on their bedrolls. All smoked and talked. An occasional bottle of vodka made the rounds but none of the men seemed drunk. A great many of them looked forlorn and lost in their thoughts about an endless trip across the Russian steppe, with the possibility of war waiting for them in a far-off land.

Ivan found the contingent of replacement officers with whom he was to travel and stood on the outskirts of the group with his family. A squadron of Cossacks laughed and chatted nearby. They had turned their horses over to the handlers and endured their inspection on foot. Most were heavily armed with sabers, pikes and either a pistol or a carbine, a short rifle that could easily be fired and reloaded while on horseback. Among them a ragged Russian priest leaned against a wagon and stared at Ivan's family. He was emaciated and dirty; his greasy beard and slick-looking hair shone in the weak rays of the sun. A wooden crucifix dangled from a cord around his neck. Ivan heard some of the Cossacks refer to him as "Father Grigori." Despite the cold the priest was lightly clad and seemingly unaffected by the temperature.

"That is one problem that Russia would do well to get rid of," said Mikhail with distaste. "We have too many of these self-styled priests, ignorant fellows from the country, illiterates, who inflict themselves on the people. Many are drunken and lecherous but perhaps they are accepted by the peasant conscripts for that very reason. They have never brought us good and never will."

The day before, the tsar himself, riding a great black stallion, had reviewed these troops on Red Square. His family and other royalty followed in carriages. The empress had a great supply of tin pictures of St. Seraphim, a hermit monk and great healer of the eighteenth century, who had just been canonized. Aides handed them to the tsar, who in turn gave them to officers and men at random. Some of the men regarded Seraphim's image with suspicion. "Why not icons of St. Nicholas?" many wondered. "He is our patron saint, the tsar's namesake and known to bring good luck to Russia. What kind of luck can this new saint bring us?"

Seraphim or Nicholas, it did not matter to most. God would go into battle with the Russians. Other longhaired, bushy-bearded and militant priests were scattered among the crowd of soldiers. Some were attached to the Cossack cavalry units, others marched with the infantry, or rode with the artillery wagons and the supply units. The priests carried banners and icons for the glorification of Holy Russia. The area around the station rang with the singing of hymns and mass prayers as the various priests urged their particular units to drown out the others.

Porters carefully loaded portable altars and crates of icons onto the freight cars. These were the inspiration of the Tsar's aunt, the Grand Duchess Elizabeth Federovna, who had paid for them.

A few days earlier, Tsar Nicholas had attended a mass prayer in St. Petersburg to pray for victory in the coming war against the Japanese. After the service, he stood for a long time in the window of the great White Hall as thousands of cheering and banner-waving citizens sang hymns. Forgotten were all the internal troubles besieging his country. His people were united. They were happy. Russia would win the war and then all would be right with his reign.

Not all Russians were as optimistic. General Mikhail Dragomirov, the grand old man of Russia's army, its leading strategist, feared for Russia's future. *Our army is untrained. Our supply lines trail across the vastness of Siberia over a railway that is not even complete.*

Like a bunch of fools, we think that our Te Deums will save us. They will attack us with artillery that no prayer can stop. Dragomirov, alas, was too old for active service, and the younger generals thought him to be an out-of-date old fool, and they were glad that he was given no real voice in the running of the war.

CHAPTER 18
ACROSS SIBERIA

Ivan, caught up in the excitement, could hardly contain himself. Visions of glory filled his head, thoughts of winning great distinction in battle. He looked around the crowd hoping against hope that Tatiana would somehow show up and bid him goodbye.

Finally, the captain in charge of the young replacement officers told them it was time to board. Ivan kissed his sister first, a brotherly peck on the cheek, then his mother, where he lingered a bit longer. He faced his father, uncertain of how he, as a young lieutenant going off to war, was to act. His father took the decision out of his hands, hugging him fiercely and kissing him wetly on both cheeks.

Boris said, "Be careful of yourself, Ivan. Thank God that the tsar has gotten an appointment for you as aide for General Baron Petrov. You should be safe there and able to write. Perhaps the general will even permit you to keep in touch with an occasional telegram."

"Yes, Ivan, we love you and will pray for you every day," his mother said as she dabbed her eyes. His sister stood by, paralyzed by sadness at the departure of her brother. She had never imagined a life without him. *Why did he have to go off to war?* she wondered. *There are plenty of men who could go in his place*.

All this emotion embarrassed Ivan, and he gave a great sigh of relief as he picked up his bag and climbed aboard. He went into one of the carriages reserved for junior officers and found a seat near a window where he could wave goodbye to his family. The young officers around him were in high spirits. Two or three passed around vodka as they smoked and told each other how they would win glory against the Japanese.

Ivan looked around the car to see if he recognized anyone.

"Family seeing their baby off to war, eh?" said a voice across the aisle.

Startled by the remark, Ivan looked and saw a fair-haired lieutenant, a few years older than himself smirking at him. The man sat with the dirty priest he had noticed in the train station, and they were sharing a bottle of vodka.

"My name is Ivan Medved," Ivan said, offering his hand.

"Ah, the little prince," was the reply. "I heard the son of one of the tsar's advisors would be among us real warriors. I am Arkady Gross," he said. "I come from a long line of fighting men and mean to be a hero in this war against the monkeys. That is, if we can get them to fight us. What do you suppose you are going to do, little prince?"

"Please call me Ivan," Ivan replied. "I am to be on the staff of General Petrov."

"Well, Ivan, there is a real combat assignment for you. You will be a dog-robber for a general, while the real men fight the war."

"I will serve wherever I am assigned," said Ivan. He turned away and dug a book out of his pack in order to end the embarrassing exchange. Arkady Gross said something in a low voice to his companions that caused them to snicker.

Here I am, Ivan thought, *in my first few minutes on the train, and I have already had to admit that I will be assigned to the general staff while others will serve on the battlefield.*

A long blast of a whistle sounded, and the train began to move with a great clattering of cars as it pulled out of the station and slowly picked up speed. The engineer wanted to cover as much ground as he could while the train ran on the stable roadbed of European Russia. Once he reached Siberia the train would slow to a crawl. And he knew there would be interminable stops.

When a porter called the officers of Ivan's car to supper they rose and packed themselves into a dimly lit officer's dining car. The senior officers had already eaten, and the remaining fare was bleak. Black bread, borscht, and some potatoes were all that were offered. Ivan sat at a table for eight arranged lengthwise along the car and was relieved to see that Lieutenant Gross was not among his messmates. Introductions were made all around and one of the young men produced a bottle of vodka, which he generously shared with his companions as they toasted the tsar, victory, and their families.

After the bottle had made the rounds a slight, sickly-looking officer sitting on Ivan's right said, "I overheard your conversation with Gross. Do not pay any attention to him as he is just a blowhard who tries to intimidate everyone around him. He and I served together in a regiment at Minsk, and he is just a cruel bully. If you stay out of his way, he will pay you no mind." The speaker had deep-set eyes that gleamed from the vodka. He parted his hair in the middle and it was too long for a soldier. His high-pitched voice sounded like it belonged on someone ten years his junior. "Oh, by the way, I am Constantine Pokrovski," he said. "Please call me 'Conya.' What is your name?"

"Ivan Medved," Ivan said.

"Ah, yes, Medved, one of the more interesting Russian names. It means 'bear' or really, 'honey eater.' The bear has become a symbol for our country. Indeed, Ivan, you do not look much like a bear," he said laughing. "You are too blond and too thin."

Smiling at the joke, Ivan said, "No, I am not a bear at all, just an officer who wants to serve the tsar."

"Yes, but your father is a prince and well known as one of the men who tutored the tsar. Could you have not gotten a good job at court?"

"Yes, but I wanted to do something on my own, achieve some good without my family's influence." He did not mention his secret ambitions.

"But did I not hear you tell Gross that you were to be an aide to General Baron Petrov?" Conya asked.

"Yes, I met the tsar before I left St. Petersburg," Ivan said, "and he arranged it as a favor to my father. But it will be just temporary, until I can ask the general to send me to a fighting unit. I hope it will be soon after we get there as I am sure that we will beat the Japanese quickly and I do not want to miss a chance to serve in combat."

As the conversation began to die many of the young officers, feeling tipsy from another bottle of vodka, swayed back to their compartments and tried to gain some fitful sleep amid the unaccustomed rocking and unfamiliar sounds of the train. Some of them, overcome with motion sickness, could be heard vomiting in the lavatory.

The next morning, after a long night of restless sleep, Ivan roused himself, managed to wash his hands and face and shave. Then he walked down the cars, rocking from side to side with the motion of the train, to the dining car for breakfast. As he entered the compartment a voice said, "Ah, the young prince, who is going to win the war by giving General Petrov good advice."

Ivan looked around and saw Arkady Gross sneering at him and whispering to his comrades. Some of the other young officers laughed. Unfortunately, the only available place was across from Gross. Ivan almost turned back to his sleeping car but decided not to be bullied into foregoing breakfast and reluctantly took a seat across from Gross. Determined not to be drawn into an argument he said, "Good morning, Arkady, did you sleep well?"

"Well enough on this rocking boat of a train. How about you, Ivan, did you have sweet dreams of life at the army headquarters?"

"I did not dream at all," muttered Ivan. He concentrated on his meager breakfast and tried to ignore his tormentor.

Several officers left the table and Constantine Pokrovski came in and sat at one of their places. "Good morning one and all," he said. He looked a bit green with hangover. Manners prevailed and Ivan introduced Constantine to Gross.

"We have already met," said Gross. "Brother Constantine and I have served together and often frequented the same bars. What was that woman's name in St. Petersburg, Conya? The one I took away from you when you were drunk."

"Oh, her," Constantine said, "she was not anyone important."

"You seemed to think she was important at the time, my friend. I seem to remember that you were about to challenge me to a duel over her," Gross said.

"I had a bit too much vodka, that night, Arkady. I do not duel. For one thing they are illegal."

"Was it because they are illegal or because you heard that I had already killed two men? I may be the best pistol shot in the army. If anyone wants to duel me, we can find a way, right, Ivan?"

Ivan did not reply.

"I would just as soon forget the whole thing," replied Constantine, looking even sicker than before.

"So be it, for now," said Arkady as he rose to his feet and started back to his compartment.

After he went through the door to the next car, Ivan poured Constantine another cup of tea and said, "So, tell me about our friend?"

"He is the son of a minor official from Yekaterinburg," Constantine said, "He gets along with few except those who lick his boots. He is an excellent shot and what he said about killing two men might be true. He is also a liar and a thief and a womanizer. He seduced a major's wife in St. Petersburg and bragged about it. He only avoided a duel there because the major was a coward. Later he was accused of raping a general's daughter, but they could not make the charge stick. He was not court-martialed but he was passed over for promotion to captain and transferred. My advice is to stay clear of him or ignore him as best you can. How he has remained in the army is anyone's guess. I suspect that he has volunteered to go to Port Arthur in order to try and save his career."

As Ivan rose to leave, he noticed that the small locket with Tatiana's photo was missing from the table where he thought he had laid it. He did not wear it but he carried it with him so he could open it from time to time and look at her picture. Oh, well, perhaps he had left it in his bag. Upon returning to his compartment he searched his possessions but had no luck finding the locket. Finally, he asked Constantine if he had seen it.

Constantine said, "Yes, I did not pay much attention to it but I saw you put something made of gold in front of your plate when you sat down. But then Arkady started in and I forgot about it."

"Do you suppose he stole it?"

"I would not put it past him but, whatever you do, do not accuse him of it. He will bring you more trouble than you can bear. It is only a locket."

"Yes, but in it is the only picture I have of Tatiana, the woman I love."

"Do not jump to conclusions, Ivan. Think about where else it might be. If you accuse Arkady, you must be prepared to fight him."

Ivan again searched his bags, turned out all the pockets in his clothing, but to no avail. After a few days of agonizing, he finally told Arkady that he had misplaced the piece, described it, and asked if he had seen it.

"A locket?" Gross asked, "What would a soldier be doing with a locket? I did not see it and have no idea what you are talking about. Surely you do not think that I had anything to do with its disappearance."

Ivan did not reply.

Several days passed. Each day, at odd times, Constantine would disappear for a while with no explanation where he was going. Sometimes he missed meals, even though he was not in his sleeping compartment at mealtime either. In the evening, he always seemed to have a bottle of vodka, some champagne, or tobacco, or some edible delicacy. Since he and Ivan were in adjoining compartments, he shared generously. Ivan several times asked him about his source of supply. Constantine was vague, saying he bribed this porter or that, or a supply sergeant. He also gambled in the evenings and was usually successful whether at dice or at cards. One of the men he won from was Arkady Gross, who at one point accused him of cheating. Conya confided in Ivan that Gross was just a terrible gambler and always had been.

On the fifth day of the trip Constantine pulled him aside and said, "Arkady has your locket. I heard him talking about it to one of his friends. He was trying to sell it to replenish his gambling money."

"What am I to do?" said Ivan.

"I will tell you what, I will see if he will sell it to me. He owes me enough money that he may be willing to use it to settle his debt."

"But Constantine," Ivan said, "the locket is mine. No one should have to buy it back. I am going to have to confront him."

No," said Constantine, "that is the worst thing you can do. Do this. Tomorrow morning at breakfast engage him in an argument. Nothing to get him too excited but enough to keep him occupied. I will see what I can do."

"But what…?"

"Don't ask, just keep him occupied."

The next morning, although there was a choice of seats in the dining car, Ivan picked one at a table where Arkady held court. He seemed surprised to see Ivan sit across from him but said, "Gentlemen, I give you the princeling," as Ivan sat down.

A couple of minutes into his breakfast Ivan interrupted a story Arkady was telling to ask, "Tell me, Lieutenant Gross, how a man from such a remote place as Yekaterinburg managed to get an army position in St. Petersburg."

Unused to being interrupted, Arkady's jaw dropped. He stared for a long minute at Ivan and said, "Where I come from is no one's business. Nor how I got to St. Petersburg. My family has been in the service of the tsar for many years."

"My, that is a long time," said Ivan, knowing that Arkady knew that Ivan's family had been in the service of the tsar since the founding of the Romanov Dynasty in 1613 and at the court itself since the Napoleonic War, and were now members of the aristocracy.

"Do not get smart with me, princeling," Gross said. "One need not be an aristocratic brat to have served the tsar long and well."

"Yes, but what did your family do? How did they serve?"

Ivan had unknowingly hit a nerve. He was not to find out until much later that Arkady's family was indeed undistinguished and he had gotten an Army commission and a favorable posting through the influence of his uncle, his mother's brother, to whom a member of the aristocracy was greatly in debt. Moreover, his grandfather did serve as in the army but he was a supply officer, not a warrior.

"Let us just say that they fought for the tsar in many wars." And with that Arkady launched into a long tale of how a supposed forebear had valiantly served in the Crimean War and was at the battle of Balaclava where the Russians slaughtered the British in the Valley of Death. No sooner had he finished that story than he began another tale of how his great-grandfather had helped drive Napoleon from Russia. He was long-winded and held the attention of his sycophants who hung on every word.

Before Arkady finished the story, Ivan looked over his shoulder and saw Constantine beckoning him from the end of the car. Ivan mumbled an apology and left. He followed Constantine back to his compartment and when they shut the door Constantine handed him the locket.

"But how did you...?"

"Don't ask."

That evening at supper, Ivan again sought a seat near Arkady. As soon as he was seated, he casually fingered the locket and then placed it squarely next to his plate where he could keep an eye on it. In the midst of conversation, Arkady's eyes shifted to the tabletop and froze on the locket. He met Ivan's eyes with such a look of hatred that Ivan almost became afraid. Arkady's story remained unfinished. He staggered to his feet and walked to the end of the car without comment. At the door he turned and once again fixed Ivan with a feral glance that said, "I am going to get you, little boy."

Ivan avoided Arkady as much as possible after that.

Another person whom Ivan avoided was Father Grigori. The priest could be smelled from a dozen feet away, there were usually bits of food in his beard and his fingernails were always black. Moreover, he always seemed to be drunk. He would rail about the importance of God to Holy Russia's cause and buttonhole various officers and sharply question them about their beliefs. He talked incessantly about the Japanese "monkeys" and the "Zhid", or Jews, and the English and he loudly prayed for unpleasant deaths and eternal suffering in hell for the entire lot. He was popular with

Arkady Gross's group. He was their court jester and they laughed at him behind his back. The priest fawned over Arkady Gross, and always had something amusingly outrageous to say about the officers who were not a part of Gross's entourage.

For nearly two weeks the train crept across Russia, crossing the low-lying Ural Mountains and then into Asia and the Russian steppe. Mile after mile, day after endless day, was stripped from their future as the train slowly made its way across the lifeless landscape, discharging steam into the air, ash and human waste between the tracks. The wheels skimmed the rust from the surface of the tracks and for a moment the rails glowed dark blue in the train's wake until the patient rust returned.

The odor of unwashed bodies, dirty clothing, the latrines and poorly cooked food permeated every car in the train. The food had gradually evolved from its humble beginnings to a fare that was barely edible. Several days in a row, the only fare offered was shchi, watery cabbage soup, and tough Russian black bread.

Finally, the train stopped at the small city of Irkutsk, the last major settlement before the train reached Lake Baikal, the world's deepest lake. The stop was a scheduled one. It was at Irkutsk that they would take on coal and replenish their provisions. The food improved a little, but the foul odors still stalked the cars.

Irkutsk was also a good place for the train to pause while the senior officers calculated the conditions at Lake Baikal itself. A squadron of mounted Mongolian cavalry joined the train at Irkutsk. The Mongolian border lay not too far from Lake Baikal and these men were mercenaries who had signed on to fight for the tsar. While the train waited, many of the enlisted men and some of the officers snuck into the city to take advantage of the brothels and barrooms.

Here, also, the soldiers who were to join the Siberian army departed the train.

After the pause, the train resumed its journey and soon reached the western shore of Lake Baikal at the village of Listvyanka. Russian engineers had not yet been able to blast tunnels through, or lay rail bed around, the tall mountains surrounding the lake and it was necessary for the troops to be carried across on its surface. In fair weather, steamers ferried men and cargo across to the eastern shore, where they boarded another train and continued their voyage across the remainder of Siberia. In the winter, they crossed the lake on the ice. This year the Russian winter howled down from the Arctic Circle earlier than usual. When the train reached Irkutsk, the senior officer passed word through the cars that there would be an indefinite wait. The surface was frozen enough to prevent the steamships from running but not frozen enough to permit marching across the ice. The train sat still for nearly another week, until the steadily plunging temperature froze the lake enough for transit across its surface.

As they waited another storm roared out of the north, with a fury rarely found anywhere on earth except Siberia. The temperature dropped to minus thirty degrees on the thermometer, and the forty-knot winds drove the chill factor even further down the scale. It was so cold that urine froze before it hit the ground.

Then there was the snow, great sheets of it, driven horizontally across the flat and barren steppe until it met an obstacle against which it could cling and build. In this case the obstacle was the railroad line and the train itself. Soon the train was buried in a huge drift. The soldiers huddled around smoky, poorly fueled stoves, and most wore all the clothing they possessed. After forty-eight hours at gale force, the winds dropped to nothing but the snow continued.

When the wind stopped, the snow piled up on all sides and formed a cocoon around the train, which made it warmer although the outside temperature remained well below zero. The snow paused after another day and a half and the landscape became a still, white mass, unbroken as far as the eye could see. A cold, hostile sun illuminated the earth. The train had to be uncovered before completing the last few miles of its journey. Battalions of enlisted men were pressed into service with shovels to free the train from its frozen cloak. That done, the train proceeded to the shores of the lake.

Then there remained the most difficult job of all, the task of traveling across the lake to board another train on the other side. The soldiers unloaded and harnessed hundreds of horses to sleighs to ferry goods and equipment across the frozen surface. Then they unloaded ton after ton of supplies from the train and piled them onto` the sleighs. The men would walk.

The officers and men set out in groups of one hundred. One officer marched at the head of each party of enlisted men and another at the rear to keep stragglers moving. Ivan drew the duty of marching in the rear of his group.

The day before they were to set out, Ivan listened as the major who was appointed to lead the formation shouted out instructions to the men. "We will be led by guides across the narrowest part of the lake. The distance is about twenty miles. Every four miles there are shelters where we will take twenty-minute breaks. The shelters are out of the wind but cannot be well heated for fear of melting the ice beneath them. However, each will have samovars over small fires to provide tea."

The winds rose and fell without warning as the first groups crossed and found that the ice was not uniformly solid. Men, sometimes groups of them, strayed off the route, fell through the ice where it was thinnest, and were lost.

Ivan's group started out on the second day. By this time, earlier parties had trampled a path in the snow but the going was still slow and the wind picked up again. Like beasts of burden, carrying their arms and equipment, the men marched head down with their faces covered except for their eyes. Even when no more snow fell, the wind drove that already on the ground across their path and reduced visibility to a yard or so. In single file they trudged, at times the visibility so poor that each man hung on to the equipment of the man in front so his way would not be lost. Even so, small groups in the column lost track of the men before them, wandered off in the wrong direction and were never seen again.

Because of the uneven pace, the column suffered from the concertina effect. Gaps would occur in the column and those behind them would have to increase the pace to catch up or risk being lost. By the time the movement reached the tail of the column the hindmost soldiers were running as fast as they could in a desperate attempt to not be left behind. Then when those in front slowed down, all behind them jammed up until the column was a compressed mass and those in the rear stood still until the front of the column stretched out again. All soldiers knew about the concertina effect and knew how to avoid it when they moved over simple terrain in clear visibility. Under the conditions on Lake Baikal the effect was impossible to prevent. Ivan moved continuously, shouting at his men, "Keep an even interval! Keep an even interval! You must keep moving or you will freeze." It required all the strength he could muster to keep going and he envied those at the head of the column.

Despite Ivan's efforts, frostbite claimed soldier after soldier. Noses and fingers had to be covered or rubbed frequently to keep the circulation going. Toes were another matter. The Russian soldiers wore felt boots over their regular footwear. Though warm, they were difficult to walk long distances in and clumsy to run in. Moreover, when those at the rear of a column worked up a sweat from running to catch up and then paused, their toes were in danger of freezing no matter what.

Ivan's group reached the first of the shelters. Most of the men threw themselves onto the ground and rested. Some lined up at the samovars for tea. Ivan and the officer who headed the column circulated among them without pause. "Take your shoes off and dry your feet and let as much moisture as possible out of your boots. It is the only way you can keep going." Only a few men took the advice. Most just looked at the officers with faces of despair as they prepared for the continuing ordeal. They reluctantly got to their feet when ordered to do so and filed out of the shelter. Some refused to leave until threatened by court martial and imprisonment.

The horse-drawn sleighs were faster than the walking soldiers, traveling along their own parallel path a few meters away. Every man on foot regarded at the sleighs with longing. At one point Ivan thought he saw Arkady Gross and Father Grigori perched atop one of the sleighs as it passed, but they were so bundled up that he could not tell for sure.

It took Ivan's party nearly thirty hours on their feet to walk the twenty miles across the lake. They reached the small town of Tanhoi on other side of the lake and stumbled into the passenger cars of the train that awaited them. These trains and the rail bed material that supported them had been sent on a long voyage by sea to Vladivostok. Because of the difficulty of supplying the eastern portion of the railroad with rolling stock, the cars for this portion of the voyage were fewer in quantity, of inferior quality, and not well maintained. But the crowded, poorly heated and lighted cars seemed a luxury compared to the frozen wasteland the soldiers had just crossed. Two days later the train reached the town of Chita.

Luckily, coal was abundant in the Russian Far East and in northern China, and the authorities stockpiled plenty of it along the remainder of the route. The only stops the train made between Chita and their destination were brief ones, just a few hours to take on coal. The men ignored the smoke from the stoves and were a solemn and stoic lot for the remaining days of their trip. The Russian soldiers debarked at the Chinese village of Nanshan. They were all grateful to be off the train although the smell of smoke and unwashed bodies continued to cling to them. They marched the fifteen miles from Nanshan to Port Arthur, too exhausted to give much thought to the war ahead of them.

CHAPTER 19

PORT ARTHUR, PART 1

Upon reaching Port Arthur, the NCOs quickly formed the new arrivals up and they marched off behind guides sent by General Petrov's headquarters. The replacement officers waited in small groups until they were told where to report. A captain circulated among them calling out names and sending the new officers to their various units. They engaged Chinese coolies to carry them to their destinations in rickshaws. The captain gave each rickshaw puller a piece of paper with the passenger's destination written on it in Chinese. Many of the pullers were illiterate so a Chinese assistant shouted the destination at them in their native language. Ivan's name was near the end of the captain's roster and most of the other officers were gone when he found a rickshaw to take him to the headquarters of General Baron Anatole Petrov, the Governor-General of Fortress Port Arthur. The coolie gestured for Ivan to board and then loaded his baggage around him. He picked up the handles of his primitive vehicle, took a deep breath and began pulling his load through the muddy streets. It was slow going at first until the rickshaw gained some momentum. Then it seemed to fly over the ruts and potholes. The rickshaw man was short, slight and dressed in rags and Ivan wondered where he found the strength to pull his fares. The scene around Ivan fascinated him and all the activity fueled his imagination.

Port Arthur was a wild and wooly town, reminiscent of the growing western cities of mid-nineteenth century America. Native Chinese mixed with Europeans and Asians of a dozen nations. Livestock roamed everywhere on unpaved streets. Open sewers ran odorously. Ramshackle, hastily constructed buildings leaned at angles and many seemed ready to collapse. The town boasted dozens of saloons and brothels. Tens of thousands of cases of Russian vodka could be seen stacked at the railway station. There was a traveling circus, music halls, gambling dens, opium emporiums, sleazy hotels, and restaurants of both good and of doubtful quality. Yankee trader Enoch Emory, who had made a fortune with a chain of grocery stores in Russia, built a major emporium there that was popular with the wives of senior officers. In the midst of such chaos, the Russians busily constructed a support establishment for the year-round port. Workmen laid the foundation for an elaborate Russian Orthodox cathedral to meet the requirements of the Russian God.

Grim, bare hills, that boasted little vegetation any time of year, silently looked down on the port. With few local foodstuffs, the port depended on the Trans-Siberian Railroad and ships from abroad to supply their needs. Nearly 40,000 Russian soldiers and sailors crowded the city and thousands of Asian workers, fortune hunters, gamblers, grifters, and mystics from many nations supplemented the military population.

The city had a denser population than the districts of Moscow with which Ivan was familiar. The crowds were mostly male. Small formations of men and individual soldiers strode through the streets. Sailors on shore leave staggered between the many saloons and lined up outside the brothels. Cossacks galloped through the streets. Of the women he observed, a few who were well dressed and accompanied by servants, and often bodyguards, visited the stores and emporiums scattered among the more distasteful establishments. Others, prostitutes of the lowest type, advertised their wares with revealing clothing and lewd glances at the servicemen in the streets. The higher classes of whores did not have to advertise themselves in the woman-starved city. The men who could afford them knew where they were and kept them busy.

Ivan reached the headquarters and presented the letter from Moscow to a clerk who in turn gave it to a personnel officer. He then waited while an aide got a minute of the general's time and consulted with him. After a wait of nearly an hour, the aide finally told Ivan, "The general will see you now."

An aide ushered Ivan into the general's office, where he stood at rigid attention, saluted and reported. He hoped the general would not notice that his uniform bore ample evidence of the long and difficult voyage across Russia.

The general, a thin man of about sixty, looked up from Ivan's file on his desk. "Good to see a young Medved out here, Ivan. Have a seat and tell me how things are with your family." Ivan seated himself gingerly on the edge of a hard chair that faced the general and began to relate what he knew of his family and St. Petersburg. Petrov had the reputation of being a strict disciplinarian and he looked the part. Worn thin with drink and rather uncouth of body and posture, his clean-shaven head appeared to have been polished. Enormous eyebrows overshadowed his deep eye sockets and his waxed mustache twitched above his thin lips and goatee when he talked. Petrov had been wounded in the Russo-Turkish war as a captain and later commanded a large international force during the Boxer Rebellion in China. Rumor had it that he carried off dozens of cases of precious loot as personal booty from the conflict. It was well known around Port Arthur that the general received a forage allotment for six riding horses and twelve carriage horses. Since he only maintained two riding horses and six carriage horses, the remainder of the allotment went into his pocket.

Ivan began with a brief summary of what he knew about society in Moscow and St. Petersburg, and after a few minutes he noticed that Petrov's eyes were taking on a vacant look. Ivan quickly wrapped things up by saying; "I just hope I can be of service to the tsar and, of course, to Your Excellency."

"Well, I suppose I can find place for a bright young lieutenant on my staff as a junior aide. My wife is here and requires a lot of attention, poor dear, that I do not have time to give her. I am sure she will keep you busy. Report to Major Sakharov." With that dismissal, Ivan saluted, did an about face, and left the room to find the major.

Major Sakharov was a thin pale man with lank hair that fell about his eyes. He unsuccessfully tried to imitate the mustache and goatee of his general, but his facial hair was patchy and shapeless, and his goatee rested on his chin like a thin bundle of twigs. The little moustache ends, although reinforced with wax, drooped, giving him a permanently sad expression. "I think, Medved, that I will send you up to see the general's wife. She has need of an aide and someone to run her errands and to escort her about town. As the commanding general's wife, she is entitled to a junior officer as an aide. The young lieutenants I sent before you have not lasted very long. She has already fired several and several more have requested transfer to combat units. Perhaps she will find you more acceptable since your father is a prince and advisor to the tsar."

"Major, if there is something else I could do, please do not send me there." Ivan had visions of what his friend Constantine, and, even worse, what his enemy Gross would think if they found out about his assignment.

"You are here to serve, Lieutenant, and if I think and the general thinks that you can best do so by helping Madame Petrov, then you will do it. Besides, if you keep her occupied and happy, she will stay out of the general's hair, not that he has that much," he added in a whisper, "and mine. You can take the rest of the day to get settled in the junior officers' headquarters barracks and then report to me at 0700 tomorrow morning. In your best uniform, and it had better be clean. I will send word to Madame Petrov by runner that you will report tomorrow. That will be all."

Ivan left the major's office and a clerk told him where he would be billeted. He found the barracks and unpacked his clothing and equipment in a dirty little room with one small window. He inquired of an orderly who gave him some bedding of questionable cleanliness and a small oil lamp.

The next morning, having breakfasted, shaved, and done his best to come up with a clean uniform, Ivan reported to the clerk outside Major Sakharov's office. The major kept him waiting again for nearly two hours and then simply took him outside, pointed to a large house on the hill behind the headquarters, and said, "On your way, she is expecting you."

Disconsolate, Ivan trudged up the hill to the house. He just raised his hand to tap on the door when a maidservant opened it. The girl was young, about sixteen, and pretty in a hard sort of way. "Lieutenant Medved? Madame Petrov is awaiting you." The maid showed Ivan into a large sitting room overlooking the harbor where the maid said. "Lieutenant Ivan Medved, madam," and quickly curtsied and shut the door behind her.

"Come in Ivan," said the fortyish but handsome, buxom woman who remained seated, "I am Madame Petrov. Pour tea for us and sit and tell me of the latest in St. Petersburg and Moscow." Ivan carefully poured and as he handed her a cup he smelled a thick cloud of stale perfume that surrounded her. Then he sat in a comfortable chair across a low table from her. Madame Petrov kept him busy for the remainder of the morning asking this question or that about Moscow society and the grand balls in St. Petersburg. Ivan had just about exhausted his limited knowledge of such affairs when there was a soft knock on the door. The maid appeared with the announcement that lunch was served.

"I have asked our cook to provide a little something special for a special guest from St. Petersburg. Please help me up and escort me to the dining room."

Ivan rose, took the lady by her arm and let her guide him to a well-appointed dining salon. He was surprised to see the spotless linen, polished silver and gleaming glassware. He noticed that Madame Petrov leaned into him a little heavily and pressed a large breast against one arm. Ivan immediately felt his loins stir even though the woman was far older than he and he did not feel particularly attracted to her. Her perfume made him a bit light-headed as he steered her to her chair and took a seat opposite.

"I hope the champagne is cold this time," she said to the maid.

"Yes, Madame, I put some on ice early this morning." The maid served them silently, poured champagne and left the room. Madame Petrov gulped rather than sipped her champagne and halfway through luncheon called for a second bottle, she having consumed nearly three quarters of the first.

Madame Petrov completely dominated the conversation and relieved Ivan of a responsibility to keep it going. As her tongue loosened from the wine, her chatter slowly turned from how grand it was to be married to a Baron who was also a military governor, to talk about the poor quality of social events in Port Arthur and then to how lonely and abandoned she felt most of the time. She looked woefully at the second empty champagne bottle and Ivan worried for a moment that she would order a third. Finally, she put her hand over her mouth and lightly belched and then yawned. "I am afraid it is time for my afternoon nap, Ivan. The rest of the day is all yours. Do what you like and I will see you at ten o'clock tomorrow morning."

Ivan retraced his steps down the hill and spent what remained of the afternoon wandering the bleak streets of Port Arthur, orienting himself to its atmosphere and geography. At about dark he wandered into one of the better-looking restaurants to order a meal. He had no sooner been seated than he heard his name, "Ivan Medved, how are you doing?" He looked up into the smiling, thin face of Constantine.

"Conya, join me for supper," he said. His friend sat down at Ivan's table and ordered vodka for them both.

Constantine said, "I am assigned to the 5th East Siberian Regiment under Colonel Tretyakov. He is a man with a real soldier's reputation. All his officers and men love him and say he is the best regimental commander here. How did you fare? Are you really with General Petrov's staff?"

"Worse than that, Conya," Ivan said, "I have been assigned as a junior aide and all that I have been given to do so far is to look after Madame Petrov."

"That cannot be too bad, Ivan. Tell me, does she look as good as I have heard?"

"Well... I suppose so. Maybe she was beautiful in her youth, but her looks are slipping and she looks her age, above forty, I would guess. I suppose that she is good looking if one likes older women. How am I ever going to face St. Petersburg society again when they learn that all I did in the war was to look after a woman?"

Constantine immediately changed the subject and began talking about assignments of the other officers they had met on the train. "Your friend, Arkady Gross, has also been assigned to my regiment, but to another battalion and I have only seen him once. Hopefully I will not again. He asked me if I had anything to do with the return of your locket and I suspect he knows that I stole it back from him but cannot say anything about it."

The evening wound down as two friends finished their meal, exhausted their material for gossip and had vodka toasts—to their families, to the tsar and victory, and then parted company.

CHAPTER 20

PORT ARTHUR, PART 2

The next morning Ivan repeated his reluctant journey up the hill. This time a four-horse carriage and driver waited in front of the house. The maid told him to wait, that Madame would be right there.

Preceded by the familiar fog of perfume, she soon appeared and said, "Good morning, Ivan, I hope you are ready to see the sights of Port Arthur."

Ivan said that he was and helped the lady into the carriage. They sat opposite each other as was proper. After Madame Petrov settled into her seat, she issued a curt order to the driver, a Russian enlisted man. He draped thick woolen blankets across their legs and climbed up into his seat. As the carriage got underway, she snuggled deeply into her furs and pulled the blanket up to cover more of her body. It was cold but sunny, and Madame Petrov directed the driver around the city, stopping to point out such things as the old Chinese wall, the Russian ships in the harbor, most of which she knew by name, and several of the more respectable business establishments. At 1:00 p.m. she ordered the driver to pull up in front of what she said was the best restaurant in the city. Alighting from the carriage, she tightly grasped Ivan's arm and guided him into the dark interior. As they as a waiter seated them, Ivan became aware of a raucous group nearby. He looked, and there sat Arkady Gross and several of his friends. Among them was Father Grigori who roughly pawed the heavily rouged woman sitting in his lap. Gross pointed to Ivan and the general's wife and said something that Ivan could not catch but at which the table erupted in laughter, laughing with the harsh, loud and insistent voices of crows. Ivan reddened. He looked at Madame Petrov and saw that she was closely examining his face.

"What is wrong, Ivan, you look sick?"

"It is nothing, Madame Petrov, I am just getting used to the light in here."

The general's lady scanned the menu, made several recommendations, and insisted that Ivan order for them both, adding that champagne would be nice. Their lunch arrived and Ivan sat through the interminable meal, just nibbling at the food on his plate and scarcely aware of his conversation with Madame Petrov but attuned to the loud vodka-fueled conversation from Gross's table.

When Ivan and Madame Petrov finished their meal, again with two bottles of champagne, which Madame Petrov drank the bulk of, Ivan was dismayed to find the Gross party still there.

As they passed by the table on the way out, Arkady said, "Well, if it is not my good friend, Lieutenant Medved. And with a beautiful lady, too. Please introduce us, Ivan." He punctuated this with a short laugh made bright by scorn.

Ivan had no choice but to make introductions to Madame Petrov who looked at them all with grim, unfocused eyes and merely nodded. Ivan was grateful that she did not try to speak. She ignored Father Grigori, who lurched over and grabbed her hand and wetly kissed it. She fixed a bemused expression on her face and made a valiant but unsuccessful attempt to smile. The corners of her lips turned up but the center of her mouth looked like she had just bitten into a lemon.

"I am sure, Madame Petrov," said Arkady as Ivan made their excuses, "that taking care of you is a most important job for the war effort." His comrades rolled their eyes, clearly stretching the boundaries of their self-containment to avoid laughing.

"Goodbye, Arkady," said Ivan as he took Madame Petrov by the arm and guided her out the door.

On the carriage ride back to the house, Madame Petrov insisted that Ivan sit beside her and when the carriage left the center of town, she lightly placed her hand on Ivan's thigh.

Day after day Ivan reported to the house on the hill, always to do the same thing. They would have lunch, or tour Port Arthur or just sit overlooking the harbor and chat while she swilled champagne. Madame Petrov's behavior became more bizarre. Sometimes she appeared to have been drinking before he appeared. She drank champagne the whole time she was with him, always guzzling it like some men guzzle beer. When drunk she boldly flirted with him, touching him and telling him how handsome he was. He thought that nothing grew stale so quickly as her perfume.

One afternoon after lunch, Ivan noticed that the maid had served the meal and then left the room. She did not clear the dishes from the table as usual and the house was unnaturally quiet. Madame Petrov shakily got to her feet. "None of the servants will be here for the rest of the afternoon, Ivan. There is just you and me." She walked around the table, leaned over and kissed him soundly on the mouth. Ivan was terrified.

"Madam Petrov, you are the general's wife!" he said, "What are you doing?"

"Anatole is so busy," she breathed, "that he never has time for me. I am so lonely. Come Ivan," she said as she grasped his hand and tried to lead him from the room.

"I cannot, I just cannot," he protested.

Anger shone in her eyes. "Either you will and no one will know, or you will not and I will tell my husband you tried. He will probably have you shot."

She rubbed her leg between his and kissed him again, trying to pull him to the back of the house. Ivan did not know what to do. Just then he heard the brakes of a carriage squeak outside. Madame Petrov froze. "Someone is here. Hurry, back into the dining room." They no sooner were seated and were trying to look casual when General Petrov strode through the door.

"Hello, my dear, hello lieutenant. Just finished lunch I see." His bug eyes took in the two champagne bottles and then fixed a hard stare at Ivan. Turning back to his wife, he said, "Maria, how many times have I got to tell you not to drink during the day? And two bottles, too! That will be it for today, Lieutenant. I think you should report back to Major Sakharov in the morning."

Ivan walked back down the hill to his quarters, weighted down by the messy events with the general's wife that clouded his future. He felt depressed as never before and spent a sleepless night expecting that the worst kind of discipline awaited him the next day. How would his parents take the news that he could not even succeed as an aide to the general, not even the general but the general's wife, for God's sake?

Before the light of day began to illuminate the sky, he gave up on sleep, got out of bed, shaved, and put on his best uniform. He went to the officer's mess but found that he was not hungry. He had but a single cup of tea for breakfast. Then he waited until he knew the general staff would be at work, trudged across the parade field to the headquarters, and tentatively peered through the door of Major Sakharov's office.

Sakharov looked up from his paperwork with a sour expression on his face. "Another failure," he said. "What is it about you young officers that I send to Madame Petrov? What can be so difficult about that woman?" It was clear from his voice that he did not really expect an answer. He gave Ivan a long look. "Anyway, the general wants you out of headquarters, letter from St. Petersburg be damned. He said to post you to an infantry unit. You will not be there long before you will wish you had not messed up a good comfortable assignment in the rear."

"If I may, sir …" started Ivan.

Sakharov gave him a sharp glance. "Yes?"

"Is there any chance that I could go to Colonel Tretyakov's 5th East Siberian Regiment?"

"I do not see why not." the major said, "There is as good a chance to get shot with the 5th East Siberian as anywhere. Tretyakov is a fighting colonel. Report there immediately."

In the dim light of the overcast day, Ivan, his gear in a waiting rickshaw, reported to the 5th Regiment Headquarters. The regimental adjutant was just going to lunch when Ivan caught him. "Hmm, a new lieutenant. I will assign you to the 1st Battalion," and he gave Ivan directions how to get there.

Before he departed for his battalion headquarters the regimental adjutant told Ivan to report to his new colonel. Colonel Nikolai Tretyakov was a tall slender man, balding with a sharply pointed mustache and a closely trimmed beard. He did not look like an officer in the tsar's army. His tunic was unbuttoned, his shirt was wrinkled and unclean, and mud and horse manure clung to his boots. His office was austere, the walls undecorated except for a holstered pistol that hung on a peg behind his desk. He regarded Ivan closely, his unsmiling eyes intent as he scanned the young lieutenant from his polished boots to his well-tailored uniform. "There is nothing in your brief record except your performance at the academy and it appears that you did well there, Lieutenant Medved, but you have been on Petrov's staff and that sort of duty has ruined many a promising officer before. Tell me, did Major Sakharov assign you to my regiment, or did you volunteer?"

"I volunteered, sir," Ivan said. "I wanted very much to get out of headquarters and get into the battle when we eventually fight the Japanese. And I heard that this was a real fighting regiment."

"This *is* a fighting unit, Lieutenant Medved," the colonel said. "The only thing that matters to me is how you perform on the battlefield. Being the son of a prince will not prevent me from relieving you of command and sending you back to Moscow in disgrace if you fail to live up to my standards. I recommend that you get out of that fancy uniform and get into something more appropriate for an officer in the field. Do you understand?"

"Yes, sir," Ivan answered meekly.

With that, Tretyakov grunted and dismissed him.

Ivan had no idea to which of Tretyakov's units his friend Constantine was assigned but when he reached the 1st Battalion area and found the officers' quarters, he scanned the list of names posted on a bulletin board and was happy to find that he would be in the same company in the same battalion as his friend Constantine. He was unhappy that he was in the same regiment as Arkady Gross but at least was not in the same battalion. That meant that he would see Gross from time to time but not have constant contact with him. When he first ran into Gross at the morning's formation Gross said, "Well, our little princeling has come to join the fighting troops. Was Madame Petrov too tough on you?" Ivan made an effort to ignore the remarks but his ears burned when some of the troops in the ranks heard Gross and sniggered.

CHAPTER 21

WAR

February 8th was a cold; peaceful night and a light snow fell on Port Arthur. A band played on the battleship *Tsarevitch* and some sailors sang an evening hymn. The sounds of their voices drifted across the water to the town. Searchlights casually swept the sea around the quiet fleet as most of the crews prepared to bed down for the night. Two Russian ships on picket duty finished their periodic patrol to the harbor mouth and slowly drifted toward their anchorages. Sleepy lookouts scanned the area behind the returning ships and wondered if a long line of unidentified vessels, which they could only make out dimly, could be real. The formation was real, a squadron of ten Japanese destroyers steaming at low speed so their funnels gave off no sparks and traveling in blackout conditions. They came on, one behind the other, in a straight line, directly at the anchored Russian ships in order to keep the Russians from easily determining their number.

At ten minutes before midnight, Captain Asai, the commodore of the squadron gave the order to attack. The Japanese increased their speed to full and "crossed the T." Some split left and the others right, turning their broadsides to the anchored Russian fleet. All launched torpedoes. Once the torpedoes were on their way, the Japanese opened fire with their big guns. The battleship *Retvizan* took a torpedo below the waterline and soon began sink. Armor-piercing rounds struck the cruiser *Pallada* amidships, and she immediately heeled over. Japanese guns shattered the bulkhead and armored deck of the *Tsarevitch*, crippling the most powerful battleship in the Russian fleet. The explosions completely carried away her steering compartment and left her adrift. A great deal of shouting and ringing of bells accompanied the confused crews as they staggered to general quarters. Before the Russians could recover and return fire, the Japanese vessels turned and steamed out of the harbor unharmed.

On shore, bugle after bugle sounded the alarm. General Petrov, still in his nightshirt and groggy from sleep, refused to believe the Japanese were attacking him. "They would not dare!" He finally awoke to reality but issued contradictory orders, which further confused the situation. Officers and men ran willy-nilly through the darkness, trying to find out what was going on and getting to their posts. There was a great deal of firing from the Russian shore batteries, and from their undamaged ships, but they shot at ghosts. The Japanese ships had disappeared into the night— out of sight and out of range.

As dawn broke over the port, Admiral Stark, the Russian naval commander, conferred with Petrov and told him he was taking the rest of his fleet to sea to prevent the Japanese from bottling him up if they returned. His ships called general quarters, built up steam, and had guns at the ready as they moved out toward the open sea. Awaiting them they found a formidable Japanese force of six battleships and nine cruisers. An exchange of fire killed about 150 sailors on each side and damaged several Japanese and Russian ships. The Japanese quickly gained fire superiority and forced the

Russians back into Port Arthur, then bombarded the town with thirty twelve-inch shells, terrifying the population. The Japanese blockaded the Russian fleet in the harbor and their powerful force patrolled the entrance to the Port Arthur like Dobermans.

In Moscow, the tsar and tsarina had just returned from the opera and were stepping down from their carriage in front of the royal apartments in the Kremlin when a military aide rushed up and told the emperor there was an urgent telegram from Port Arthur. The tsar moved out of the chilling wind and into the entrance of the palace, where he read the telegram as the aide held an oil lamp. His face turned white and his shoulders slumped as he read of the disaster to his navy, and the pounding of Port Arthur by Japanese naval gunfire. He looked grimly at Alexandra and the couple went to the royal apartments where the tsar spent a long night conferring with his military advisors. Two days later, the Japanese made it official and declared war on Russia. The tsar dithered for another week before declaring war on Japan.

Colonel Nikolai Tretyakov's 5th East Siberian Rifle Regiment held a line on a narrow three-mile-wide isthmus at Nanshan, fifteen miles northeast of Port Arthur. His unit was in a tenuous position. He had helped build this position four years ago but at the time the Russians thought they would only have to defend it against the militarily incompetent Chinese. He knew he was spread thin against the Japanese and was refused reinforcement. His superiors did not think that the Japanese would be any more formidable than the feckless Chinese from whom they had seized the territory. At the same time that Tretyakov heard of the naval attack on Port Arthur, his outposts alerted that him the Japanese were patrolling the area to his north and were a threat to Nanshan. He desperately redoubled the efforts to reinforce his defensive position.

The ground he defended was a slight ridgeline that bisected the peninsula. His enemy's main forces lay a few miles to his north, but he could easily see their outposts less than a half-mile away. It seemed like there were one or two new outposts every morning. He was well aware that the Japanese could throw up earthworks with astonishing speed and were preparing their own lines of defense. He had no doubt that his enemy carefully watched him.

Between the two forces sat a flat, marshy plain. Summer would bring millions of mosquitoes and make the soldiers on both sides miserable. This no-man's-land was generally treeless, and Tretyakov instructed his engineers to topple and burn the few trees that remained to deny his enemy cover if they should attempt to attack him across the marshy area. When it rained the marsh was a sea of mud, impossible to cross quickly. Tretyakov prayed for continuous rain in the warm months to come. But now snow cloaked the area and the water in the marshes was frozen solid. Most mornings he could see footprints in the snow where the Japanese had run night patrols up to the edge of his fortifications. None of his sentries ever reported seeing the enemy.

The Russian colonel put hundreds of Chinese coolies to work fortifying his positions. The laborers were thin, impoverished men who had been unemployed, and nearly starved. Most worked barefoot in the bitter cold or wrapped their feet in whatever rags they could find. They hacked away at the rock-hard ground, preparing fighting positions a shovelful at a time.

Colonel Doi of the Japanese Army had planted spies among the Chinese laborers, who reported the location of the Russian trenches and gun positions. The Russians attempted to insert spies of their own among the many coolie gangs and other Chinese working around the Japanese, and the Chinese laborers happily took their money. But the Japanese paid better than the Russians, and many of the spies who were paid by the Russians were paid at a higher rate by Colonel Doi's staff. The Russians got little useful information and a lot of disinformation; stories planted by the Japanese to mislead them.

Kenji Dainichi labored among the Chinese coolies working on Nanshan for the Russians. His colonel was happy that the lieutenant could speak Russian and chose him for this assignment as a spy. The strenuous labor Kenji's Russian masters assigned him quickly hardened his body and he learned enough Chinese language to understand and carry out the shouted orders of the Chinese supervisors. The supervisors knew who he was and what he was there for and were instructed to let him do what he wanted, but to appear to treat him like any other coolie. Day after endless day he worked with pick and shovel in the frozen earth to help with the Russian earthworks. The coolie boss allowed him to work nearest the Russian overseers, where he could eavesdrop on their conversations. He could not halt his labors too long nor get too close, but he did manage to pick up snatches of conversation from time to time. His most valuable contribution was to map the Russian earthworks, which he did with a pencil and thin paper at night by firelight after sunset. Every day or so another Japanese, disguised as a coolie, would make his way into the workers' camp and collect Kenji's drawings and notes. The coolie boss, under instructions from Colonel Doi, would also shift him around to various places in the position so he could broaden his knowledge. The Russians did not notice him. All the Asians looked the same to them.

Tretyakov instructed his officers and men to not only supervise the Chinese but to work alongside them. The more hands at work, the better. Ivan Medved pitched in vigorously and worked side by side with his soldiers. He and Constantine numbered among the few officers who did.

Arkady Gross took the opposite approach and spent most of his time standing off to one side and smoking and regaling his clique with more tales of his adventures. He and his followers took care to keep a pick or shovel nearby so if the colonel approached they could pretend to be working. They rarely supervised the Russians under their command and they certainly wanted no part of a bunch of dirty and ragged little yellow coolies. Leave that to the non-commissioned officers.

In the evening, Ivan would go the rude officers' quarters in the rear, clean up and write letters to his family. He did not join the other officers in their drunken bouts over cards. For one thing he realized the seriousness of the position at Nanshan. For another he was simply tired from his labors and needed rest. Finally, he wanted to avoid all possible contact with Arkady Gross. Once or twice a week Constantine would come up with a small bottle of vodka, and the two friends would smoke and talk.

Constantine asked, "What happened between you and this girl you mentioned--Tatiana was her name, was it not?"

"I knew her as a child in Moscow," Ivan said, "when she was just another young girl. I lost her when she moved to St. Petersburg and then found her again and fell in love with her. Unfortunately, I found that she had taken up with an unsavory group in St. Petersburg and was doing things that made me uncomfortable."

"Oh?"

Ivan said, "She began hanging around with a crowd of people who want to bring Western democracy to Russia. I could not make her understand that Russia is Russia and has always had a tsar and will always have one. Then she became more radical and began talking revolution. Revolution! What nonsense. And to talk that way to me! My family has been close to the royal family for generations, and she brings that sort of thing up to me. And then finally, in her last letter she told me that she loved me but that she had taken up with another man...one of her revolutionaries. I love her too, although I am heartbroken over her behavior. I may have lost her but I cannot stand the thought of losing the photograph of her in the locket, although it is painful for me to look at. I have not heard from her since we left St. Petersburg. But my sister, Natalya, has written and said that they visit with each other from time to time. I am torn between trying to get her out of my system and hoping somehow that I will see her again. Sometimes I wish Natalya would never mention her again. Also, I am worried about what their seeing each other will do to the reputation of my family."

"Do you love her still?" Constantine asked.

"Yes, I suppose I do."

"You know, Ivan, Russia has been ruled by a tsar since Rurik, over 1,000 years ago. Many things have happened then. Many people in other European countries have gotten their freedom and are able to vote for those who rule them."

Ivan said, "Yes, but Alexander II freed the serfs in 1861 and now all Russians are free."

"They may be free," Constantine replied, "but they do not have the right to vote for a government. They have no representation when it comes to taxes and laws. They must just do as the tsar tells them to do and pay their taxes whenever they are due, no matter how poor their harvest or whether they are starving or not. The government prevents them from moving to the cities, and those who manage to make it to a city anyway are exploited by the factory owners."

"You are starting to talk like a revolutionary, Conya. Are you one?

"No. I am just anxious to see a better life for the average Russian. The majority of Russians are peasants, liberated from serfdom by the Tsar Liberator forty years ago. Now we have sixty million people from eighty-seven ethnic groups who live in a half million villages sprinkled across our country Most toil as sharecroppers on land held by the aristocracy and the rich, like your family. Their numbers increase inexorably, and they outgrow the ability of their farms to feed them. More and more of them try to come to the cities but there are not enough jobs for them. Other than army officers like us, the only people who are free are members of the aristocracy, and then the merchant princes. They are the worst of all. They squeeze the peasants and workers for more wealth, while all the time they live in great mansions and spend vast amounts of money on their personal pleasures.

"I am not saying that we should get rid of the tsar, but we should think about adopting something like in England, or America or France, where the poor have a chance to get ahead. In England, they still have a monarchy but the people are much better off because they have a voice in the laws and in the amount of taxes through their election of representatives in parliament."

"Someday a future tsar may grant these favors," replied Ivan. "I think that our tsar is a good man and he loves his people. But Russians, Conya, are not English. We are Russians, dwelling on the eastern fringes of Europe. Although few in this day and age want to recognize it, we are Asian as much as we are European. We are not yet ready for the kind of government that the English have. The Russian people have always had strong leaders because they need them."

Constantine shook his head, "We have to change, Ivan. My cousin's family joined a peasant commune when I was a small boy. The idea was that each person would work according to his ability and each would receive according to his needs. They would share everything-- labor, tools, crops, and animals. It was an ideal but one that did not work because the villagers could not get along on an equal basis. It might have succeeded if it were under the control of a strong central authority. Maybe you are right about that. But life remained desperate, and the villagers would fight over a few kopecks or a bottle of vodka. There has got to be something better for Russia's people. Most are illiterate. Perhaps education would make them able to resolve their differences and get along without the need for a strong authority."

Several times Kenji Dainichi noticed the young blond Russian officer working alongside his men and after seeing him a few times realized, to his great surprise, that it was Ivan Medved. He was amazed how tough this son of a prince looked. He noticed that Ivan not only labored with his men, but also allowed them to take a few minutes' rest every hour to regain their strength and smoke a bit and talk. Once he identified Ivan, Kenji made it a point to try and draw near to the Russians in this group. Ivan treated his men better than most of the Russian officers treated theirs and the Russian soldiers in turn were kinder to the coolies. Ivan, Kenji noticed, always checked to see if his troops and the Chinese coolies who worked with them had plenty of water and got a meager meal at midday. He yelled in Russian at the coolie boss one time when the boss struck a man who had fallen and spilled a load of dirt he carried. The coolie boss could not tell what the Russian was saying but he knew by Ivan's actions that the Russian did not like it. Kenji understood and although his face remained impassive, was impressed by the young man's care for his men. The coolie boss was impressed, too, and never struck another coolie again while Lieutenant Medved was around.

Colonel Tretyakov's position on the isthmus bothered him for more reasons than the inadequate number of troops he had been allotted to hold the line at his front. Not only was he to defend the Nanshan hills, Petrov also ordered him to garrison and hold the small walled Chinese town of Chin-chou to his north. Deep bays indented the coastline on both sides of the peninsula at Chin-chou, and Japanese naval gunfire could support their infantry if they decided to attack this position.

Colonel Tretyakov went to see his superior, General Foch. "General, I must have reinforcement. There is no way I can hold that line against any sort of determined Japanese attack with an under-strength regiment. You have several battalions sitting around and not doing anything. I need at least one; two would be better. And not only must I have men, I must have more artillery ammunition."

Foch blinked at the aggressive tone of his subordinate. "You are out of place, Colonel. You have more than enough troops to defend that position. If you are really worried about it then why do you not leave two companies on the line and die with them when the Japanese come? You can send the rest of the men back to me and I will use them as they should be used. As far as artillery ammunition is concerned, the answer is no. Make do with what you have. The rest will stay in strategic reserve and will be sent to you if needed."

"General, I need more men now!"

Foch said, "I just told you why you cannot have any other troops. Do your job with what you have, or I will relieve you."

"Then, General, would you please give me permission to move to a position further to the south? One that is more easily defended."

"That, too, is out of the question, Tretyakov! Do you understand what a catastrophe it would be among the Russian troops if we showed fear of the Japanese? This is the tsar's army and any Russian soldier is worth ten of them any time. You are a Russian officer and must not move your lines back. You have enough men and artillery to repulse any Japanese attack and make them pay a high price for their actions. Once they have met the Russian bayonet, they will give up the whole idea of trying to take Port Arthur."

Colonel Tretyakov left the general's quarters and stormed back to his position in a black mood. *Incompetent bastard.* he thought, *He is the most worthless son-of-a-bitch that ever shit between a pair of boots. If he had any real experience in combat, he would realize that he is foolishly endangering Port Arthur with his stubbornness and desire to have the last word.*

Reaching his lines, he toured them once more looking for places where he might be able to better use his limited resources. On the eastern side of his line he had laid minefields and strung barbed wire but he had not enough of either to cover his entire front. On the western portion, he relied on muddy ground to slow a Japanese attack. He prayed for rain and warmer weather. If the marshes remained frozen it would be easy for the Japanese to cross them.

Colonel Tretyakov decided to make an offensive probe to try to learn something about the Japanese disposition of forces. Leaving about a third of his units in place, he made a reconnaissance in force. He sallied forth with two of his battalions of infantry, with a battery of horse-drawn artillery in his wake. But he had no reliable map, and his force pretty much marched around in circles. The Russians had brought no survey party with them to Port Arthur, and they only had one copy of an outdated and inaccurate map of the area. Even it had somehow been misplaced. The Russians bumbled about the hillsides, making no real contact with the Japanese, and returned to camp after encountering only a little fire from Japanese-led Chinese guerrillas. Tretyakov returned to his position without having learned anything about the enemy. Ivan's company marched as rear guard for his battalion, and he and his company commander were just as confused as anyone about where they had been. The fire from the Chinese guerrillas was the only excitement of the day, and because the enemy had caused no Russian casualties, it only confirmed the Russians' opinion of Japan's soldiers.

One of the better Russian generals, Roman Kontradenko, was shocked at Foch's refusal to grant Tretyakov reinforcements and appealed to Petrov. Petrov, no strategist himself, told Kontradenko that he would not countermand an order from one of his field officers, in this case General Foch. Kontradenko had no choice but to tell Tretyakov that he would have to be prepared to defend Nanshan to the last man.

Others had different views. General Alexei Kuropotkin, another able commander who had suffered in the past at the hands of fools like Petrov and Foch, realized the danger of the Nanshan position and stated that if attacked, Tretyakov's force should be withdrawn early rather than be destroyed and let their artillery fall into the hands of the enemy. Petrov regarded him as an unbridled pessimist and refused to consider his advice.

Not only could Tretyakov not get any additional troops, but he also continued to worry about supplies of artillery ammunition. His batteries had an average of fewer than twenty-five shells per weapon. Behind Foch's back he quietly appealed to all the commanders he knew, but they were unwilling to give up ammunition from their own stocks. He received no additional shells.

The colonel drove his men like slaves, scrounging additional barbed wire for entanglements and timber and sandbags for roofing over trenches and fighting holes, leaving slits for their own weapons to fire and reducing the size of the targets for the enemy. For over three months they labored over their defenses, but their positions were still far from complete.

CHAPTER 22
GROUND ATTACK

As spring began, Colonel Tretyakov got his wish and the marshland in front of him lost its icy cover and once again became muddy. The seasonal rains began. Sometimes, when the sheets of rain were as opaque as a theater curtain, he worried that the Japanese would attack right through it, using the rain for cover. His lookouts huddled in the downpour, each clad in his own misery and sodden clothing and dreaming of comfortably sitting before a fireside or sleeping snugly under warm, dry blankets. The colonel himself and his officers strode the line night and day under all conditions making sure that the sentries remained at their posts and awake. The rains had an unexpected result. When they slackened enough for the colonel to see the field before him he was shocked to discover that most of his mines had been uncovered. The dirt on top of them had simply washed away. They had not been placed deep enough during the hard digging of the winter and an attacking force could easily avoid most of them.

The Japanese, too, had been waiting for better weather and they began their attack that morning with two of General Nogi's three divisions. It started with an artillery barrage. Even to the initiated, exposure to artillery is terrifying. And it was. The massed artillery pieces sounded like thunder in the distance as the rounds left the tubes. A second later, filling the air with the howl of banshees, they flew toward the Russian fortifications and they impacted on the Russian lines, throwing great fountains of mud into the air. Showers of deadly, red-hot, razor-sharp shell fragments flew off in every direction shredding any human flesh in their path. The Russian soldiers knew that in an instant that just one of these fragments would erase anything they had ever been or would ever be. The shells that hit bunkers directly collapsed them, usually killing all their occupants. Others exploded in the trenches, killing those inside by blowing them to bits. Some Russians escaped harm from the flying steel but were buried alive and smothered to death when bunkers and trenches collapsed on them.

An hour into this airborne hell, the Japanese infantry advanced behind its screen. They came across in a frontal assault without regard for the Russian artillery and machine guns that tore through their ranks. A few met death when they tripped mines. Many more saw those that had been exposed by the rain and avoided them. Those who had to attack through the mudflats had the worst of it. They found themselves in sucking mud up past their ankles that slowed them down and made them an easy target for Russian marksmen. If a man slipped and fell, and many did, he often required the help of a comrade to regain his feet. The Japanese line staggered and swayed and the assault was ragged. A cloud of gun smoke hung over the Russian lines and another followed the Japanese as they struggled up the slope toward their objective. When the Japanese got within two hundred meters of Russian lines the Russian soldiers rose up over the lip of their trenches. Sergeants adjusted the fire of their machine guns and other men began picking off individual Japanese with their rifles. The machine guns, their snouts protruding out the slits of the bunkers, cut through the uneven Japanese lines like scythes and left windrows of dead and dying, the dead in grotesque postures impossible in life, the wounded silent, screaming or sobbing, each finding his universe compressed to the world within his own skin. Russian artillery, which had previously been dueling with the Japanese guns, shifted its fire to the advancing troops. It would continue to fire right up until the enemy was within fifty yards of the Russian trenches.

The Russian weapons mowed down row after row of Japanese in a fury of hot steel and still they came on. After three hours of slaughter, it became obvious to the Japanese that they were getting nowhere. Their bugles blew retreat and they retired back to their positions. Russian marksmen continued to shoot them down as long as they were in range. The field looked like a slaughterhouse, with bodies, body parts, weapons, and equipment everywhere. The Russians held fire as Japanese stretcher-bearers searched for wounded on the field. They carried off the wounded. The dead they left to rot on the battleground. The stench of their rapidly decomposing bodies would turn the air into a foul perfumery within a day.

After the Japanese battle plan was set, Kenji's role as a spy was unnecessary and a few days before the attack he was sent back to his company, the unit in which he commanded a platoon alongside Katsuke Nogi, General Nogi's eldest son. Kenji was pleased and surprised to find that Taro had been transferred into the same company. His old comrades Hiroshi and Yukio were in the next company over. All the young lieutenants got along well enough in their companies although Kenji was quietly in a near-panic, worrying about how he might behave under fire.

When his unit moved forward in the attack his mouth was so dry he could not spit. He thought that no amount of water would ever be enough and he would never think of life in the same way again. Russian bullets seemed to be everywhere, snapping past, sounding like drops of water hitting hot grease, and their artillery rounds rained death from the skies. The sheer numbers of Japanese casualties nearly paralyzed Kenji. The hardest thing for him to bear was the sight of his men, men he knew well, who went down but he could not stop to help because of his orders to press on with the attack no matter what. Those who had been mutilated by Russian artillery made him sick; body pieces and intestines lay everywhere. Some of these remains looked like they had never been part of a human being but could have been the offal of any animal from an abattoir. Kenji's hesitation slowed his unit down although they continued to advance tentatively. Sergeant Iwao respectfully suggested that Kenji pick up the pace, to act more aggressively. Twice a runner came from his company commander telling Kenji to get his platoon moving and stay in line with the others.

After the Japanese retired from the field and regrouped, Kenji was called to Captain Nakayama's presence, where the latter screamed at him for not keeping up. "You are a soldier! You are an officer in his Imperial Majesty's army! You were highly regarded at the military academy but this is not the academy, it is combat and combat is about killing and dying. You are the son of a soldier and the grandson of a soldier and you must have the bushido spirit. You must go into combat determined to win or die. There is no alternative. Do you understand?"

All Kenji could do was nod. His face reddened and his ears burned with embarrassment.

Captain Nakayama dismissed him with an angry "Get out of here. I do not want to set eyes on you again until I see you on the objective or until I see your corpse."

When Kenji rejoined his company, he noticed that Sergeant Iwao would not look him in the eyes. That evening he reluctantly confided his fears to the younger Nogi. "Dainichi-san," the other replied, "everyone is afraid in combat, even though dying for the emperor is the most glorious death a man can have. You must learn to control your fear and must never hesitate on the battlefield. Your men must never, ever see you in doubt. If you falter, they will falter too. It is giri, responsibility. Without giri we are nothing, we are no better than the animals. When fear tries to find lodging in your heart, remember the emperor, think of your father and your grandfather. Do whatever you have to do to keep a clear head and accomplish your mission. Remember what the poets say, 'Life is just a summer night's dream.' No matter what you do, life will be brief. It is in your death that you will become immortal as a soldier of Japan. Here, take this."

He handed Kenji a hakimachi, a warrior's white headband with the characters for giri inked on it. Kenji reminded himself that there was no stronger responsibility in Japanese society, whether military or civilian, than the concept of giri. It influenced family obligations, business deals, and military responsibility. It was the reason that Momoko could never marry him.

"Thank you, Nogi-san. I will remember what you say." Kenji tied the hakimachi around his head and rejoined his men.

In the middle of the night, barking dogs alerted the Russians that their enemy was once more on the move, this time against the Russian position at Chin-chou, just north of Tretyakov's main position. General Nogi had changed his mind and decided to capture this town first. He had to cut off the possibility of the Russians sending reinforcements down the railroad toward his rear.

Kenji, much heartened by his talk with young Nogi, led his platoon from the front. It was a dark night and once more raining heavily and the only way the soldiers could avoid getting lost in the pitch-blackness was to close ranks and advance nearly shoulder to shoulder. The men, burdened with heavy weapons and ammunition, fell often in the cold and slippery mud. As they neared Chin-chou, Russian searchlights suddenly picked out their ghostly formations advancing through the night and storm.

Four Japanese sappers volunteered to swim across the river that ran past the east side of Chin-chou, work their way around to the front, and blast open the front gate of the wall that surrounded the Russian-held town. Each man stripped down to a loincloth, and with a mine strapped to a kapok float, slipped into the river upstream of the town. As they floated downstream a Russian sentry spotted them and sounded the alarm. Russians poured small arms fire down on the swimmers. First one, then another, was killed. The other two, one of them slightly wounded, reached the gate and attached their mines to it. They lay next to the gate, pulled fuses and matches out of heavily oiled cloth packets, attached the fuses, and lit them. The fuse of one of the mines was too damp; it smoked for a bit but failed to go off. The other exploded and reduced the gate to smoking piles of rubble. Both of the sappers died in the blast. As the debris settled, Kenji and the other officers blew whistles that sent their infantry pouring through the gate and into the town. The fight went on for nearly an hour, the Japanese and Russians tangling with each other with small arms, bayonets, and hand to hand. By midnight Chin-Chou was in Japanese hands. Then General Nogi turned his attention back to Nanshan.

Daylight saw the appearance of Japanese ships on Hand Bay to the Russian's east. The Japanese had now added their naval guns, guns that outranged anything the Russian had, to the fray. Once more the Japanese artillery punished the Russian position, concentrating on Russian artillery. Once more the Japanese formed up behind their artillery screen and advanced.

As their infantry drew closer, the Japanese artillery stopped pummeling the Russian artillery and shifted their fire to the enemy trenches. The Russians were lined up in their trenches shoulder to shoulder, ignoring the Japanese fire as much as they could, pointing their long rifles down field, and once more killing Japanese by the hundreds as they struggled through the muddy flatlands and over the bodies of their fallen comrades. The defenders managed to slow the attackers and then halt them. But they could not drive them back.

Colonel Tretyakov's fifty artillery pieces could not effectively counter the fire of nearly two hundred on the Japanese side. One by one the Russian artillery batteries fell silent as they took hits from the enemy or ran out of ammunition. By noon they were all out of action.

The last battery to fall was manned by a single artilleryman, Alexei Ivanov, a talented, courageous, and experienced sergeant of artillery. For nearly two hours he labored alone. He would move to one gun, painstakingly load, sight, and fire it, and then move to the next gun and repeat the process. He used a different gun for each round, hoping to keep the Japanese from discovering that he was all alone. Though blackened, sweating, thirsty, and tired, and suffering from minor wounds, he moved tirelessly among the big guns doing his best. With only one Russian gun firing at a time, the Japanese regarded it as more of an annoyance than as a threat to their advance. Eventually the Japanese artillery commander had had enough and ordered it to be taken out. The Japanese concentrated their fire on the crippled artillery position, and finally a direct hit on Ivanov's position killed him.

Despite the complete loss of their artillery support Tretyakov's men continued to fire mercilessly with machine guns and rifles. The Japanese attack faltered and once more they withdrew to reorganize.

Colonel Tretyakov was afraid he would not hold against another Japanese assault. He sent an aide galloping back to General Foch's headquarters, to beg for reinforcement and additional artillery support. The general grumpily roused himself from his luncheon and walked outside where the noise of the artillery had been faintly heard all morning. All he now heard was a few desultory shots. "It sounds to me like the Japanese attack has been contained. That means that you need no reinforcements. As to artillery, tell Colonel Tretyakov to submit a written request for his needs and I will see to it later today or in the morning."

"But, General," the aide replied, "it is just a lull in the fighting. The Japanese artillery has ceased because they are nearly on our position, and ours has ceased because we no longer have any ammunition. Nor do we have any artillery men left."

"Nonsense. I know the sound of a completed battle when I hear one. Now get back to Tretyakov and tell him I want a full report." With that Foch took his time finishing his lunch before going back to his headquarters, where he told an officer to send a messenger to General Petrov informing him that the attack had been contained and all was well.

At his headquarters Petrov called his staff together and broke the good news. "We have contained the monkeys," he declared. "They have probably learned their lesson and will not attack again. I would not be surprised if they sue for peace soon. Now let us break out the champagne and celebrate. I shall send a telegram to the tsar informing him of our victory."

The Japanese were neither defeated nor contained. They had withdrawn only temporarily and busily reorganized to press the attack.

With no Russian artillery to worry about, General Nogi ordered all three divisions forward in a general frontal assault. When Kenji got the word to attack once more, he donned his hakimachi and gathered his men. His speech was as much for himself as for his men. "We are short of ammunition. That matters not. We will become human bullets. No matter how bad the Russian fire, we will continue to advance. We will not stop for any reason, not to help wounded comrades nor to dress our own wounds. If you are able to move forward, then you will move forward no matter what. We will not stop for the minefield nor for the mud. We will reserve our ammunition and only use it when we have clear targets. We will advance on the Russian position with fixed bayonets at the ready, and when we reach their position we will attack with bayonets and with our remaining ammunition."

Kenji hoped that he had planted courage into the hearts of his men and in his own heart. His platoon moved into attack formation and with thousands of other soldiers once more started up the slopes to Nanshan. Remembering what young Nogi had said and his duty, he was determined that fright would not slow him down. He gritted his teeth and led his men forward.

When they got to within five hundred yards of the Russian position, they started to die. Just a few at first but as they got closer the Russians killed more of them. Hundreds fell in the mud, their bodies destroyed by the constant storm of Russian rifle and machine gun fire. Still they came on.

Not far from the rear of the Nanshan position General Foch had six battalions of fresh troops. Once more Colonel Tretyakov sent an aide back to plead for reinforcement. He needed two battalions, immediately. Once more he was refused.

Finally, about 6:00 p.m., two companies, a third of what he asked for, showed up. They came with instructions from General Foch that they would be used in the rear and deployed only when needed. Ignoring his superior, Tretyakov immediately threw them into the fight on the western side, the most endangered part of his line.

The Japanese waded through pools of water up past their ankles or through the damnable sucking mud, but they kept coming. Tretyakov ordered his troops on the western side to counterattack where the Japanese appeared to be strongest. Ivan's company was in the battalion ordered into the attack. They formed up and moved down the slope toward the advancing Japanese. Combat was like nothing he imagined. Rather than leading a glorious attack from astride a magnificent horse, he was tired, filthy, and frightened, and slogging through mud toward an enemy that appeared to be unconquerable. And he was on foot.

General Foch finally woke up to the potential danger of the Japanese attack and sent a staff officer up to take a look. When the officer reported back what was happening, the general dithered for over an hour before reluctantly permitting Tretyakov to retreat.

General Foch's order to retreat failed to reach the dauntless Tretyakov but it did get to some of his troops on his western flank, including those involved in the counterattack. Enough of these men turned their backs on the enemy and headed south to doom the Russian effort. Ivan's battalion commander, uncertain of what was going on, ordered a retreat to the Russian trenches.

The Japanese sensed that confusion was rampant within the Russian ranks and taking advantage of it they pressed the attack. As they neared the positions, the Russians who remained on the line had a turkey shoot. Each rifleman downed many Japanese before he was overwhelmed.

In the vanguard of the 4th Japanese Division on the western flank was the company of Katsuke Nogi and Kenji Dainichi. Kenji was emboldened by young Nogi's courage and his example. Nogi was right. He could be afraid but must not let fear control him. He thought of the emperor, his father, his mother, Momoko, and the code of bushido every time he began to falter. Men fell around him but he stayed in the attack. Just as his company covered the last few yards to the Russian trenches the gunfire intensified. Young Nogi went down with a wound to the chest. Blood and air bubbled from under his tunic.

Kenji immediately took charge of Nogi's troops as well as his own and could not help pausing to look at the fallen officer.

Nogi knew he was dying. "Dainichi-san, I will never see Port Arthur. Please take my sword from me, a gift from my father, and wear it for me into Port Arthur. My spirit is in this sword."

The young Nogi gasped a last frothy breath and was still. He lay there, his sightless eyes staring at the sky. Dainichi unbuckled his friend's sword and tucked it into his belt next to his own. Then he hurried to catch up with his men who had continued the advance.

His company reached the Russian trenches and jumped into them to take on the Russians in hand-to-hand combat. Those on both sides who still had ammunition expended the last of it at close range. Many more had only the bayonet and they used it until they fell.

Kenji, enlivened by the heat of battle, used all the bullets in his pistol, then drew his sword and rushed into the melee. The first Russian he ran towards fired at him with his rifle and missed. Kenji was on him in a blur of motion, in a macabre dance of death, as if directed by a grim cosmic choreographer. With a swing of his sword, the man was nearly decapitated. Then he ran another through, swiped at a wounded Russian trying to rise from the ground, and went after his next opponent. He heard a gasp and scream to his side and turned to see one of his sergeants impaled on a Russian bayonet. Before the man could withdraw his blade and attack Kenji, Kenji swung at the man's arm and lopped it off at the wrist. His next swing was at another Russian, this one an officer with a pistol who was firing at one of the other Japanese. This time the sword struck the man's head and partially opened his skull. Brain matter and blood flew everywhere.

Had he been able to stop and think about it he would have realized that he was doing what his kendo masters wanted him to do. He was one with the sword. The combination of adrenalin and blood lust kept him moving. He was breathing hard and fast, but it seemed that no oxygen was reaching his lungs. His mouth was dry as if he had never had a drink of water in his life, just as it had been on the attack on Chin-chou. But this time he was inspired by the thirst and driven forward.

Roused by his aggressiveness, his men carried their portion of the hill. In the gathering darkness, they began to search out and capture or kill the Russian survivors and consolidate their position.

On the objective, Sergeant Iwao regarded his lieutenant and then nodded and grimly smiled to himself.

Many small groups of Russians who had not gotten the word to retreat held and most died to the last man. Ivan, Constantine, and four of their men were among those holding on. Ivan had been hit twice and his wounds were painful, but comparatively minor. One of the four men was dying and the others, except Constantine, were wounded. Their dead comrades surrounded them.

As they saw shadows moving towards them in the deepening twilight, the wounded Ivan whispered, "Constantine, help turn me over so I can face them better."

Constantine did as asked, and immediately Ivan opened fire with his revolver at the enemy, expending all his rounds. Then he fainted from the pain.

The Japanese charged the position, overran it, and began shooting the survivors. Constantine was lightly wounded in the final attack but pulled the body of one of his men over him and played dead as the Japanese moved on. Several times he was kicked during the night as the Japanese roamed the battlefield making sure there were no survivors. Beside him, he could hear Ivan's ragged breathing. At dawn things were quiet although Constantine could hear voices speaking Japanese in the distance. He crawled out from under the stiff corpse of his sergeant and looked around. Seeing no one, he checked Ivan's body and found he was still breathing. He splashed some water over Ivan's face and began to dress his wounds.

Ivan finally awoke, saw he was with Constantine. "Where are we?"

"We are behind Japanese lines," Constantine said, "They have captured Nanshan. Our forces cannot have retreated too far and we must try and reach them."

CHAPTER 23
CAPTIVITY

Ivan passed out again and was awakened several hours later by pain. He could tell that he was lying in some sort of building on a damp, dirt floor. Other than that, he had no idea where he was or why he was there. He was wet and cold. He felt his wounds and decided that though they were painful, they were probably not life-threatening. He lay there in total darkness for a few minutes and then struggled to pull himself up into a sitting position. The smell of other human bodies, feces, urine and mold lay heavy in the air. Ivan lay back down and stared up at the blackness for an interminable time until he drifted off again. He awoke again to see pale daylight seeping through cracks in the walls. He could faintly hear voices outside the hut but could not tell what they were saying. As he sat up again he realized that he was in one of the crude shelters on Nanshan that had been built by the Russians. For a moment he thought that they had repulsed the latest Japanese attack. But if that were so, why was he here, on the floor, cold and without medical attention? The floor was muddy, and wind whistled through the cracks in the wall. In the dim light, he saw a rat that was regarding him curiously about a foot from his face. He swiped at the animal with his hand and was rewarded by a sharp pain up his arm from his wounds. The rat squealed and scampered off into the darkness. The shadow of another rat passed across a crack in the bottom of the wall.

Then he heard a man softly moaning a prayer in Russian and another whimpering. He fell back again and for a moment Ivan thought that this was just a bad dream, that the Japanese attack had never happened. His wounds told him otherwise. He tried to sit up again but the pain was too much and he fell back. He finally struggled up to rest on his elbows. By this time the hut was faintly illuminated by weak sunlight coming through its single window and he saw that it was packed with other wounded Russians. Constantine lay on the ground near him and was either asleep or wounded so badly he could not reply when Ivan tried to speak to him in a whisper. He never knew if he got an answer because he drifted off into a fevered sleep that was interrupted an eternity later by voices speaking Japanese. The door to the hut had been flung open and a shaft of bright sunlight divided the room in half. Two Japanese soldiers passed from man to man and handed each prisoner two small balls of rice and a small wooden bowl of thin, cold soup. It was the first thing Ivan had eaten in two days and it easily went down and gave him a bit of strength. He soon fell back to sleep but awoke several times during the night. His fever broke sometime before morning, and he slept better. When he awoke, he looked for Constantine but did not see him. He wondered if his friend had been there at all or whether he was the product of a dream. The next morning, after once more having been served rice and soup, a small group of Japanese officers entered the room. He did not recognize his captor until one of the officers spoke to him in Russian. "Good morning, Lieutenant Medved, I hope you are feeling better."

"Where am I?" asked Ivan. And then, "Kenji, is that you?"

"You are in one of your old buildings on Nanshan hill which is now in the hands of our Imperial forces. And yes, Lieutenant, I am Kenji Dainichi. Your friend who was captured with you told us who you were last night. It may have been the only reason my men did not shoot you. Not that we are in the habit of killing prisoners, but we captured you in the heat of battle, the blood of our soldiers was running hot and anything could have happened.

"We are a long way from Moscow. We finally took Nanshan from you, but it cost us over 700 killed and 5,000 wounded. We have no idea how many of your men were lost and will probably never know. Your dead and ours will be thrown into a common grave and if we can find enough wood, will be cremated. Otherwise, we will just cover them over.

"While you were passed out our doctor looked at you. Your wounds may be painful but unless disease sets in they are not fatal. With a little luck we will be able to arrange a prisoner exchange with your generals and you will be paroled back to your people. Under the conditions of parole, you must agree to not fight any longer. If we cannot reach an agreement, you will remain our prisoner until we have won this war. Do you understand what I am telling you?"

The news of the fall of Nanshan had reached Port Arthur at about 11:00 p.m. on the night of the attack and panicked the population.

The remnants of Colonel Tretyakov's 5th East Siberian Regiment staggered back toward Port Arthur struggling with a slow passage through the mud that sucked at their boots. They were a ragtag bunch. Many had lost their weapons or left them behind in their eagerness to get away from Nanshan. Their clothes were ragged and muddy and they were starving. Their defeat humbled them although they had fought with courage and determination.

As the Russians retreated, they performed a crude triage on their casualties. The lightly wounded, those well enough to walk, had to stumble along on foot, often supported by one or more of their comrades. Others, who had wounds they would probably survive but who were incapable of walking, were carried. The sucking mud made their evacuation difficult. Because there were no stretchers they were carried on their blood-and-mud-soaked blankets and it took four to six men to carry each of them. Even then, their progress was slow. The makeshift stretchers were often dropped and sometimes when traversing hills, the casualty simply slid off into the mud. These accidents were accompanied with screams of pain from the wounded and much cursing by the casualty bearers. Those marching behind the fallen makeshift stretchers simply flowed around them, eyes averted from the pain and suffering of their comrades.

Those who would probably not survive were simply left on the field to die. In some cases their comrades shot them in order to relieve them of their suffering. Colonel Tretyakov and his officers knew of these mercy executions and said nothing.

It took nearly two days for the column to crawl back the fifteen miles to Port Arthur and they had to constantly remain on the alert in case the Japanese decided to capitalize on their victory and press on toward the port by attacking their rear.

General Nogi had no such intention. The capture of Chinchou and Nanshan insured that no more supplies or reinforcements would reach Port Arthur by rail. With supplies cut off by land and with Japanese warships patrolling the mouth of the harbor, he knew that he had achieved strategic supremacy. He could afford to wait. Every day the town went without replenishing its supplies, the Russians grew weaker. And every day the Japanese grew stronger.

Colonel Tretyakov hoped that rescuers from the garrison town would meet them en route and bring them food and help them with their casualties. His hopes were in vain. General Petrov's staff recommended that a relief force be sent out but the general was in such a rage over the Japanese capture of Nanshan that he forbade it.

The ragged and demoralized force finally found and entered the Russian lines. They had fought bravely and cost the Japanese nearly 6,000 casualties but by this time they looked like a disorganized mob of derelicts. The only food they had for the two days it took them to reach Port Arthur was some bread.

General Petrov, dressed in his finest uniform, was waiting for them red-faced with fury and surrounded by his aides and staff, each turned out as for inspection. Spotting Colonel Tretyakov, the general sent an aide galloping up to him and ordered the colonel to form up the remains of his regiment. The colonel's subordinate units were intermixed, and it was a difficult process. Slowly and painfully, they sorted themselves out and fell into ranks. They were a sorry sight-- starved, many were wounded, and all were filthy and weary.

The general, nearly apoplectic with anger, slowly rode back and forth in front of their ranks on his horse looking down at them. "You are nothing but cowards! You are dogs and traitors! You are blackguards! You should be ashamed of yourselves. I will have the whole lot of you court-martialed and shot," he repeated over and over. Then he turned away from the exhausted men, rode back to his headquarters and ordered Major Sakharov to prepare court-martial proceedings for all the officers. He dithered and wrung his hands for hours before finally sending a telegram off to the tsar, informing His Majesty of the loss of Nanshan. In order to save his own skin, he told the tsar that his men had fought bravely but vastly superior forces overcame them. He promised to retake Nanshan within three days.

The tsar was saddened by the loss of the position, but he believed Petrov's claim that Nanshan would soon be retaken and took comfort in the report that his men had fought with courage. After all, the enemy were Japanese. Soon they would feel the wrath of the Russians and give up their attempt at capturing Port Arthur.

By return telegram, the tsar praised the Russian soldiers and ordered that all wounded from the regiment who stayed in the ranks be decorated with the Cross of St. George.

When General Petrov read the telegram from the tsar he exploded. "The Cross of St. George! For these cowards? I shall be court-martialed first!"

His adjutant, Major Sakharov, tried to calm him. "General, it is the tsar's wish that these men be decorated. You cannot directly disobey him. It is important that these cowards not be rewarded and we must carry out the tsar's wishes and, at the same time, not encourage this sort of cowardice."

"Mm, you are right of course. Check with the quartermaster and see if we even have any of the damnable decorations with us."

The quartermaster reported that they had about thirty Crosses of St. George in supply. The number of wounded at Nanshan who stayed in the line was about three hundred.

General Petrov quietly awarded about half of the decorations on hand to officers on his staff, those he liked who had seen no action at all. The remainder he reluctantly and randomly pinned on a pitiful few of Colonel Tretyakov's men. The colonel, who had done everything he could to save the position, received nothing. The men were mystified and dejected at the reception they received after such a bruising battle and the thoughtless and random award of an important medal. Some who had fled the line were rewarded and most who had fought bravely were passed over.

Kenji was ordered to question the Russian prisoners and gain as much information as he could. The Russian prisoners in one hut were separated from the prisoners in the others so none of them had any idea how many of them had been taken prisoner or who their fellow prisoners were. They were allowed out of the huts and into the prisoner compound yard for a half hour every day, but at a different time from the prisoners in the other huts. The only contact came at night when the prisoners used the latrines. Only one prisoner from each hut was allowed to use the latrine at one time, but this was only sporadically reinforced because of the laziness of the guards. During these brief and furtive contacts, some information managed to get from one group to another. The result was often rumor that swelled and became more inaccurate as it was passed from prisoner to prisoner. Constantine had originally been in a different hut but the first night he found out in which hut Ivan was kept and just moved in after dark one night after visiting the latrine. The Japanese enlisted man who counted the prisoners each morning simply figured that he had made a mistake when he counted the prisoners before. Anyway, what difference did it make?

Every morning Kenji would begin his rounds just after sunrise and question one prisoner after another until after sundown. He moved from hut to hut and selected those he wanted to talk to and each was taken to another, cleaner, hut where Kenji could interrogate them outside of the earshot of their comrades. With some he spent just a few minutes and with others an hour or more. He dictated, in Japanese, his findings to an enlisted man, a scribe who made notes. At the end of each day, Kenji examined the notes, looking for important information he could pass up his chain of command. He also looked for inconsistencies that might tell him that one prisoner or another was lying.

During his first interrogation of Ivan he said, "We do not mean to harm you. You are, after all, a fellow officer and we will not mistreat you as long as you cooperate. You and I have much to talk about. I am one of only a few Japanese who has any knowledge of Russia or your language, so you may expect to see much of me."

Ivan immediately went on the alert, afraid that he would tell his enemy something of value. During the first session, he said little. After a few moments, Kenji realized that Ivan was not going to say anything important. He rose, bowed to Ivan and left. After a few sessions Ivan became used to Kenji's visits and began talking to him but was careful to keep the conversation to non-military matters. One day Kenji said, "Do you play chess?"

"Yes, I do," said Ivan.

"Then tomorrow I will bring the equipment and we will have a game."

When he showed up the next afternoon, Kenji had a small chess set with him, which he set up. He offered Ivan a choice of white or black and Ivan demurred. "Well, since chess is the Russian game," said Kenji, "perhaps you would be kind enough to give me the advantage of playing white?"

"Gladly," said Ivan.

The game proceeded quietly, and Ivan won the first one. He played white the second game and lost, and then he won the third.

He wondered how a Japanese could become a good chess player. Both the young officers approached the games as a surrogate for the Russo-Japanese War. They had no way of knowing it, but the back-and-forth contests were a prophesy of the battles the two powers would fight over the next forty years. For the time being they caused Kenji and Ivan to reflect on the current conflict between the two great empires and their own small roles in it. For different reasons, each felt like a pawn in the overall scheme of things.

It was a great relief to Ivan that games were played quietly, with concentration and little conversation. This allowed him to forget his captivity and forget the possibility that he might be giving away Russian secrets. Every two or three days, Kenji would show up with the chess set and they would play one or more games. He would casually ask questions about the Russian Army. Ivan found these easy to deflect or to answer vaguely. Kenji did not seem at all to mind. When not asking questions, Kenji mostly talked about Japan's destiny in East Asia and the futility of Russia's position.

He always spoke in a soft, polite but firm monologue, "You see, Ivan, Japan is an ascendant power. We mean to win this war against you and drive you from Port Arthur. It is our proper role to rule this region of the world, and we will. Russia has enough internal problems and should really concentrate on them rather than trying to expand even further..."

One day a match was going Kenji's way and Ivan feared he was trapped and was desperately looking for a way out of a possible checkmate. After a long pause, Kenji broke Ivan's concentration and startled Ivan by quietly listing the Russian order of battle, the strengths and weaknesses of the Russian commanders, their morale and their offensive and defensive doctrine, and the hopeless predicament that Ivan and the other prisoners found themselves in.

"So, you see, Ivan, the position of the Russian forces in Port Arthur is as bleak as your situation on this chessboard."

Ivan went pale and could not help blurting out, "Where did you get such information?" he asked.

"Friends of yours told us."

"What friends?" he asked, completely losing his concentration on the game.

While still talking, Kenji moved a piece on the board and said, "Check." Ivan scarcely noticed.

"Two of your lieutenants have been cooperative. One's name is Gross, Arkady Gross. He has been most helpful to us. Since he has told us most of what we want to know, why do you not tell us the rest? We reward Lieutenant Gross with better food, some of your captured vodka and an occasional woman from Chin-Chou. The other of our informants is a man that Gross tells me is your friend Constantine."

Ivan stiffened with the news and replied formally, "I am sorry, Lieutenant Dainichi, but what others tell you has nothing to do with me." He turned away from Kenji and seeing that his situation on the chessboard was hopeless he turned his king over on its side and said, "I resign; you have won the game. But just wait, we will win this war." At that Kenji silently collected the pieces, stood and bowed and left the room.

That night Ivan brought up the subject of talking to the enemy with Constantine.

"Yes, I talk to them, but I tell them nothing but lies, things to mislead them."

"Are you sure, Constantine? Dainichi seemed awfully certain he was getting something of value from you and he is not stupid."

"Nor am I, Ivan. I just mix a little bit of harmless fact with a whole lot of fiction. They will never know the difference."

"Why do you just not say anything at all? I do that and they never bother me."

"That is because Dainichi knows you from before. Probably he thinks that the way to handle you is to not pressure you but to try and draw out some facts through casual conversation. I act weaker than I am and he thinks that I *am* weaker and will cooperate for a little food or vodka. He gives me the food and vodka but I only tell him things that will deceive or confuse him."

"Do you swear you are giving him nothing of value?"

"I swear."

"Okay, then, but be careful. No telling what he will do if he finds out you are lying to him."

"I am always careful, Ivan, you know me."

Ivan knew that Conya was anything but careful and he worried about his friend.

As Ivan's wounds healed and he grew stronger he began thinking of trying to escape and get back to Russian lines. He quietly broached the subject with Constantine.

"You are mad, completely mad," said Constantine. "You, or we, could never get to Port Arthur. It is fifteen miles away, and there is nothing but Japanese between here and there."

"Yes, but we must try," said Ivan. "The Japanese have taken Nanshan and cut off the supplies from the Trans-Siberian Railway, and General Petrov is going to need all the help he can get to win it back. With no supplies coming overland by train and with the Japanese blocking the harbor we will sooner or later run out of food, ammunition, and all the other things we need." The more Ivan talked, the more adamant Constantine became.

Constantine had been questioned for an hour or so every two or three days just like all the other Russian officers. He was a good actor and when he pretended to give useful advice to the Japanese in exchange for favors they believed him. The food and vodka they gave him was most welcome and sometimes he was able to carry some of it back to his hut and share with Ivan. One day he was escorted into the interrogation room to find that Arkady Gross was there with Lieutenant Dainichi. Gross had his usual grin and seemed to be a bit drunk.

Kenji addressed Constantine. "So, Lieutenant Pokravsky, I believe you know your compatriot Lieutenant Gross?"

"Yes, I do."

"Gross tells me that you have been lying to us about many things. I didn't know whether to believe you or to believe him, but we have spies among the Chinese who are working as laborers behind the Russian lines, and they have confirmed that he is giving us useful information while you, on the other hand, have been lying to us. How could you do such a thing? An officer and a gentleman! It would not be so bad if you were like your friend Medved, who refuses to tell us anything, but you have lied to us simply to get a few favors. It is disgraceful conduct for a warrior, and I am not sure I can even regard you as a warrior after such behavior. I am sentencing you to five days in the box with only water. We will let you sit in your own filth for a while and see if you do not learn to appreciate the privileges you receive as an officer."

Constantine was marched to a small wooden box in the center of the compound. By this time every prisoner knew what it was for. They had seen others forced into the little structure and then heard the moans and pleas of those who had been imprisoned inside. The box was a cube, three feet by three feet by three feet. To shove a man inside, the guards removed one side, pushed the prisoner into the foul-smelling cube, replaced the side, and bolted it shut. A four-inch hole in the top permitted the guards to look down on the prisoner and to hand down water once a day. The guards were not permitted to say anything to the prisoner. The prisoner could neither stand, nor lie down. All he could do was sit with his knees drawn up before him. There was no floor in the box, so he sat in mud laced with urine and excrement.

When Constantine did not return that day, Ivan began to worry. The night passed without his friend. The next afternoon Kenji showed up with the chessboard for a game. Midway through the game Ivan asked, "Lieutenant Dainichi, I wonder if you know what happened to my friend Lieutenant Pokravsky?"

Kenji had been waiting for the question. "Ah, yes, Lieutenant Pokravsky. He has misbehaved and is being punished. You will see him again in a few days." Kenji was clearly not in the mood for additional conversation and shut it off.

CHAPTER 24
ESCAPE

Four days later Constantine reappeared. He was filthy with matted hair, his watery eyes rimmed with red. He was freezing cold, and he stank of human waste. "They put me in that small wooden box. I was not allowed bathroom breaks and ended up sitting in my own shit and piss. They gave me water once a day but no food at all. All I could do was crouch there with freezing rain dripping through the hole in the top and wait for the period to be over. It was an eternity. Dainichi says that he might send me back there at any time if I do not cooperate with him. He thinks that I have learned my lesson and will be more pliable, more cooperative now that I have been softened up. I cannot bring myself to talk about the Russian forces, but I am not sure I will survive another session in the box. I will kill myself rather than go back there. You are right, we must attempt to escape."

Ivan and Constantine made their plans carefully. Ivan's wounds continued to bother him a little and he walked with a slight limp but he thought he was well enough. For a week they saved a small portion of their meager rice ration, and they found an old vodka bottle in which they could carry water. The resourceful Constantine somehow managed to steal a pair of pliers with a cutting edge that they thought they could use to cut through the barbed wire surrounding the prisoner compound.

Although Constantine was in trouble with Kenji Dainichi, he was still able to move about the inside of the prisoners' compound during their half-hour break time in the daylight and observe what was going on. Ivan did the same. They agreed that the best time to go would be about 11:30 p.m. The Japanese guards changed shifts at midnight and they thought that the out-going sentries would be impatiently waiting for their reliefs and not so vigilant. And the two decided that they would go on the first night that the moon was right. They needed a "thief's moon." A full moon would allow the Japanese to see them more easily. On the other hand, in the dark of a moonless sky they might lose their way. They chose a night with the moon a little over a quarter full.

On the night they chose, the sky was unblemished by clouds. When the time came, they rolled their blankets into what might, to casual inspection, be themselves on the floor where they normally slept. Then, one at a time, they stole out the door of their hut and moved toward the latrine to the east, intending to use it for an intermediate objective and observation point between the hut and the wire. They stealthily got to the latrine just as the door banged open and out came Arkady Gross buttoning up his trousers. He took one look at them and immediately became suspicious.

"What are you two doing here, together?" he demanded.

"Hold your voice down, Gross," whispered Ivan.

"Why are you whispering? Are you trying to escape? You are trying to escape!" he said and lowered his voice. "You must take me with you."

"No, Arkady, you cannot come with us."

"If you do not agree to take me, I will start shouting right now and you will be captured and punished. Just imagine how long you will have to spend in the box for this, Pokravsky!"

"We must take him, Ivan, I could not stand any more time in the box," whispered Constantine. Realizing that he was in a bad situation either way, Ivan reluctantly agreed.

"Okay, Arkady, but you follow my orders."

"Lead on, princeling. Maybe some good will come of knowing you yet."

The three young officers crawled to the edge of the fence, Ivan first and Constantine bringing up the rear. Ivan tried the pliers on the wire. The tool was old, rusty, and undersized for the task and he had to worry the wire back and forth, shaking it for some dozen yards before it finally gave with what seemed in their imagination to be an ear-spitting twang. It had taken nearly five minutes and all his strength to cut through the one strand of wire. He had a dozen more to go at ground level before they could crawl clear. Sweating in the cold night, Ivan inched forward and worked on the second strand, and then the third. As he was working on the fourth the hinge on the pliers gave way, rendering them useless. What to do?

Crawling up alongside Ivan, Constantine brought with him a three-foot-long metal stake that he had found. He moved up to the next strand and pried it up until his comrades could just inch their way under it. Then they turned and held it while he moved under. It was slow going. At some points the wire was so taut at ground level that it would not raise high enough. When this happened, they had to move laterally to the right or left and find a place where it was looser. Several times they snagged and tore their clothing. When Ivan and Constantine planned this effort, they had imagined that their passage through the wire would take half an hour. Instead, it took over five hours. The sentries who had gone on duty at midnight were relieved at four a.m. Their relief seemed to be more active than those who had been on duty before them. They patrolled in a wider circle but none came close to the portion of the wire that the Russians were attempting to pass through. At what Ivan estimated was about five a.m. they finally crawled under the last wire. They faced Hand Bay to the east. The plan was to move across the railway tracks that followed the contours of the bay and then, using the tracks as a guide, move south and hopefully away from the Japanese and into Russian lines.

Ivan halted them a hundred meters short of the tracks and whispered, "Wait here" He moved at a low crouch to the rail bed. He could see pairs of Japanese sentries to the north and south and could hear them talking. When he moved back to the others he whispered, "There are sentries in both directions. We will have to be careful crossing the tracks. I will go first." He reached the tracks and rolled over one rail, then across the ties and over the second rail. Constantine followed, hardly daring to breathe. They waited and waited for Gross. "Gross! Gross! Where are you?" After a long minute, Ivan said, "I am going back to look for him."

"But Ivan--" Constantine began.

"Shhh!"

Ivan crawled back across the tracks and found Gross shivering in the darkness on the far side. "What is wrong, Gross? It is going to be light soon and we must get moving."

"I cannot do it. I just cannot do it. Go on and I will take my chances."

"Make your own choice," said Ivan and again rolled over the tracks. He and Constantine had moved no more than a hundred feet or so before they heard Gross call out in broken Japanese. The guards immediately converged on his position from both directions, weapons at the ready and excitedly talking. When they reached Arkady one of them clubbed him with a rifle butt. He was partially stunned but was able to point in the direction of Ivan and Constantine, and through sign language explained to them what was going on. He tried to tell the Japanese that he was forced to accompany the pair, a story he would repeat to Dainichi the following morning.

Luckily for the two Russians, the quarter moon had set, and the night was now the dark before the dawn. The Japanese fired a few volleys in their direction and then began pursuit on foot. Shortly after, the sky in the east began to turn silver-gray, and the sun was about to crack the horizon. Ivan and Constantine found themselves in a draw at the edge of the bay. They crawled under some brush and covered themselves at the limit of the beach where the incoming tide would cover their footprints. They lay motionless, hearts beating furiously, as they heard the Japanese thrashing through the brush around them. Just as they were about to be discovered, the searchers changed direction and moved away. The morning sun crossed the sky above them, alternating with light rain, a sun that did not warm and a rain that did not refresh. They lay there shivering and exhausted for the entire day. They could hear search parties of Japanese shouting to one another, but none drew near.

When night fell, they began moving again. The bay curved around to the west at this point, just south of the Chinese village of Ta Lien Wan. The fingernail moon arose early and glowed like a sliver of ice. They approached the village in the dim light, moved carefully along the shoreline and saw half a dozen small fishing sampans on the beach. “Come on, Constantine, we can steal one of the boats and make our way past the Japanese lines, perhaps as far as Dalny, which hopefully we still hold.”

They took the boat nearest the water and dragged it into the sea. At the first noise of the boat being moved a chorus of dogs began baying and several Chinese and a pair of Japanese soldiers rushed down to the shore to see what was going on. The Japanese spotted them and opened fire. Neither Ivan nor Constantine was hit, but the boat took a small bullet hole below the water line, and immediately began leaking. The boat was without oars but had a couple of long poles. The two men stood up in the midst of enemy fire and poled through the shallow water for all they were worth. Finally, they faded from sight of shore and except for a couple of wild shots the firing ceased. They poled their way through the night, first westward and then south.

When the sun once more threatened to expose them, they pulled into another cove for the day and covered the boat with brush. Ivan told his friend, “Sleep for a while. I am going to look around.” He moved cautiously inland a few hundred yards and found a small rise from which he could look both north and south. When he looked south, he was shocked to see the Rising Sun flag flying over the town of Dalny. Several Japanese vessels dotted the bay next to the eastern side of the peninsula. It would be impossible for them to pole their small craft through them. This meant that they would have farther to go, and they would have to travel by land and cross a broader part of the peninsula in order to safely pass Dalny.

Ivan returned to the place where he had left Constantine, lay down, and got a few hours of troubled sleep. When they awoke they ate the last of their rice and drank the last of their water. At dark they headed west and then south past Dalny. They heard patrols of Japanese around them in the night but none came close. At dawn they crawled into the center of a field of wild millet that was several feet high and slept once more. Two dawns later, the sun illuminated earthworks to their front on which they could see a Russian flag flying.

They stood up and, waving their arms, began to move toward the position. A shot rang out and then another and then a whole fusillade. They hit the ground hard and crawled away fast. One of Ivan's old wounds opened and began leaking fluid. Constantine was hit in the head, and blood cascaded down onto his uniform. Ivan rolled over on his back, removed his coat and when the firing ceased, stood and began waving it back and forth and shouting in Russian as loudly as he could. This time the Russians in the position held fire and about twenty Cossacks galloped forward in their gaudy uniforms, sabers drawn and pistols at the ready. They quickly circled around the pair and finally, when they became convinced they were dealing with fellow Russians, hoisted them behind two of the riders and galloped back to the position. Constantine could barely hang on to the Cossack in front of him, his blood streaking down his face and onto his clothing and the back of his rescuer.

When they reached the lines, they were immediately taken to the hospital. Colonel Tretyakov came in and questioned Ivan closely about the Japanese as the doctors dressed his wounds. Conditions in the Russian hospital were appalling. They were little more than butcher shops. There were more sick and wounded than there were beds, and many lay on stretchers in the hallways. The poorly trained doctors lost as many patients as they saved.

They kept Ivan overnight, and the next morning he decided that he was well enough and declared himself ready to leave. They showed him where to clean up and gave him a cleaner uniform, one that had been taken from a dead Russian lieutenant. There were a few blood spots on it, it was worn and was too big, but it was better than the rags in which he had escaped. When he inquired about his friend, he was told that Constantine's wound was serious, and he may have suffered some damage to his brain. It was not known if he would live.

CHAPTER 25

ST. PETERSBURG: NATALYA

While Ivan was at war in the Far East, his sister Natalya had regained a tenuous contact with Tatiana. It came about because Pyotr Bolkonsky became personally interested in the young aristocratic woman. Pyotr's motives were both practical and sexual. He knew that it would be a real feather in his cap among his fellow revolutionaries if he could subvert the daughter of a prince into joining the cause, thus providing an important link for obtaining information about the aristocracy. And Tatiana had remarked frequently on Natalya's beauty. "If I am successful at subverting her and somehow become personally involved with her then, well. . ."

For Natalya's part, forming a tentative friendship with lower class members of Russian society who wanted to fundamentally change the country was a chance to do something thrilling, and somewhat wicked, that would relieve the sameness of her day-to-day life of privilege. Certainly it could not hurt anything, not seriously damage the established order of things. Tatiana thought of it as a chance to maintain a link to some of the most pleasant memories of her childhood when she and Natalya had been the best of friends.

Shortly after the friendship was renewed a period of several weeks passed when Natalya did not hear from Tatiana, and Natalya began to wonder if she had been arrested. The Okhrana had raided one of the locations where her father Vladimir and his group met. Fortunately for the revolutionaries, a spy, an undercover comrade among the police, tipped them off, and they dispersed just hours before the raid. Unfortunately for the revolutionaries, the Tsar's secret police found a roster of the members of Vladimir's group. Once again, the movement's informant within the Okhrana told them of this and each fled one step ahead of the police. Not long after Tatiana and her father had moved, Vladimir found new employment with new papers, and they changed their surname again. Vladimir talked of leaving St. Petersburg for another city but decided not to go. St. Petersburg was the center of the revolutionary movement, and he was determined to be part of it no matter the danger.

A few weeks later Tatiana sent a note by a street urchin to the Medved mansion to tell Natalya that she was okay. The note also suggested that the two resume meeting now and then for tea. It also cautioned her that they would have to be even more careful than usual. If Natalya was interested, the note said, she should show up at a certain restaurant at a certain time and date. When the date came, Natalya managed to slip out of the Medved mansion without a chaperone and walked to nearby Bolovsky Square, where she hired a small carriage to take her to the restaurant. The place was a shabby affair, in a bleak neighborhood, and she hesitated.

"Miss, I have better things to do than wait. I need to find another fare," the driver said as he scowled over his shoulder.

"All right, but here is another ruble if you will wait for a few more minutes."

"I will, but hurry."

The moment she alighted from the carriage, the driver spoke to the horses, snapping the reins, as he grinned and thrust her coins into his pocket. The carriage trundled away.

She looked around for another carriage, but none was in sight. Stranded! Nothing to do for it now. She resolutely strode through the door and scanned the room for Tatiana. The owner took in her clothing, gave an obsequious smile, bowed over his soiled apron, and declared himself at her service. She chose a table that looked a bit cleaner than the rest and was located where she could see the entrance. As the anxious owner pulled out her chair, she asked him for a pot of tea. It arrived quickly, along with a cup that was none too clean. The owner poured tea for her, but she had no intention of drinking from a dirty cup. The tea, untouched, rapidly cooled.

She waited about twenty minutes and did not notice the scruffy looking young man who rose from a table in the rear and slipped out the back door. This man whispered to a young boy who waited in the alley. The boy walked down the alleyway and around to the front of the restaurant where he lifted his cap and scratched his head. Tatiana spotted it and strode into the restaurant. A floppy hat covered her head, a scarf covered her neck up to her chin and she was garbed in the unremarkable clothing of the poor. She looked around, saw Natalya, approached her table and sat down.

"Natalya," she said, "I am so happy to see you." The owner hurried over to take their order. Tatiana demanded, and got, clean teacups, and the two gossiped through three cups of weak tea until Tatiana said that she must go. They promised to meet again.

Whenever Tatiana was free from her duties and Natalya could get away from the Medved home they would meet. Sometimes Tatiana would bring along Pyotr whom she introduced as her lover.

Natalya asked, "Are you going to get married?"

Tatiana and Pyotr both chuckled at the question. Pyotr said, "Marriage is such a bourgeois concept, Natalya. In the New Russia, marriage will not be necessary. It will be a universal comradeship and men and especially women will be free to love whomever they like, whenever they like. Just think, we will be free economically because we will have seized all the wealth for the people, and we will be free in our personal relationships. We will also be free of God and religion. Christianity, all religion, is but an invention of the privileged classes to keep us in line and give us false hope. The real, and only, paradise will be created here on earth: by us."

With the "lover" comment resonating in the back of her mind, Natalya regarded Pyotr with a critical eye. He was a serious and good-looking young man. A bit smaller than what Natalya considered ideal but handsome, nonetheless. Although she paid little attention to his speech, a tingle of naughtiness ran up her spine as her thoughts of him became more personal.

Pyotr had a roving eye. He gave every passing young woman a careful look and continuously flirted with Natalya. Tatiana not only seemed to not mind, she seemed to encourage it. She would make flattering remarks about how good Natalya looked to Pyotr and make comments, some embarrassingly intimate, about not only Pyotr's good looks but also his prowess as a lover. Natalya, whose knowledge of sexual matters was limited to the sparse information she had gotten from her mother, found herself awash with sensations that were both mentally and physically erotic. She was familiar with masturbation.

In their meetings with Natalya, Pyotr and Tatiana talked about many things, but mainly the conversation revealed an obsession with bringing good to Russia, and they inundated Natalya with propaganda about the "movement." They began by pointing out to her the absolute poverty of most Russians and how the aristocracy and the wealthy merchants mistreated the common people. They pointed out examples of orphans, cripples, and beggars in the street as they walked with her through the toughest part of St. Petersburg to see the worst slums. Although she had heard about the problems of the poor, this was the first time that Natalya had seen poverty and suffering up close. On one hand the poverty touched her heart. On the other hand, the sight of the impoverished and the conditions in which they found themselves physically repelled her. Finally, she decided, she had no intention of giving up her privileged status.

At each meeting Pyotr became more physically familiar with Natalya. In the beginning, he kissed her hand and complimented her on her looks. Then he began to embrace her when they met and kissed her on both cheeks. She had never been kissed in public, except by members of her immediate family. When Pyotr hugged her she tried to hold back from his embrace so that her breasts did not touch his chest, but his grip was strong and he would press his whole body against her from groin to chest. Once or twice she felt what she thought what had to be an erect penis pressing against her, and she blushed bright red with embarrassment. Tatiana always looked on with a sort of amused detachment.

One day Tatiana frankly asked Natalya, in front of Pyotr, if she was a virgin. Natalya turned red and stammered that it was not the sort of thing she wanted to talk about. *Especially in front of a man*, she added to herself.

"Pyotr is a wonderful lover," Tatiana said matter-of-factly. "You could do worse than lose your virginity with him."

Without a word Natalia stood up, left the restaurant, and found a carriage to take her home. She went to bed early that evening and masturbated twice while thinking of Pyotr.

Despite her anxieties Natalya could not resist the invitation to have tea with them a week later. Neither Pyotr nor Tatiana brought up sex at that meeting or at the one after that. Eventually Tatiana returned to the issue but she talked about it in broad terms. Natalya began to think that Tatiana was patronizing. Nevertheless, she was surprised that the absence of conversation about sexual matters seemed to heighten her anticipation and she discovered that she had a secretly held desire to return to the subject. Terrified to broach the subject herself, she squirmed impatiently with desire and curiosity in Pyotr's presence.

The subject of their meetings became equally divided about the need for change in Russia and the needs of the human body for sexual relief. They discussed the latter subject in objective terms. Tatiana's philosophy was that sex was a normal appetite, like the need for food and water and that one should feel no shame but should satisfy that appetite now and then for one's mental health. Natalya wondered how such an intimate subject could be discussed in such cold, objective terms.

Finally one day, while drinking his second cup of tea, Pyotr looked at her and said with an amused look on his face, "Well, Natalya, are you ready to lose your virginity yet?

"Yes, I am." She replied.

The suddenness and directness of her reply startled all three of them.

"Well, now," said Tatiana, "let's finish our tea and go to our place."

They strode through the crowded streets of St. Petersburg until they came to an unkempt, poor-looking apartment building. As the three of them started up the stairs, Natalya said, "Are you coming too, Tatiana?"

Tatiana laughed and said, "Of course. Maybe I'll even participate."

This declaration startled Natalya. She had never heard of such a thing but was determined to go through with what she had begun.

The small one-room apartment had only one bed. A tiny window in the back illuminated the room. Tatiana locked the front door while Pyotr led Natalya to the edge of the bed, sat on it and began unbuttoning her dress.

"But it is so light in here," said Natalya.

"All the better for us to see what we are doing," Pyotr replied with a grin.

Natalya was embarrassed. Not even her own mother had seen her nude since she reached puberty.

A half hour later, Tatiana sat next to her and stroked her sweaty brow. "How was it, Natalya? Did it meet your expectations?"

"It hurt so much."

"That is only the first time. From now on it will be all pleasure."

Then Tatiana took a wet cloth and cleaned up the blood and stains.

After a few minutes rest, Pyotr mounted Tatiana and had sex with her too.

CHAPTER 26

PORT ARTHUR UNDER SIEGE

Port Arthur was in shock. The Japanese capture of the railway had cut off the primary source of resupply to the beleaguered Russian forces and the townspeople. Many Russian officers lost control of their poorly disciplined soldiers and entire units disintegrated. Drunken soldiers and sailors staggered from building to building, indiscriminately looting. General Petrovdid his best to cut off vodka to the army, but it was the one commodity that was not in short supply and it found its way into every unit. The highly vaunted Cossacks were the worst offenders. They had not proven their worth in battle and seemed uninterested in doing so. The priest with them, Father Grigori, was the worst of the lot and was rarely seen when he was not drunk or near a whorehouse. Usually both.

On the 15th of August, Kenji was showing several lieutenants in his company how he would conduct the final campaign to take Port Arthur. He sat on an old wooden artillery ammunition crate, using a stick to outline his strategy in the dirt, and drawing rough diagrams and explaining the logic behind his ideas. The others, faces creased in concentration, listened attentively. The young officers did not notice the two soldiers who approached them and shifted from one foot to another, reluctant to interrupt the exercise.

Finally, during a pause, one of the runners asked, "Sirs, which one of you is Lieutenant Dainichi?"

Kenji looked up and said, "I am."

"Sir, General Nogi wants to know if it is true that you speak Russian."

"Yes, I do."

"The general asks that you report to his headquarters."

Kenji quickly changed into a cleaner uniform and buckling on his father's sword strode off with the runner over the muddy and bumpy ground toward the Japanese headquarters.

General Nogi was entertaining a group of war correspondents, mostly Europeans, in a large building, a former Russian warehouse, when Kenji arrived. The reporters cradled glasses of champagne in their hands, part of the booty the Japanese had captured from the Russians. One of the Europeans, Alfred Addington, did a double take at Kenji's approached, and recognized the young Japanese officer as one he had met on the ship going to Russia. He discreetly waved and smiled at Kenji but Kenji was too preoccupied to notice. He stood on the outskirts of the group as the runner approached General Nogi, saluted, and said a few words to him. Nogi turned to Kenji and started toward him, giving instructions to an aide to keep the champagne glasses of the reporters full, "to warm the hands." The general took Kenji by the arm and led him to the one-room unpainted shack that he used as his headquarters.

"Lieutenant Dainichi," the general began, "it is good to see you again. We are far, far from the academy and are in the world of warfare. I expect that you are living up to the high expectations we had of you as a cadet. I have a most important assignment for you. I want you to help me compose a document to be addressed to the Russians. Tomorrow, I want you to carry a flag of truce into the Russian position and ask them to read it. The document will offer them a chance to surrender Port Arthur without further bloodshed to either side. It should be evident to them that their position there is hopeless and that the port will eventually fall into our hands. Our sources tell us that Port Arthur is in a shambles, food and ammunition is running out, and the population is out of control. Surely they will see that they cannot possibly win and will give considerable thought to my proposal."

With that, the general removed the maps from his small table and furnished each of them with a Western-style pen, a bottle of ink, and a sheaf of blank paper. General Nogi slowly composed his message, pausing after each sentence to pass the paper for Kenji's comments and for him to translate and copy the text into Russian. From time-to-time Kenji made suggestions for additions or deletions and most often the general nodded his assent. Nogi stated that he did not wish to appear to be contemptuous of or insulting to his enemy. Rather he wanted to present, soldier-to-soldier, a proposal to General Petrov that would end the bloodshed. The exercise was a real struggle for Kenji. Although he could speak and read Russian fairly well, it was something else to write something out and be certain of its accuracy. He labored over the Cyrillic characters and the Russian grammar to get it just right and several times had to stop and begin again on a new sheet of paper.

After several hours, the two came up with the rough draft of what the general wanted to say. At that point, the general told Kenji to make two clean copies of the document in each language, one for himself and the other to be delivered to the Russians.

"I must attend to other duties," he said. "Copy the documents and make sure they are absolutely correct. Then find me and read it to me in Japanese for my final approval. It must be ready first thing in the morning."

Kenji did so that evening and reported to the general's headquarters at first light. He found the general in a staff meeting and stood in the doorway until he caught the general's eye. Nogi excused himself, took Kenji by the elbow, and led him outside. The general read the document carefully, rereading parts of it, and nodded in approval.

Kenji listened carefully to the general's final instructions, which included the admonition to just deliver the letter to the Russians and to not engage in conversation with them. "You will be accompanied by Major General Kawamoto to show rank and demonstrate our respect for the Russians as professional soldiers. Kawamoto does not speak Russian, so any conversation between him and our enemies will have to be translated by you. You will translate whatever is said faithfully and without your own interpretation or comments. I also want you to remember as much of the conversation as you can so you and General Kawamoto can report back to me and each of you can give me your reports. Do you understand?"

Kenji said that he did.

The General dismissed him and returned to his staff meeting.

The morning dawned foggy and cold with little promise of improvement. When Kenji reached the headquarters, a major from General Kawamoto's staff met him and introduced him to the general. The general skeptically eyed the small junior officer and told him to mount up so they could get going. Kenji had to get a leg up from a staff member because the stirrup was too high for him to get a foot into. The general shook his head at the sight of an officer of the emperor's army having such a hard time mounting a horse.

The general, Kenji, and an aide who carried a white flag on a long staff, proceeded slowly through the fog toward the Russian lines. The fog worried Kenji. The Russians might not see the flag of truce until General Kawamoto's party was in easy gunshot range of their lines. They would also be within earshot, which was both good and bad. The Russians might shoot at the sound of their approach but on the other hand, Kenji might be able to shout at them and be understood.

The Russians heard them coming before they could see them and they loosed an ineffective fusillade at the noise. The rounds passed by harmlessly and impacted far off to one side. The riders slowly pressed on until Kenji thought they were fairly close and then he suggested to General Kawamoto that he and his aide stay where they were while he rode ahead to get the Russians' attention. He slowly walked his horse through the fog, shouting in Russian, "Flag of truce! Flag of truce! Please get one of your officers."

After much delay and a couple of wild shots from the Russian lines, a voice answered. "I am Captain Piatiev, what do you want?"

"This is General Kawamoto's party," Kenji said. "He is an emissary from General Nogi and wishes to speak with General Petrov under a flag of truce."

"Stay where you are. I will find out if the general wishes to see you."

The trio dismounted and stood by, shivering in the cold for nearly three hours. The sun was a pale-yellow disk beyond the fog, but by mid-morning the fog cleared enough for the Japanese and Russians to see one another. Each side regarded the other curiously.

Captain Piatiev finally reappeared, accompanied by a major general from General Petrov's staff.

"What did you come here for?" the general demanded.

"We have a message for General Petrov and for him only," said Kenji.

The Russian general, whose contempt for the "monkeys" would admit no other possibility than the message was a Japanese surrender, said, "All right, follow me, but you must be without arms."

"We are unarmed."

The party rode to the Russian headquarters where General Petrov made the Japanese wait another hour. The general was informed of the Japanese delegation and, he too, thought that if it were not a proposal for a Japanese surrender that at least it would be a proposal in which the Japanese made some major concession. They could wait. Perhaps that would make them easier to negotiate with.

General Petrov's aide, Major Sakharov, appeared and said that he would personally deliver the document to his boss. Major General Kawamoto reluctantly agreed and passed the document to the aide.

General Petrov wanted Major Sakharov to read the document first and summarize its contents and then he, the commander of all the Russian forces, would decide whether he would deign to reply to the entreaty. Major Sakharov read the document and turned white. The last thing he wanted to do was present the proposal to the mercurial General Petrov. When the general at last shouted for Sakharov to come in and give him a report, the major slipped through the door and said, "I think, sir, that you had better read this for yourself," and he handed Petrov the document.

The general read only the first paragraph before he flew into a rage. He tore the paper in half and then into small bits that he contemptuously threw on the floor, and then he paced the room, shouting, "No! No! A thousand times no! I will never surrender His Imperial Majesty's forces to these little yellow bastards. Tell them no and send them back to their lines. I should shoot them and send their corpses back!"

The major got out of the general's office as soon as he could and confronted the Japanese delegation. He toned down the general's message, saying only that the Russian commander had rejected the proposal and would not meet with General Kawamoto. Kenji grimly translated the Russian general's reply to General Kawamoto, who did not comment. Then the Japanese delegation bowed as one, and without saying another word, retrieved their horses, mounted, and rode back to their own lines.

General Kawamoto and Kenji immediately reported to General Nogi, who listened attentively and asked no questions. He thanked them for their effort and then returned to the work at hand.

Shortages of supplies began to affect the Russian soldiers of all ranks and most civilians. The merchants were the only exceptions. They hoarded their supplies with the expectation of getting rich by controlling the flow of goods and gradually increasing their prices to whatever the market would bear. Clothing was scarce, so the Russian soldiers took to wearing Chinese clothing along with their ragged uniforms and even conical straw hats. The effect would have been humorous if it had not been so pitiful. Boots and underwear could not be found at any price. Meat, salt, fresh vegetables, and sugar were scarce. Alcohol was never in short supply. Great stores of vodka and champagne remained. Those who could not afford the prices of the merchants made their own liquor. In all cases it was a strong drink and sometimes it was deadly, causing paralysis or death. The prostitutes stayed busy. They rented out their bodies for whatever they needed to stay alive.

The Russian God was everywhere. Priests had brought hundreds of icons and they held services daily, for those so inclined, even on the front lines. Father Grigori held them for the Cossacks, although his services were generally incoherent and he attracted but a small following.

A few neutral merchant ships managed to run the Japanese blockade. General Petrov stubbornly refused to take supplies from them on the grounds that he would be displaying a defeatist attitude and a siege mentality. He would not let down his sovereign. He kept insisting that he would break out of the Japanese encirclement, crush the enemy, and take back the railroad. As his rants grew in frequency and intensity and some of the general's staff officers and subordinates wondered if he had gone insane. But he held the ear of the tsar and he was still in charge.

The merchants of Port Arthur were not so fastidious about where they got their supplies and bought from the blockade-runners at exorbitant prices, prices that ate their way into the consumers' remaining funds. Most of the goods were purchased by other civilians, those who could afford them.

Ivan had completely recovered from his wounds and returned to full duty in Colonel Tretyakov's regiment. Constantine, not so fortunate, was getting around on crutches but he apparently had brain damage and was confined to the Port Arthur hospital. Ivan went to visit him and found that his friend had lost the use of his right arm, which dangled and swayed uselessly when he walked. He had a pronounced limp, and although he was mentally alert he had difficulty talking and it was an effort to make himself understood when he spoke.

Tretyakov's regiment was assigned to hold Hill 203, a key point in the Russian defense. He drove his men in the preparation of its defense with the same vigor with which he had fortified Nanshan. This time he was given more artillery shells and was promised reinforcement when needed. If Hill 203 fell, Port Arthur would be threatened as never before.

While the tsar's soldiers suffered from lack of clothing and hunger, great quantities of woolen coats with fur collars reached the Japanese, and each Japanese soldier had at least two blankets. They were preparing for a long campaign.

Few Russian soldiers had more than one blanket and some had to wrap themselves in their greatcoats and make the best of it. Ordinary comfort items and necessities were hard to find. Cigarettes, soap, and toothbrushes were generally not available at any price. General Nogi made sure that these items were furnished to all his soldiers but he kept supplies of alcohol for his men far from the front lines and only available in limited quantities in the rear.

Nogi began his assault three days after General Petrov rejected his surrender proposal. He avoided fancy tactics and threw his men at the enemy in frontal assault after frontal assault. For days, the battle seesawed back and forth. Positions were taken by the Japanese and retaken by the Russians. Rotting corpses and hideous parts of bodies covered the ground to such an extent it was nearly impossible to walk on the battlefield without stepping on the remains of a soldier from one side or the other. Four days later no Russian position had been taken and held and yet the Japanese had lost over 18,000 men killed and wounded.

By the end of the month Nogi realized that the mere expenditure of lives would not win the day. He set tens of thousands of men to digging trenches toward the Russian lines, laying them out in a zigzag fashion in order to contain blasts and minimize the number of casualties whenever a shell landed in one of them. The Russians kept up a nearly continuous artillery fire, collapsed trenches, and killed thousands of enemy soldiers. Yet the Japanese dug on. They carried their dead and wounded to the rear, dug out the collapsed sections of the trenches and inched their way inexorably toward the Russian lines. As they grew closer the Russian artillery's ammunition stocks reached a critical point and they were forced to ration their rounds. With the diminution of enemy fire, the Japanese progressed at a faster rate.

Kenji's company, along with all the others, became labor battalions. Kenji worked alongside his men, often wielding pick and shovel with them. The earth they took from the trenches they used to fill sandbags, and these they placed along the rim of the trenches to add further protection. Then, with great effort, the Japanese dismantled and brought ashore naval guns to join in the bombardment of the Russians.

Foreign observers, mostly military men and correspondents had flocked to China to cover the war in Port Arthur. Most came from Europe and America, and some of them were military figures in their own right. General Nogi frequently entertained them but politely reminded them they were there only because he permitted them to be. He kept a tight gag order on them and forbade them to send their news of the war to the outside world because he feared that information useful to the Russians might leak out.

The correspondents had gained a great deal of respect for Nogi during the war and did not violate his trust. He was congenial with his foreign guests and nearly every day he served them lunch or at least champagne. The exigencies of commanding the Japanese force generally prevented him from joining them at lunch but he tried to always greet them and make them welcome. The General was self-effacing, and he always wore the same, simple uniform, a black tunic with neither rank insignia nor decorations, white breeches and highly polished boots. With his close-cropped gray hair and neatly trimmed beard he was an elegant, gentlemanly figure. He frequently laughed with the correspondents but some of them noted that his laugh was only seen on his lips, and that dark thoughts wintered in his eyes.

CHAPTER 27

THE FALL OF PORT ARTHUR

General Nogi wanted to seize Port Arthur in time for the emperor's birthday on November 3 so he launched another assault on October 20th. The emperor's birthday came and went and still the Russians held on. The new assault cost the Japanese another 5,000 casualties.

Then, in the middle of November, eleven-inch siege guns manufactured by Krupp in Germany arrived and the Japanese set them up on the hillsides around Port Arthur. They poured thousands of rounds into the Russian defenses and at the remnants of the Russian fleet that they kept penned in the harbor. The terrified townspeople, starving and dirty, had to dig their own shelters. Most dug bunkers beneath their buildings and lived underground in the dark. Others used the rubble from destroyed buildings to build miniature forts.

In the meantime, Japanese sappers busily dug and tunneled, working with the industry and attention to detail of a colony of ants. One at a time their trenches drew close enough to the Russian lines that they could tunnel under them. The Russians feared the Japanese would fill the tunnels with dynamite.

The other Nogi son, the second and the general's favorite, was killed on November 30. He was shot through the head after carrying a message to the front. General Nogi was dozing in his chair when a staff officer approached him with the news.

Nogi asked, "Was he killed before or after he completed his mission?" Upon being told that his son had been killed on the way back to his regiment after having completed his mission, the general said that he was glad that his son's task had been completed. *I often wondered how I could apologize to His Majesty and to the people for having killed so many of my men...but now that both my sons have been killed...*

The staff officer noted tears in the general's eyes, tears that would not fall, and quietly asked what should be done with the body.

"Cremate it. Turn it into ashes."

Moments later, Nogi's aide told him that General Oseko waited to see him. General Oseko's 7th Division, 8,000 strong, had arrived from Japan only a week earlier and was immediately fed into the attack. The Russians slaughtered them in great numbers and the division failed in its attempt to take Hill 203 although it had tried for several days running. "General Oseko, you have failed in your mission to take Hill 203. I am going to relieve your unit and assign another unit in your place."

Oseko turned pale with shock. "I beg of you, sir, to reconsider. It is a good division and would like the honor of carrying Hill 203 where so many of our brave soldiers have already fallen for His Majesty."

"How many men do you have left, General?"

"Fewer than a thousand, sir. But they are gallant as demonstrated by the fact that nearly ninety percent of their comrades have fallen."

Leading a thousand men in an assault to seize an objective that eight thousand men had failed to carry was a suicide mission. But General Nogi recognized the imperatives of personal honor, bushido and giri.

"Very well, General. If you want to lead the attack and redeem your honor, who am I to stop you?"

The next day General Oseko's ragged 7th Division spearheaded the assault. The Russians slaughtered them to a man. The general lay among the dead.

With the fire of the Krupp guns reducing the Russian fortifications to mud and rubble the Japanese slowly took one position after another around Hill 203. They paid dearly for each advance. The Russians lay prone, shoulder to shoulder, firing at the oncoming enemy in great volleys that sliced through the Japanese formations, leaving great rows of shattered flesh. But on the Japanese came, in one wave of violence after another. When they broke into the Russian lines the fight became one of the Russians' favorite weapon, the bayonet; cold steel against cold steel, bayonet against bayonet penetrating flesh, sending soldier after soldier on both sides off to meet his god. The Russians threw them back.

But the artillery barrages continued. By mid-afternoon on the fifth day the Japanese fired over 1,000 rounds at Hill 203, which Colonel Tretyakov's men stubbornly defended. The Japanese attacked again. Under the combined pressure of the artillery, and the infantry attack, the Russians lines began to crack and small bodies of them fled from the hill, leaving mounds of casualties behind them. The Japanese took part of the hill but the Russians held the rest.

Tretyakov, wearing a silver cross around his neck, stood near one of the casualty dressing stations on the rear slope of the hill. All around him lay Russian corpses and unidentifiable hunks of flesh and bone. The stench was horrible and disease from the decaying corpses swept through the ranks of both armies.

Tretyakov stopped the retreat through sheer force of determined personality. He ignored the fire and strode back and forth in his lines, "Soldiers of Russia," he called out, "we must retake this hill. The whole of Port Arthur depends on it."

He rallied the unwounded and walking wounded to conduct a night counterattack to recover the portion of the hill that had fallen into Japanese hands. In the pitch-black night they charged up the slope, struggling against the rifle and machine gun fire and grenades that the Japanese rolled down on them by the hundreds. They found the ground so choked with the dead that they could hardly move forward. Ivan led his men gallantly and without thought to his own safety. The only way the Russian soldiers could know they were attacking their objective was to charge directly at the muzzle flashes of the Japanese weapons. With fixed bayonets, determined looks, and fiercely beating hearts, they stumbled slowly upward.

Ivan stepped in the stomach of a disemboweled soldier. It was too dark to tell if the man was Russian or Japanese. Ivan's foot became tangled in the greasy entrails, and he fell face down onto the rotting body of another soldier. He worked himself free, pulling off a loop of intestine that had captured one of his boots. And then he continued upward. Men, he was not sure who, fell on either side of him. He yelled for the Russians to keep going.

By this time the attacking units were so mixed up in the confusion of the assault that Ivan was not even certain if any of those who heard him were from his unit. It did not matter. He urged them on anyway. Finally, the Russians reached the last few yards and as if from one throat yelled, "God save the tsar!" and assaulted right into the position. Soldiers, Japanese and Russian, shot, stabbed, clubbed, choked, and bit in a frenzy of violence. Men fell on both sides, but the Russians prevailed and the position was in their hands once again.

Their superhuman effort proved too much for the Japanese who retreated down the hill. This time it was the Russians' turn to roll grenades down on their enemy. They also kept up a fusillade of small arms and machine gun fire until all movement ceased and the battlefield fell silent except for the moans and the screams of the wounded.

But the Japanese were not finished. On the morning of December 1st they concentrated all their might against Hill 203. Once more the large shells burst among the defenders. This time the gallant Tretyakov was seriously wounded and carried to the rear. The loss of his leadership had a profound effect on the morale of the Russian troops.

Voices cried out, "Tretyakov is down, the colonel is down!" As the word of his injury spread through the ranks, one Russian soldier after another lost the will to fight. As evening fell, Japanese infantry stormed the hill and carried it. Ivan Medved was among the seriously wounded. A rifle bullet clipped the corner of his head at just the height of the bridge of his nose and neatly took his right eye with it. One of his soldiers wrapped a dressing around Ivan's head and led him to the rear just as the Japanese gained the hill. With their commander out of action, and most of their officers and NCOs dead or wounded, the Russians were forced to withdraw. Ivan was one of the casualties who made it to the rear. Many were left behind in the dark and confusion.

At General Petrov's headquarters that night the Russians held a council of war. Some of the generals advised surrender. Others, ignoring the losses from shellfire and scurvy, said that if they killed all the horses they could survive on horsemeat for a couple more months.

"When the ammunition for the big guns goes, we still have our small arms, when that goes, we have our bayonets," declared Petrov. "We will discuss surrender no longer."

Rations were soon down to half a pound of biscuit, a quarter pound of horseflesh, and two ounces of vodka per man per day.

On December 15th the burst from an artillery round killed the competent General Kontradenko, one of the few Russian officers universally admired by the men. This further damaged Russian morale, and Petrov appointed the incompetent General Foch to replace him.

General Petrov tried to cover all the possibilities. Without telling his fellow officers, he sent a telegram to the tsar that said, "We cannot hold out for more than a few days. Am taking measures to prevent a street massacre."

Then, two weeks later: "Great Sovereign! Forgive! We have done all that was humanly possible. Judge us, but be merciful. Eleven months of ceaseless fighting have exhausted our strength. A quarter only of the defenders, and one half of them invalids, occupy eighteen miles of fortifications without support and without intervals for even the briefest repose. The men are reduced to shadows." At the same time he sent an officer under flag of truce to Nogi arrange to the surrender.

Nogi, who rarely took to his bed, was once more dozing in his chair when an aide came to tell him the news. "Send for young Dainichi. I want to make sure I understand what the Russians are offering me."

General Nogi had held up receiving the Russian party until Kenji arrived. The general listened to Kenji's translation of the Russian proposal and then left his staff to arrange the terms for surrender. The Japanese general demanded and got an unconditional capitulation. He agreed to parole officers who voluntarily signed an agreement to not participate further in a war against Japan. They would be allowed to leave with their personal effects but all their horses would be the property of the Japanese army. Prisoners would be exchanged immediately.

After the two sides agreed to the terms, General Nogi wrote his last poem of the war:

His Majesty's millions conquer the strong foe.

Field battles and siege result in mountains of corpses.

How can I, in shame, face their fathers?

Songs of triumph today, but how many have returned?

Once the word of surrender spread through the ranks the Russian troops dropped their arms and looted the town in a drunken orgy before the Japanese occupiers arrived. Russian officers saw the futility of dealing with the problem and hid from it. The Japanese occupied the town and restored order but not until everything of value had been stolen or destroyed.

Finally, Nogi met Petrov himself. Petrov, in a state of shock, was gray of complexion and his hand trembled. Nogi bowed to the Russian general and praised the general's conduct and the bravery of the Russian soldiers. He declined Petrov's offer of his sword.

The Japanese headquarters in Tokyo immediately telegraphed their congratulations to General Nogi. First came a message from General Yamagata, a man who had once demanded Nogi's suicide. His congratulation was not effusive, but it was nonetheless larded with admiration. He conveyed the thanks of the emperor and said that the Japanese victory dominated the headlines of every newspaper in Japan and that people were celebrating in the street, ecstatic and proud that they had won a victory over a European power. General Nogi's name figured in all the celebrations and one government official after another praised his leadership and courage.

The emperor himself sent a telegram off on the heels of General Yamagata's. With royal reserve, the emperor praised the courage and determination of the Japanese soldiers and sailors and thanked General Nogi personally for his service. Another private telegram, for Nogi's eyes only, expressed the emperor's sadness and condolences over the loss of both of Nogi's sons. Nogi read the telegrams impassively. Then he passed the word to his subordinate commanders and his staff to send the praise from Tokyo all the way down the ranks. Cheering and joy rapidly spread through the ranks of the Japanese soldiers. Those who had lost comrades in the campaign felt that the sacrifices of their friends had been worthwhile, that they had died in the most worthy cause there was—in service to the Emperor of Japan.

The Japanese Navy immediately took over the port.

At this same time, orderlies delivered mail from home to the Japanese soldiers. It was the first news they had received since the siege began, and they eagerly opened the letters from their families. The letters that were meant for those who perished in battle sat in sad piles in the various headquarters. Kenji received a bundle of letters, from his mother, from Momoko, and from his uncle Genichi. Kenji opened the ones from Momoko first and then arranged them in the order of the dates that Momoko had written at the beginning of each. As he read one and then another his emotions spun off into a downward spiral. Each of Momoko's letters revealed yet another level of pressure that her father applied to her to marry Kozo Shimada. Her father's main reason, she wrote, for insisting on the match, was because of the prospect of greatly expanding his business. Momoko seemed to have lost her status as her father's favorite child and she wondered if his affection was a sham all along. Did he really love her all these years or was he was really just grooming her to be a bargaining chip, one that was to be spent for commercial purposes? He constantly reminded her of her duty to her family. "Giri, giri, giri," was the endlessly repeated mantra of his arguments. "You have been raised in luxury and it is your responsibility to preserve that luxury and make sure it is passed down to our future generations," he insisted.

In the last letter, Momoko announced her capitulation. "Kenji, if only you had been here to give me strength. I don't even know if you are still alive or have perished in the great battles we are hearing about. I weep when I think of you. I do not have your courage and can no longer stand up to my father. I will be married to Kozo by the time you receive this, if you ever do. It is unlikely that I will ever see you again, so this must be goodbye."

The news shocked Kenji even though he had known all along that events might take this turn. He rapidly read his other letters, scarcely understanding what they said. His mother and his uncles expressed their pride in his service, hoped he was still alive, and promised to say prayers at the Yasukuni Shrine for him if he had fallen. Almost as an afterthought, his mother confirmed the news of Momoko's betrothal to Kozo Shimada. It was difficult to tell from her letter whether she was saddened or pleased by the news.

In order to take his mind off of events at home, Kenji busied himself with the reorganization of his company. There were new soldiers, replacements, to be melded into the ranks; enlisted men to be promoted to replace their fallen NCOs; and the selection of those who would garrison Port Arthur. Kenji's unit was among those slated to go home. Kenji volunteered to remain in Port Arthur. With the loss of Momoko he had no reason to return so soon.

Part of the garrison's duty was the restoration of order in the city. And part of the restoration process was the care and feeding of their Russian prisoners. The Japanese opened the rail line that they had cut off and permitted supplies from Russia to once more flow into the port. And they began to allow the Russians to send their wounded troops and their paroled officers back to their mother country. The remainder of the captured soldiers would remain in Japanese custody until the war was over. The first to embark were the wounded.

Kenji wondered if Ivan had survived the battle. Whatever time he could spare from his duties, he spent riding among the defeated Russian and asking of Ivan Medved. He finally found him in one of the Russian hospitals.

Kenji approached Ivan's bed, noted his heavily bandaged head, bowed, and said, "Well, Ivan, the Russians fought bravely, and none more than you. The war is over now. What are you going to do?"

"I don't know, Kenji. Even if the war were to continue, I have given my word that I will no longer fight in it. And I am not sure I have the heart for it anymore."

"Why do you say that, Ivan?"

"So much that I saw was wrong. Colonel Tretyakov was, and will always remain, my hero, but most of the others…there was so much incompetence. So many generals hold their positions not because they are military leaders but because they were from the nobility. The whole system is rotten to the core. I don't see how we can ever expect to win a war or to be a modern military power as long as a man is recognized for this birth and not for his ability. Then there were the supply shortages. Even before the trains stopped, we were plagued with shoddy equipment made by people who made millions of rubles. And they were mostly nobles, or merchants who were supported by nobles. Finally, there were the priests. Some of them were as bad as the incompetent generals. Many were sincere but too many of them drank, whored, lied, and stole, and obviously their influence with God did not do us any good. I just do not know what to think except that we were betrayed by the aristocracy, the merchants, and the church."

"It sounds to me that you have been thinking too much. I suppose that we will never see each other again then, my friend. Please give my best to your family, especially your lovely sister."

"That is very kind. I will do that, Kenji. Who knows? Perhaps we will meet again someday, and we can resume our chess games."

As he left the hospital, Kenji thought, *Everything that I learned from Araki and Minobe is true. The Gods are with us. Russia really is a weak nation and Japan is destined to rule East Asia. The future for our Empire has never looked brighter. I wonder where the next challenge will be.*

For Ivan, the return trip to St. Petersburg was a sorry affair. On the way east, the officers and men had been elated, thinking that they had a chance to win the short and victorious war the tsar desired. The long weeks on the train, the long weeks of poor food, cramped compartments and problems getting across Lake Baikal, were all acceptable as long as they thought that they were serving a cause that was noble and good. Traveling westward was another matter. Most of the soldiers, particularly the officers, were in a state of shock over their loss and mourned their comrades and their fallen troops.

Ivan's wounds were no longer painful, and he was getting used to seeing with one eye. He was able to join the other officers in the dining car. Meals were sorry affairs. The food was still bad and the atmosphere was even worse. In addition to their shame at having lost Port Arthur, the officers felt a strong apprehension about how they would be received at home.

The ice across Lake Baikal was frozen solid and the weather cooperated so they traversed the lake without too much trouble. Like most of the wounded, Ivan was spared the march and rode a sled. However, they had no sooner reached the western shore than the weather turned bad again. The train managed to reach the city of Irkutsk. And while they paused for two days to take on coal and provisions, an arctic storm hammered them and kept them in place for over a week.

While they waited, a number of new wounded Russian passengers boarded the train. The officers, all of whom had been in combat with the Siberian army against the Japanese rear, but had missed the fighting at Port Arthur, crowded into the dining car at mealtime and asked the Port Arthur veterans about the battles they had been in. Few of the veterans of Port Arthur wanted to talk about it and they generally ignored the newcomers.

Among the new passengers was Baron Ungern. Tales of his cruelty during the Siberian campaign abounded and rapidly swept through the ranks of the passengers. One story had it that he had taken over a Japanese train and, being short on fuel, had tossed live Japanese prisoners into the firebox to keep it running. He was courageous, though, and wore the St. George Cross on his tunic. Most officers avoided him except when forced by circumstance to be in his company. They reported that he still had a fixation about Mongolia and declared that he would rather be the new Khan of that desert country than anything else in the world. One officer observed that Ungern wore madness like the sheen of oil on a placid pond. Ungern had been only slightly wounded but was one of the officers chosen to return to St. Petersburg and brief the general staff on the campaign in Siberia.

Ungern had ignored Ivan on the trip out, when he had made up part of Arkady Gross's retinue, but now he went out of his way to introduce himself. He knew that Ivan was a fellow member of the aristocracy and thought that another noble would be more likely to talk to him about Port Arthur and to listen to his fantasies.

"I am happy to make your acquaintance," Ivan said politely. "But as you can see, I did not come out of this war unscathed. I would prefer not to talk about it."

After several more attempts at getting information from Ivan, Baron Ungern finally gave up and launched into his own monologue. "I was impressed by the Mongols. What warriors they are! I am not surprised that they conquered all of China and Manchuria and a great deal of Russia. They are an independent people but in search of a bold leader. Why, an experienced military officer could come to lead them and become the next Khan of Mongolia. Just think, wouldn't being a successor to Genghis Kahn be a wonderful thing? You and I should leave the tsar's service and go to Mongolia and become famous generals." As he talked the glow in his eyes grew brighter and brighter.

Ivan soon began to wonder if the baron was a madman, but he nodded politely. Since he did not reject the man outright, he found himself subject to his rants all the way across Russia. He could not help wondering the fate of a man like this.

CHAPTER 28
REVOLUTION AT HOME

"Arrrrgh! Arrrrgh!" Nina, who was making up Natalya's bed, stopped and heard it again. "Arrrrgh!" It sounded like her mistress was vomiting in the bathroom. She stood still and listened but heard only the sound of water running and the flushing of the toilet. Natalya shakily emerged, her face gray and ghastly.

"Mistress, are you well?"

"It's nothing, Nina, but I am feeling a bit tired this morning. I think will go back to bed for a while. Please go on and take care of your other chores and leave me alone."

After the maid quietly closed the door, Natalya returned to bed, pulled the bedding up to her chin, and cried until she exhausted her reservoir of tears. Then she slept.

"Natalya, Natalya!" Her mother's voice pulled her upward and out of the troubled blackness until she broke through the surface of a deep sleep and awoke.

The fuzzy image of her mother's face gradually gained focus and she saw a face contorted by emotion. Anger? Fear? Motherly concern? Natalya could not tell, but the look made her afraid. Nina stood beside her.

"Natalya, you missed breakfast and Nina said she heard you vomiting. Are you sick? What is wrong?"

"It is just a little upset stomach, Mama, nothing for you to worry about. I had some milk last night that smelled a little odd. I am sure that was it."

Natalya thought that she had never seen her mother look so intently at anything. "Well, if you say so but if you are not perfectly well by tomorrow, I am going to call Doctor Orlov." Marina left the room thinking, *Oh, God, please God, no! Don't make it that, anything but that. It would ruin us. I knew that sooner or later she would cause us trouble, but please, God, not that.*

Natalya kept to her room the rest of the day, leaving only for dinner, which she barely touched. The next morning she vomited again.

She exited the bathroom to find Nina standing just outside the door. The maid gave Natalya a look. "Mistress, we both know what is the matter, and it is my duty to tell your mother."

"Please, Nina, don't tell her. I'll find a way out of this, I just need some more time."

"No. mistress. I must tell her. If she finds out that I know I could lose my job. I do not want to be sent back to the country estate and have to milk cows for the rest of my life."

"What can I do to persuade you to keep quiet, for just a little while? I'll give you anything I have."

Nina shrugged. "For one of your gold bracelets I could throw it out of my head for a while. You don't want me to grow a long tongue."

"Nina, I will give you my biggest gold bracelet. It is worth hundreds of rubles. But you can't wear it here."

"I know, but it could become my dowry and would help me find a good husband so I don't have to make beds and clean up after you."

"Thank you, Nina, thank you."

That afternoon Natalya sought out Tatiana. "What am I to do, Tatya? I just missed my third period and think I am getting fatter."

"Didn't you use pomegranate, or one of the other things, every day like I told you? I know your family has the resources to buy it."

"Yes, but I could not ask for it every day. What would the cooks and my family think?"

"Very little compared to what they will think if you are pregnant and cannot do anything about it. Look, I will take you to a woman who knows how to take care of these things."

The woman's house was not far. Natalya expected a withered old crone with a wart on her nose. Instead, an attractive young woman in her late twenties opened the door. She listened to Natalya with half an ear and a bored expression.

When Natalya finished, the woman sighed, pulled a paper bag out of a drawer, and filled it with dry herbs from a large ceramic jar. "This is called blue cohosh. It will terminate a pregnancy about two-thirds of the time. You must boil a pinch of leaves in water and drink it at least three times a day. If it is going to work, it should do so in two or three weeks."

Natalya gave her hundred-ruble gold coin and her thanks.

At home, she enlisted the aid of Nina to provide her with the hot water several times a day. It cost her another gold bracelet.

Three weeks later she still felt no effect from the herbs. The vomiting had stopped, but fear and remorse nearly paralyzed her. Nina hinted that she was soon going to require further payment.

Tatiana promised to find a woman who would take care of the problem but warned her that it was risky.

"I am ready to try anything, Tatya."

Throughout the Russian empire citizens of every class trembled with shock and disbelief that the upstart Japanese had defeated the mighty Russian army. No one understood how the monkeys had won. The returning soldiers arrived home to a somber populace, a populace that was not exactly ashamed of them but avoided them whenever they could. The good citizens of Moscow and St. Petersburg were in no mood to examine their country's failures.

Those who would see an end to the monarchy were elated by Russia's defeat, which they regarded as a positive step toward their dreams of a different form of government. The more radical among them hoped for the fall and destruction of the tsarist system. The centrists wanted to see a constitutional monarchy like, say, in Great Britain.

Whispered rumors flew in St. Petersburg that an important demonstration was pending. The word began among the Russian intelligentsia and soon spread to the workers. Father Georges Gapon, it was said, would lead a peaceful march to the Winter Palace. He hoped the tsar would meet with the people who loved him and listen to their pleas for sweeping reforms. Russia, they would say, needed a representative government. The country needed peace, the poor needed bread, the peasants needed land. There was so much deprivation among the people and so much wealth in the hands of the nobles and the wealthy merchants. Surely the Little Father would understand and help his people.

In all the poor neighborhoods of St. Petersburg, workers hotly debated the issue. Many dismissed it altogether, some because Gapon's aims did not go far enough and others because they did want to oppose their sovereign. But a great number of people decided to participate in the peaceful demonstration. Morale in Russia had deteriorated since the news of the Russian defeat at Port Arthur. The tsar's "short victorious war" was supposed to take the people's minds off of the increasingly poor conditions in which the average Russian lived. The loss to the Japanese focused minds on these conditions instead.

Tatiana and Pyotr scorned Father Gapon's aims and decided to stay away from the demonstration because the reforms he wanted did not go far enough toward the total fundamental makeover of Russia that the Bolsheviks had in mind. After much discussion, they changed their minds. It was at least a first step in loosening the tsar's iron grip on the people.

Tatiana talked to Natalya about it. "You must go with us. It will be nothing but a peaceful demonstration and it will take your mind off this other thing. You will be able to see if the tsar is the lover of the people your family thinks that he is. By the way, I have found an abortionist and she will see you next week. But I must tell you again that it is risky and may involve a lot of bleeding."

"I do not care how risky it is, Tatya. I must go through with it. And I cannot go to the demonstration. My father is an advisor to the tsar. What do you think would happen if my family found out? Even worse, what do you think would happen if my father's enemies found out? He would be destroyed. The tsar would have no choice but to be rid of him."

"Look, Natalya, it is just a peaceful demonstration. There will be no violence. A priest will lead it. Probably more than one priest. Many people will participate and no one will know that you are in the crowd."

"All right," said Natalya, "I will go. But I will stop and return home at the first sign of anything that is not entirely peaceful."

On Saturday Jan 21, Father Gapon sent a letter to Prince Pyotr Sviatopolk-Mirsky, the new interior minister. In it, Gapon pleaded for the tsar to meet with his people the next day in front of the Winter Palace. Gapon was not a violent man. He did not want the tsar to be removed or to threaten his autocracy. He did want his ruler to listen to the problems of his people, directly and without the interference of his ministers who protected him and told him only what he wanted to hear. Nearly every Russian blamed their problems on the bureaucrats and said among themselves, "If the tsar only knew, he would do something about this." Gapon wanted to help the tsar understand his people better and thereby help the workers and peasants. Only the personal intervention of His Majesty would help.

Word spread rapidly, and work in the city nearly came to a standstill that day as workers stopped what they were doing to discuss the next day's march.

The morning of Sunday, January 22nd, dawned clear and cold. The sky was cloudless and the sun, reflecting off the snow-covered roofs and the ice of the parks of St. Petersburg, was blinding.

Priests, clad in their full regalia, led the procession. Some carried icons. Others bore pictures of the tsar. None of the demonstrators had weapons. Behind the leaders marched tens of thousands of workers. Their ranks became more swollen by the moment. At mid-morning they numbered nearly 200,000.

Sviatopolk-Mirsky, the Minister of the Interior, did not even inform the tsar of the imminent demonstration. Instead, he deployed fifty thousand soldiers to block their path.

Revolutionary proselytizers had radicalized a majority of the workers at the Putilov plant, and they showed up in great numbers. The soldiers stationed on the bridge that crossed the Neva River into St. Petersburg proper blocked several thousand men from the Putilov plant. The workers circumvented the troops by marching either up or downstream and easily crossing the river on the ice that covered it. They came together at the rear of the troops and marched on. The maneuver unnerved and confused the soldiers.

By mid-afternoon nearly a quarter-million Russian workers had neared the Winter Palace. They found all the streets and intersections around the palace blocked by battalions of infantry and squadrons of Cossack horsemen.

Tatiana, Natalya, and Pyotr walked in a group not far from the front of the procession. Tatiana and Pyotr walked proudly and fearlessly with heads erect, defiantly shaking their fists in the air. Natalya thought she was in the most dangerous place she had ever been. If anything were to happen, her family could not help her. She kept her head as far down into the collar of her coat as it would go and lowered her scarf to cover her forehead.

Despite shouted warnings from the military officers, the crowd crawled forward. When it became apparent that the crowd would not stop, Cossacks charged the front ranks using knouts, iron-tipped clubs, that they swung left and right. This felled some of the demonstrators with bloody heads but the remainder surged on. The knouts had not worked so the Cossacks drew their sabers. With blades flashing in the bright sun they charged once more. Their objective was intimidation, not injury, and they had orders to only use the flat of their swords and not the razor-sharp edges. The crowd marched on. The Cossacks retired behind the infantry and left the rest to them. The soldiers loaded their rifles with blanks and fired at the crowd. The marchers fell back a bit, trampling some of those behind the front ranks. Then those at the front prostrated themselves on the ground and called out.

"We beseech you, please let us pass. We mean His Majesty no harm. We only want to talk to him."

The soldiers loaded their weapons with live ammunition. When the front ranks of the demonstrators got to their feet again and inched forward, the soldiers fired into the crowd.

The rifle fire decimated the front ranks, and the crowd reeled as the soldiers worked their bolts and fired a second volley. Natalya Medved was shot through the heart and died instantly. Pyotr and Tatiana looked down at her crumpled body, turned around, and melted into the crowd, away from the gunfire. The soldiers on the flanks of the procession joined the shooting and fired volley after volley into the mass of bodies. Several priests fell, dead or wounded. The wounded Father Gapon escaped. The crowd broke up, and the demonstrators fled, splitting into smaller and smaller groups until they became only angry and confused individuals seeking the safety of their own homes.

Several hundred marchers were killed and hundreds more wounded. No one ever knew the total.

Madame Kusa, the principal soprano at the Imperial Russian Opera and the wife of a leading composer, witnessed the soldiers firing into the crowd. She shouted at an officer, "You don't know how to kill Japanese, but you are good at killing innocent civilians. Shame!"

Excitement among the revolutionaries spread to the countryside and abroad. Vladimir Lenin, from exile, said, "The prestige of the tsarist name has been ruined forever."

When Ivan alighted from the train in Moscow two weeks after the demonstration only his father and his uncle Mikhail, the priest, stood on the platform to greet him. They embraced and kissed in the Russian manner. Ivan was stunned by how old and frail his father looked. "Hello, father, where is Natalya? Where is mother?"

"Natalya is dead, my son. She and Tatiana were in a march organized by the rebel priest Gapon. She was killed by our own soldiers."

Michael said, "God will preserve Natalya's soul. I said a funeral mass for her."

Ivan stood openmouthed in shock. Then he asked, "And Mother?"

"She has taken to her bed, Ivan. She is brokenhearted, refuses to eat, and grows weaker by the day."

The three men sadly boarded the family carriage, which was decorated with black crepe, and returned to the Medved mansion.

EPILOGUE

The lookout carefully scanned the dark street. A block and a half away, a well-appointed carriage rolled to a stop. Two men stepped down and started in his direction. One of them walked with a pronounced limp. As they grew nearer, the lookout could see that the man with the limp had a useless arm that dangled and swayed with his pace. The other man wore a black eye patch. The lookout moved down the three steps to a cellar door and softly knocked. The door opened, and the murmur of voices and the scent of harsh tobacco followed the young woman with the curly black hair up the stairs. She walked to the two men, greeted them quietly and led them down the stairs and into the cellar.

AUTHOR'S NOTE

This is a work of fiction. Some of the characters and events are borrowed from real life but I have fictionalized the actions, words and events. There was a stampede on Khodynka Meadow a few days after the coronation of Tsar Nicholas II. It started with rumors that there were not enough treats for the crowd and that each of the ceramic souvenir cups contained a gold coin. An estimated 1.400 people died and thousands more injured. Because of this tragedy, the new tsar and tsarina did try to cancel their appearance at the ball given by the French ambassador that evening but were talked out of it by the tsar's uncles. The tsar and tsarina in real life conversed in English and addressed each other as Sunny and Nicky. Other than this, my portrayal of them is entirely a figment of my imagination. Sergei Witte, the finance minister and some of the Russian officers, like the gallant Colonel Tretyakov were real but fictionalized by me. Another character inspired by real-life was Baron Ungern-Sternberg, often referred to as "The Bloody White Baron," of whom I hope to have more to say in another volume. Among the Japanese, there was a real Colonel Motojiro Akashi who spied on the Russians from Moscow in the months leading up to the Russo-Japanese War. He also fanned the flames of revolution within Russia. General Maresuke Nogi was the victor at Port Arthur and lost both his sons during the campaign. He and his wife committed suicide, she by slashing her own throat, and he by seppuku, ritual disembowelment, the day of Emperor Meiji's funeral. Like I have with the Russians, I have completely fictionalized their behavior and their words. The demonstration led by Georges Gapon that ends the book was a real event and known in Russia as the Revolution of 1905. Ivan Medved and Kenji Dainichi, and their friends and relatives, are completely made up. For those interested in such things, Medved is the Russian word for bear, and the characters for Dainichi mean large sun. I have borrowed most of the other Japanese and Russian names from people I know. I hope they will forgive me.